ALSO BY ANDREW VACHSS

THE BURKE SERIES

Flood

Strega

Blue Belle

Hard Candy

Blossom

Sacrifice

Down in the Zero

Footsteps of the Hawk

False Allegations

Safe House

Choice of Evil

Dead and Gone

Pain Management

Only Child

Down Here

Mask Market

Terminal

Another Life

OTHER NOVELS

Shella

The Getaway Man

Two Trains Running

Haiku

SHORT-STORY COLLECTIONS

Born Bad

Everybody Pays

THE
WEIGHT

THE WEIGHT

ANDREW VACHSS

Pantheon Books · New York

Copyright © 2010 by Andrew Vachss

All rights reserved. Published in the United States by Pantheon Books,
a division of Random House, Inc., New York, and in Canada by
Random House of Canada Limited, Toronto.

Pantheon Books and colophon are
registered trademarks of Random House, Inc.

Library of Congress Cataloging-in-Publication Data
Vachss, Andrew H.
The weight / Andrew Vachss.
p. cm.
ISBN 978-0-307-37919-1
1. Professional thieves—United States—Fiction.   2. Criminals—
United States—Fiction.   I. Title.
PS3572.A33W45 2010
813'.54—dc22   2009050945

www.pantheonbooks.com

Book design by Robert C. Olsson

Printed in the United States of America
First Edition

2 4 6 8 9 7 5 3 1

Mom:

I know you couldn't wait any longer to be with Dad, but don't fret—I'll be with you both soon enough.

I've got a few things to take care of first.

Yeah, I know . . . I *always* did.

And *you* know . . . I always will.

THE
WEIGHT

Whatever it was the cops had snatched me up for, they had to believe I was good for it. But not all *that* good. Otherwise, why go tag-team on me?

One of the cops on the second shift was an older guy. He looked the way some people say all cops used to: tall, big hands, straw-colored hair. Back then, they'd say, cops would catch a kid doing something wrong, they'd kick him in the ass, send him home, and go back to walking their beat. They never paid for a meal, but nobody thought that was graft. Some might even take money from bookies or whorehouses. But *never* from a dope dealer.

Maybe cops were really like that once. I don't know; I wasn't around then. I only know how they are now.

I'll say this for the older cop: He dressed like a guy who lived on his paycheck. And he wasn't there to dance. He walked in with his partner, sat down, and threw his Sunday punch: "This one just doesn't look like your line of work, Sugar."

That told me he was sharp enough to do more than just check me for priors. Not by calling me "Sugar." The first pair, they'd called me that, too. Sliding it out of their mouths like they knew something dirty about me. This cop, he just said it like it was my name.

The first two cops, I think all they did was scan my record for a "Registered Sex Offender" ticket. When they didn't see one, they were out of gas; it's the only card they know how to play.

The older cop shook his head, like he was confused about what they'd arrested me for.

"I got to say, I don't like you for this one at all."

"Then what am I here for?" I asked him.

He made his eyes go sad, showing he was disappointed in me. It was a good trick. A guy who's been around as long as him, he probably knew a lot of them.

We'd already been sitting in the interrogation room for a couple of hours when he did that. Maybe it was part of his act, I don't know. But it was as clear as if somebody wrote the rules on the wall for us all to see: As long as I didn't say the magic words, we were going to play it like men. No disrespect, not in either direction.

Those magic words could only come out of my mouth. Door Number One: "I want a lawyer." Door Number Two: "Yeah, you got me."

I tell them I want a lawyer, they'd give me a look like I'd just screwed myself, cuff me back up, and have one of the bluecoats walk me into a holding cell.

But if I started talking, they'd hold off until they squeezed as much juice out of the lemon as they could. Say I told them I wanted a deal. They'd tell me that I could get damn near whatever I wanted . . . depending on what I had to trade.

The way they were working me, walking so soft, that was just to stop me from asking for a lawyer. Good cops—I don't mean like they were good *guys,* just good at their job—they think the same way we do. They know if you get all impatient you can mess every-thing up.

So they stayed decent and respectful, like I said. Not kissing my ass or anything; making it just three men, talking. The way they'd figure it, so long as they could *keep* me talking, talking about *any-thing,* there was always the chance I'd take Door Number Two. Or stumble through it.

They had to know it was a-thousand-to-one against them get-ting me to confess. And I knew it was even worse odds against me convincing them they'd grabbed the wrong guy.

A weak hand, sure. Who hits a gutshot straight-flush draw? But I wasn't drawing dead, not yet.

We each had our reasons for staying with it. They had all the time in the world. And that's how much time I was looking at.

So I had to stay to see the last card drop. Because, no matter what those sex-crimes clowns had told me, I knew this couldn't really be about a rape.

The rape they kept asking me about, it must have been a bad one. For the cops, the worst one would be if it happened to some kind of famous person. I hadn't seen a paper for days, but I knew they'd been sitting on my place, waiting for me to come back. At least six of them, round the clock. That's a lot of cops.

I didn't know how long they'd been waiting, but they couldn't have started until after I left, and that was only a few days ago.

Sending the sex-crimes cops in first, that didn't mean any-thing—it could just be a hype to get me to take my eye off the ball. Misdirection, like three-card monte. They pull you in for some-thing big, get you so scared of *that* charge that you drop your guard and give up something about whatever they're really after you for.

I knew they hadn't bagged any of the others. If they had, they'd drop their names, so I'd know they weren't just blowing smoke. Then they'd have *their* magic words. Door One: one of the other guys had turned canary, put all the weight on me, trying to cut himself a deal. Door Two: here was my chance to help myself before it was too late.

Only the second pair of cops would try a move like that. The first two, the sex-crimes boys, they mostly made speeches. Or asked me stupid questions, like a TV camera was filming them. Big guy like me, all those muscles—what happened? I'd been on steroids so long I couldn't get it up, and she'd laughed at me? I hadn't meant to hurt her, just slap her around a little, maybe? Come on, isn't that how it went down?

I yawned in their faces.

"Got nothing to say *now,* huh?" one of them had said. Like he'd just nailed me to the cross.

I wanted to ask him if that pathetic crap ever worked. What kind of chumps show you their hand first and *then* try to bluff you off a better one?

But I didn't say anything. I'm a professional, not a punk with a pistol. You'll never see my picture on a security camera sticking up a bodega. Or jacking some guy in a suit while he's standing at an ATM.

I'm a thief, and I do clean work. I don't hurt people for money, I don't set fires, I don't do any of those sicko sex things. Stuff like that, it gets spread all over: the papers, radio, TV. Gets everybody paying attention. Specially when there's big reward money out there.

A man who does my kind of work, the only way he ever gets caught is if he goes in without a plan. Or if someone rolls over on him.

You never talk about your work, period. Too many guys walking around with heavy charges hanging over them. Anyone gets caught holding K-weight powder in this state, it's the same as a murder beef. A street cop catches a guy holding that heavy, he can make the bust, but all that'd get him is another one of those "commendations" every cop has a couple dozen of. What he really wants is that gold shield, so he'd rather have that guy on the street, working for him. Any outlaw is going to be able to go places no undercover ever could. So all he has to do is listen long enough.

Guys like that, they're all nothing but rats on leashes. If it wasn't for informants, the cops would have to get damn lucky to ever make a case against a pro.

They'll pretty much always get the amateurs—the clowns who leave a trail you could follow even with one of those white canes tapping the way.

The amateurs who stay out the longest are the ones who kill for fun. A random kill doesn't even *look* like what it really is until the bodies pile up.

There's also people who get off on being a rat. Nothing in it for them; they *like* doing that kind of stuff.

So it's just as hard for people on my side of the law to sniff them out as it is for the law to sniff out a guy who does freakish stuff.

There's even people stupid enough to rat on themselves. A pro can be smart about work and dumb about other things. Say you talk about your work to your girlfriend: all it takes is for her to get mad at you one time to put a whole crew under the jail.

A few years ago, that happened to a guy I'd worked some jobs with. He was real good-looking. Smooth talker, too. Always found some girl to pick up his tabs—I don't think he ever paid rent in his life. This guy, he'd never talk about our kind of work, but any woman he ever stayed with, she'd have to know he wasn't any W-2 man. Probably helped them get over the nights he didn't come home. And explained the flashy way he always dressed, too. Whatever, they were always happy to help out with some cash while he was waiting on this big score he had coming.

Only this last one, she couldn't leave it that way. She just *had* to satisfy herself he wasn't spending her money on some other girl.

A lot of them do it now. They call it "playing detective." You know what I mean: they buy their boyfriend a cell phone and pay the bill themselves. The mark thinks he's playing her, but the person who pays the bill *gets* the bill. Which means she gets a lot of phone numbers.

So, anyway, the girlfriend, she finds a number she doesn't recognize, dials it while the guy's sleeping. Wakes him up and goes *off* on him. She's taking care of him, and he fucking *cheats* on her!?

He should've just promised her he was done with that other girl. Better yet, just walked away and not come back.

But, no, he has to be a *big* man. Throws a fistful of hundreds on the floor, tells her, "Here, bitch. Go pay your little cell-phone bill."

All their time together, she thought he was her kept boy, so seeing all that money sends her over the edge. A few minutes earlier, she was screaming at him to get out. Now she's standing in front of the door. She's got more to say, and he's going to listen to it or . . .

He should have let her scream herself dry. But, the kind of fool he is, he's got to play his role, just like he did flashing the money. Ends up banging her around pretty hard.

He's not even a few blocks away when she goes 911 on him.

They pick him up right on the street. Once they tell him what he's being pinched for, he doesn't say a word.

This guy figures, they arraign him in the morning, he takes whatever they're offering. What's he looking at . . . thirty days and some anger-management class?

But he's only in a few hours when the girlfriend waltzes in and tells the cops she's decided not to press charges. Stupid broad, she thought it was *her* case. When they tell her it's not up to her, she loses it again. By the time she's done running her mouth, they've got enough probable cause to take her home and have a look around. That was all it took.

I'll say this for that guy: maybe he played big-shot, but he paid for doing it, and he didn't ask anyone he ever worked with to split the tab.

When a whole crew gets pulled in at the same time, the first thing they do is cut you off from the other guys. There's all kinds of ways to do that.

But these cops hadn't even mentioned the job, much less any of my partners on it.

When they left me alone in the interrogation room—a lot of them try that—I had plenty of time to think.

So, when they finally came back in, I thought I'd try that same trick myself, dividing them up.

"Those other guys, they watch too much TV," I said to the older cop.

"Is that right?"

"They found my *DNA*?" I said, making a joke of it. I knew these cops must have been watching while the sex-crimes buffoons took the first crack at me.

The older guy's partner—a black guy, closer to my age; clean-cut, sharp dresser—said, "DNA doesn't lie," making his voice all deep and serious, the way the sex-crimes clown had said it to me.

"And I *still* didn't start yelling for Legal Aid," I reminded them.

"Meaning . . . ?"

"I figured—I *hoped* anyway—they'd send in the A-Team sooner or later."

"You wouldn't be stroking us now, would you, Sugar?" the older cop said.

"I'm just saying, there's cops and there's cops. I mean, come on, if they really had any of that CSI stuff, they would have shown it to me by now. Waved it in my face."

"You think that's what we'd do?"

"No, I mean those other guys. Like I said, TV cops. But I know you couldn't have anything—"

"You were gloved?" the black guy cut me off, like he just saw an opening and needed to move fast before it closed.

It was my turn to look disappointed. "That's cold, Officer," I said to him. "I thought we were going to play this straight."

"Cheap shot," the older guy said. A cop's apology, sure, but I trusted it at least enough to see if I could get *them* to say the wrong thing.

So I baited the trap: "Something's screwy here. Listen, I absolutely *know* you don't have any of that stuff. You know why? Because I know it wasn't me who did it."

"Simple as that?"

"It's the truth," I said, dropping an even bigger hint. What I had in mind, it had to be their idea. It couldn't come from me, or they wouldn't trust it.

"Let's say, just for the sake of argument, let's say you're right," the older guy said. "Say we don't have one single piece of physical evidence to tie you to the rape. That'd make it a tougher case in court, sure. But we're still holding the ace."

"I got picked out of a photo spread?"

"Got it in one," he said. Smiled a little, too.

"I don't know what to say about that," I said, real quick—before they realized they'd told me something I didn't know. I'd already been in a lineup, but I'd just been guessing about the mug-shot book.

So I kept going: "I mean, I've been in lineups where I was the only white guy on the stage, but this one was fair. Hell, a couple of those guys looked enough like me to be my twin brother."

The black cop laughed. Not the first time he'd heard that one, I guessed. "Probably so," he said. "Only thing is—"

"Yeah, I know. They were cops, right? And no cop ever did a rape."

They looked at each other for a second—just a quick glance. I was walking pretty close to the edge of their line with that last one. They must have had some way of signaling each other. Or maybe they'd worked together so long they didn't need to.

"But you didn't ask for your phone call," the black cop said. "Which means you think you've got a shot at getting us to buy your story."

Yeah, I was right—he was smart, just like his partner. Maybe I *would* get that shot. "It's no story," I said, making sure I didn't sound resentful.

"You know what would turn it for you, Caine?" the older one said. "An alibi. That would pretty much trump our ace."

I'd been hoping for something else, but I rolled with the punch, and tried again. "For you, or for a jury?"

"For *you*," he hit back. "You know there's no point giving us a piece of cellophane—that'd just make it worse. But you give us a *real* alibi, we'll check it out. Check it out deep. Turn it upside down and sideways. If there's a hole in it, we'll find it; trust me on that. But if you're telling the truth—and, like I said, I kind of think you just might be—that'd be *good* for you."

It's not just the hard eight; now I'm down to my third throw, I thought. *Why wouldn't they just ask me to take a—?*

The older cop broke into my thoughts. "Here's the good part for you, Caine. It's not only you who knows how good we'd check out your alibi—the DA knows it, too. Believe me, my partner and me tell them your alibi's rock-solid, no way those Ivy League wimps are going to take a chance on messing up their conviction rate."

"Hard enough to get them to prosecute *good* cases," the black cop said. His mouth twisted when he said that. I took it for real, not a play. Probably watched some solid cases tossed out, and he hadn't liked it much.

I remember thinking what a fucked-up mess things were. See, I believed those cops. Mostly because they weren't telling me anything I didn't know. Every pro on both sides of the line knows the DA's Office'll always deal away the courthouse on a sex crime. Specially if the woman was the wrong kind. Like a hooker, or slow in the head, or even dressed too sexy. Or maybe she had booze or drugs in her blood when they ran the tests.

The younger guy was right: the sex-crimes DAs were all about plea deals. Everybody knows they make the sweetest offers. But once they said "alibi," I was cooked.

And when they dropped that the girl had seen a photo spread, I knew this wasn't a bad-ID case; it was a stone-cold frame. I must have fit the girl's general description, so the cops showed her the mug-shot books *first*. Then all she had to do was pick the guy in the lineup who looked most like the picture.

Crooked, sure. But that old cop-trick didn't make it a setup; the photo spread did.

You know how I was saying if they *really* had some forensic stuff they'd've shown it to me? I knew the girl who got raped never got a real look at the guy who did it. There's my eyes: one's blue, the other's brown. And my hair's what they used to call "dirty blond." But my eyebrows are black like they'd been painted on with ink, so you can see the open spot in the right one, where the scar is.

That girl who got raped, if she'd said *any* of that stuff, they would have shown me her statement. Lots of big guys walking around, but how many with two different-colored eyes?

That's how I knew for sure they were measuring me for a frame—they never even asked me to step closer when I was in the lineup.

The cops had grabbed me just after I got back from a three-day-weekend job. The second I opened the door to my apartment, I knew someone had been there while I was gone.

I stopped in my tracks, spun around, and took off. If I could get to the basement, there was a chance of slipping out the back.

But they were waiting for me.

Which meant I wasn't walking out on bond, even if the real rapist walked in and confessed. When they took me, I was carrying. The worst gun charge you can draw is "felon in possession," and I qualified, both counts.

So I knew I was going down even if I beat the rape case. I don't know why it still mattered to me if these guys thought I was a degenerate. I didn't give a fuck what those sex-crimes cops thought, but these other cops were . . . I don't know how to say it, exactly. Different. More like . . . more like me, I guess. So I kept trying.

"When did it happen?" I asked.

"You don't—" the younger one started, before the older guy stepped on whatever his partner was going to say.

"Sunday night, around two in the morning," he told me.

"I was—"

"Please don't say 'home, watching TV, all alone,' okay?"

"I got a TV. HBO, Showtime, all that."

"You rolled snake eyes on that one, pal," the older cop said, almost like he felt bad for me. "Just your luck, there had to be a domestic-disturbance call late Sunday night. A *bad* one. You know it's got to be bad when two different 911 calls come in, and neither one from the victim.

"Three cars responded. The woman in the apartment two doors down from yours, she was a busted-up mess. Ambulance job—she was just barely breathing. Told the first-responders that the guy who did it to her—her boyfriend, naturally—he took off just before the first radio car got there.

"We'd gone in silent-approach, no sirens, and it worked. First we sealed off the building, then we started a door-to-door."

He talked like all real cops do. "We" didn't mean him personally; he was talking about the whole department. "You catch the guy?" I asked him.

"Yeah. Hiding in a stairwell, three flights down. Big guy, like you. But only on the outside. His hands looked like he stuck them in a meat grinder. The fucking dirtbag was moaning and crying, like he was the one who got hurt. Those kind, they're all alike."

"The girl make it?"

"Yeah. Barely. She's going to need reconstructive surgery, eat through a straw for a year."

"And she's not going to press charges, right?"

The black guy looked at me like he'd rather be measuring me for a coffin than a frame. "We don't *need* her testimony. That kind of thing, it's yesterday. Now the victim doesn't press the charges; *we* do."

I already knew that. I didn't have anything more to say. I just sat there and waited to see if they did.

The older guy broke the spell. "Thing is, we had to make sure this guy wasn't holed up in one of the other apartments . . . maybe even holding hostages.

"Everyone on your floor answered the door. A couple of them were pretty pissed off, it being past two in the morning by then. But they were all wide-awake anyway, as much noise as we were making. Only one door wouldn't open for us. The landlord passkeyed the uniforms in, seeing as how this was an emergency."

He gave me one of those corner-of-the-mouth smiles, watching my eyes. I didn't blink, but I didn't play stare-down with him, either—that's for punks.

"And your place . . . well, you know it was empty," he went on. "Looked like nobody had been there for a while. Not that it was all filthy or anything; just the opposite, in fact. You can always tell a convict's apartment. A man who's done real time, he keeps his house clean. Neat and clean. Always seem to like those studio apartments, too."

The younger cop looked calm, but his hands kept clenching and unclenching.

"Why am I telling you this?" the older guy said. He was looking at me, but I know he was trying to show his partner something.

"I don't know," I said. Honestly.

"Two reasons, Caine. One, you've been around the block. More than once. You knew your room had been tossed the second you walked in, am I right?"

I just nodded.

"Two," he said, "I really *don't* like you for this one. So just give us something that stands up. For once in your life, make a good decision. Give us that alibi; it could turn out to be the smartest thing you ever did."

"Fuck me," I said, lighting the last of my cigarettes. They'd taken them away when they booked me, but the older guy brought them back when he and his partner took over. He was smart enough to know I'd appreciate a little thing like that.

"What?" the older guy said. "You think your backdoor girlfriend's gonna deny everything, try and save her marriage, something like that?"

I just looked at the ceiling. A pack of legit smokes costs a fucking fortune in this city, but I'd be paying a lot more than that for a single where I was going.

"I'm done," I told them.

These guys were pros; they weren't going to blow a confession by talking when it was my turn. And they weren't going to get up and walk out—I still hadn't told them I wanted a lawyer. "I'm done" could mean anything. But all it meant to me was exactly what I'd said.

It stayed quiet until I finally told them, "I'll save the alibi for the trial."

"Don't be an asshole," the younger one told me. "You just as good as told us you don't *have* an alibi. And anything you can put together over a three-way phone call is never going to hold up."

"Yeah." I nodded at him. "You're right. I'm not even going to try. I mean, I don't *have* to give an alibi, right?"

"You dumb—" the younger guy started, but the older one shook his head to shut him up.

"You really *are* fucked," the older one told me. He turned a little so he could look at his partner. "Mr. Caine here, he's got an airtight alibi for when that rape was going down, Earl. Ask *me,* I'll tell you."

The younger one shot his partner a "What the fuck?" look. Me, I didn't bother. I could see the older guy had already figured it out.

"Our boy here was working when that girl got raped," the old guy said. "Him and, what, four, five other men?" he said, suddenly looking at me with cop eyes. I don't mean blue—which they were—I mean how they went from soft to ice in a finger-snap. "The drill-through job at that little jewelry store over on Eighty-ninth? They probably started real late Friday night. When Sugar opened his door Tuesday morning, he was just coming home from work."

I didn't say anything.

"Now, *that's* Mr. Caine's kind of work, Earl. Wouldn't surprise me, we find out that the owner's in on it, too. Told the papers he lost over eleven million in stones . . . which means probably more like seven. And what's a jewelry store doing in that part of town, anyway? Nobody'd go there looking for a deal on diamonds. That's what the District is for, right?"

"You're saying this mutt was part of that crew, Tom?"

"Bet my pension on it."

The younger one turned to me. "And I'm betting my partner's right. Which means you just hit the exacta, buddy. You give us the other guys in on the job with you—the owner, too—and you not only walk away from that one, but the rape charge *has* to get dropped." He made his voice sound bitter that I could get such a sweetheart deal, but I knew that was just game.

And now I also knew why this team had come in to talk to me when the sex-crimes cops were finished.

I looked at the black cop like he was a wall with last year's calendar on it. And no pictures.

"Don't you fucking get it?" he said. "If the DA's gonna use your testimony, he *has* to drop the rape charge. You can't be in two places at once."

"Ah, our boy here, he gets it, all right, Earl," the older guy said, sounding sad again. "Thing is, what he gets is that he has to *take* it."

That old cop had it right. Rules are rules. You go down, you go down alone. Walking into any joint carrying a rat jacket is bad enough, but walking out with one would be even worse—I'd never find decent work again.

It hadn't been any four- or five-man job; just three of us. I'd only worked with one of the other guys before, Big Matt. He was some kind of engineer, so he could come up with ways to get around stuff we didn't expect. He always knew what tools we'd need, too.

I didn't know the other guy, but he'd been vouched for by Solly, the planner. Him, I trusted. We went back a long ways, and I knew he'd hold my share until I finished my bit.

Any way you stacked it, I was going down. Only question was . . . for what? Yeah, they said rape, but I still didn't know anything else about what those sex-crimes guys thought I'd done.

The Legal Aid in Night Court was one of those frazzled old wrecks—dandruff all over the shoulders of his cheap suit, bad teeth, liver spots on his hands. He smelled like the holding cell I'd been waiting in. Just putting in time until he could retire. Didn't have a clue about my case, and gave even less of a fuck.

Everybody knew their role. I pleaded not guilty. Judge threw me a telephone-number bail. They sent me back to the Tombs to wait for the bus.

The lawyer they sent over to Rikers was an 18-B—the lawyers they put on a panel to take cases that Legal Aid can't handle when they're overloaded. Which is pretty much always.

A lot of fools think 18-Bs are better, being "private lawyers" and all. Truth is, that panel is loaded with losers who can't make it on their own. They get paid crap compared to real lawyers, but it's enough to buy them desk space in one of those Baxter Street dumps right behind the courthouse.

But this guy didn't look the part. A young Puerto Rican guy, all sharkskin and leather. Slicked-back hair—not cut, *styled;* gun-fighter's mustache so thin it was like two black lines over his mouth. One of those big wristwatches with too many dials.

"Hector Santiago-Ramirez," he said, handing me his card. I ran my thumb over it as I slipped it into my shirt pocket. Engraved. That's Old School. Expensive, too.

I figured he got himself on the panel to get trial experience, putting in a few years before he could grab the big-score cases. Maybe had a girlfriend who kept him looking that successful while she waited for it to happen.

"What can you tell me?" he finally said, after he saw I wasn't going to say anything.

"I didn't do it."

"Okay." He smiled. "Now give me something I can use."

"I got nothing," I told him.

"Neither do they," he said.

That one blindsided me. "How do you know? I mean, I just got here. . . ."

"They *already* talked to me about a plea. If they'd had prints, fluids, security-camera tape—anything—they'd never do that. But they're way too eager to close this one. It's like they put up a bill-board: WE DON'T WANT A TRIAL!"

"Do they ever?"

"Maybe when they have a videotaped confession, couple of eye-witnesses," he said, with a thin smile.

"So I've got a shot?"

"The victim picked you out of a lineup."

"I know."

"Huh!" he said, surprised. "You know her before or something? Please don't tell me she's an old girlfriend."

"Uh-uh."

"She put sexy pictures of herself up on Facebook or something, and the cops found your laptop?"

"I don't have a computer."

"How old are you, anyway?"

"Thirty-three."

"You've got two priors. *Violence* priors, even if one was a misdemeanor. You know what that means?"

"Yeah, I know. I lose at trial, I get maxed."

"And Strike Two on top of that."

"I know," I said, thinking back. A few years ago, I got into something. If I hadn't lucked out, I'd already have that second strike. I remembered how that snotty little ADA said "one-punch homicide" about two hundred times while I was taking that manslaughter-down-to-assault plea. He just liked the sound of his own voice—everyone had agreed to the deal before we ever walked into court.

Sure, I was a lot older and smarter than after my first fall. But I didn't have the skills to slide away from the situation while it was still just an argument, the way a *real* pro would have done. I hadn't started the fight, and I sure didn't set out to murder anyone. But I believed the Legal Aid when he said a jury would take one look at me and come back with a murder rap.

Why wouldn't I believe him? He looked scared just being alone in the room with me.

A ninety-day county slap, that was sweet enough. But them letting me plead to *misdemeanor* assault, that was pure gold. Probably helped that the other guy had a lot of priors. And a knife.

It was even fair, sort of. I *had* dropped that other guy. I didn't set out to kill him, but he was just as dead.

Only I knew it wouldn't go that way again. Even with the DA already talking about a plea, I knew I was looking at felony time. All I cared about was keeping that as short as possible without giving anyone up.

I already missed smoking—I'd had to trade my whole first commissary draw for a decent shank. Rikers is no place for a white man, especially one with no Nazi ink.

"Could I see your right forearm?" the lawyer asked me.

I pulled back my sleeve to the elbow. He motioned for me to turn my hand so he could see the underside. He couldn't be looking for track marks—otherwise, he'd have wanted to look at both arms.

"I *knew* it," he said, nodding like he was agreeing with himself.

"What?"

"No tattoo. The victim said the man who raped her had one. Big one. Right forearm. She didn't get a close look, but she remembered it had a lot of red in it."

"So I'm off the—?"

"Experienced rapists always use them. Decal tattoos, I mean. It's the kind of thing victims remember."

"Yeah. They've got an answer for everything," I told him, remembering what the black cop had said about me wearing a rubber.

"But you still want to roll the dice?"

"What's the difference?" I said. "I'm going anyway. I was carrying when they grabbed me."

"Operable?" he asked. Showing me he'd handled carrying-concealed cases before. But *telling* me something else: that the DA hadn't exactly opened their files for him, like he thought they had.

"Yeah," I said. "With one in the chamber."

"You know they're going to write it up that the safety was off, right?"

"For once, they wouldn't be lying if they did. But I guarantee you there's nothing on that gun. Brand-new. Never been fired."

"You're *sure* of that?"

"Bet my life," I told him.

That would have been a safe bet. Solly always supplied the hardware on his jobs. I remember one time when one of the crew Solly put together wanted to bring his regular carry piece. Said it was his lucky lady. "That's no lucky lady," Solly told him. "In fact, that's no lady at all."

Before the guy could say anything, Solly snatched the piece out of his hand and held it up under the lightbulb hanging in the basement where we were meeting. "What's this hold, about nineteen rounds? Where're you even gonna carry it, fucking monster like that? You're planning on a gunfight, swell. But *this* job, it goes right, nobody shoots at all."

"Sometimes—" the guy started to say.

"Sometimes isn't *this* time. That's what I get paid for. On my jobs, every man carries the same. Show him, Sugar."

I took out the one Solly had given me. Short-barreled, kind of ugly.

"Ruger in forty-five," Solly said. "Whatever you hit with this, it's not getting up. The only thing that 'lady' of yours would be good for is a firefight. You want one with a SWAT team?"

"I still don't see why we all have to carry the same—"

"Because *one* guy also carries a little bag with him. That's Sugar. Soon as you start work, Sugar puts the bag down, opens the zipper. There's two hundred full magazines in there.

"You all carry the same, so you all got your ammo supply right there. Every round checked before it went into a clip—you're not gonna have to worry about jams. Even better, nobody has to worry about what the other guy's carrying. That's because none of *mine* got a past. Pure virgins, every single piece.

"See, that's no lady you're carrying, my friend; that's a whore. And you know whores: if she'll sell her pussy, she'll sell you. Get it *now*?"

I wasn't going to tell the lawyer about that. But there was something he'd need to know. I figured I might as well get it over with. "Only thing is, the serial numbers were—"

"*Not* good," the lawyer said. "Even worse if they make a call to ATF."

"You on the panel for the Federal Court, too?"

He gave me a look. I just looked back.

"I *am* on the CJA Panel," he finally said. "But that's not the point. Whatever you know about that gun, they know, too, by now.

No matter how you play it, being caught with it wasn't a good thing for you. But it's not good *enough* for them, either."

"How come?"

"Carrying, that's a felony hit all by itself, sure. But it'd be a *long* way to turn it into another violence beef. You didn't *do* anything with that gun," he said, making it a question.

"I never even pulled it," I said. "But it was ready to go."

"Maybe someone had been threatening you?"

"That's it, all right."

He was quiet for a minute, making a thing out of reading some papers he had with him. He looked up, said: "That gun, it was a regular carry piece?"

"You mean, did I walk around with it, or just happen to have it that particular day?"

"Okay," he said. Meaning, he wanted to see if I could guess what the right answer should be. If I was going to tell a story, it'd have to be a good one.

"Ever since I started getting those threats, I never left home without it," I said. "I've been shot before; it'll be on my records."

He flashed me just enough of his teeth for me to see he took real good care of them. Then he started looking through a bunch of papers he had with him, like he had all the time in the world.

I guess he did. They pay these 18-B guys by the hour. And it wasn't like I had anything better to do.

Finally, he made a little motion for me to put my face close. He wrote something on his yellow pad. I looked: NEVER VOUCHERED is what it said, in tiny letters.

I moved my lips real slow, so I could say what I wanted without making a sound: "The piece?"

"It's not anywhere in all this," he said, running his pen over what he'd shown me. He really worked at it, crosshatching the words into a black blob, but he made it seem like he didn't realize what he was doing. "Of course, it doesn't *have* to be. Like I said, I haven't filed any motions—they gave me all this without me even asking. And now I think I see why."

"It's a card they're holding back?"

"No. Listen." He leaned toward me again; I did the same toward him. He spoke so soft I could barely hear him: "The rape, it wasn't gunpoint; the guy put a—"

"Shut. The. Fuck. *Up!*" I said. Just moving my lips like before, not making a sound. But he heard me. Heard me good.

"What's your problem?" he said, backing off. "I'm just trying to—"

"Yeah, I know. But right now I could walk in and pass any polygraph they got. Sure, the operator's going to tell me I failed, see if that gets me to confess. But *they'll* see I'm not lying. That's why I talked to the cops for so long after they picked me up. I figured, sooner or later, they'd ask me, since I was innocent and all, would I mind taking the test? I had the surprise all ready for them, but they never took the bait."

"That wouldn't be admissible—"

"I know. But it's *something*, right? They started with the registered sex offenders. Stupid fucks: every joint's got plenty of rape artists who pleaded to burglary, so there's all kinds of sex fiends who wouldn't even be on that list. I figure, if she stopped when they got to my picture, they probably didn't show her any *more* pictures."

He nodded.

"Then, when I went in the lineup, she was looking for the guy who matched the picture, see?"

"Right. And that's exactly what we'll be saying. But why don't you—?"

"It's not much, but it's *something*. If you start telling me the details, that'll mess up the test . . . if they ever decide to give me one. I don't know how the girl was raped because I didn't rape her."

He leaned forward. "Straight up?"

"Hey, the cops already *know* I'm not the guy. At least the last two detectives I talked to, they know."

"If they know . . ."

"They know because they know something else. I mean, I was *doing* something else when that girl got raped."

"Ah."

"Yeah. My alibi buys me as much time as a rape would. In *this* state, probably more."

He raised an eyebrow, asking me a question. This guy knew there's things you don't say out loud, even when you're talking to a lawyer.

"Not that," I said, drawing my finger across my throat, putting distance between myself and any homicides that might have gone down during what the cops call the "critical period" when they're investigating a murder. Probably their idea of a joke.

"So . . . ?"

"So this: if they show the girl more pictures, she might change her mind. Except for this"—I touched the scar that ran down from my forehead through my right eyebrow—"the only thing that stands out is that I'm a big white guy with two different-colored eyes. The guy who actually did the rape, he's done a lot of them."

"How could you know that?"

"How come she never saw his eyes? How come they don't have a single damn drop or fiber or hair or—?"

"A pro, you're saying?"

"There's no such thing as a pro rapist. A pro works for money."

"No offense," he said, giving me a weird look. Like what did *I* have to be offended about? He was slick about the law maybe, and he could talk some of our talk, but now he was working without a map. He couldn't know I *wanted* people to say, "Sugar's a real pro." Some people, I mean. But this guy wouldn't understand that. He didn't know the people I was talking about. He didn't know our life.

"She saw what he *wanted* her to see," I told him. "Probably one of those masks on his face. Maybe contact lenses. But how was she gonna miss a guy with two different-colored eyes, like me? So, if they were to tell her I passed a polygraph, it might be enough. Anyway, if I have to go on trial, better it's for something I *didn't* do."

He leaned closer to me. "That scar, it's not that visible, even up close. But, you're right, there's no way to miss your eyes." He touched the right side of his pencil-line mustache. Manicured nails, no rings.

"I'll get back to you," he said.

Rikers never changes. Neither do the people who keep taking that bus ride. Some worked on not looking scared, others worked on looking tough. The only guys you have to watch are the ones who look bored.

The same Inside, too. They keep you separated while you get "processed," but you could still hear voices calling out what they were going to do to you as soon as you got out of the fish tank. Some of the first-timers tried shouting back at them. Most of us knew better than to waste our breath on cell gangsters.

The first test was always Population. This time, it happened real quick. Some greasy little punk half my size says, "What they call you on the street, *esé*? In here, you got to pay to stay. Otherwise, what they be calling you is the other white meat, *comprende*?"

"Azúcar," I said, smiling at him.

"What?"

"You asked me what people call me on the street, right? So I just told you . . . *esé*."

His boys were all watching, but they weren't close enough to hear anything. Maybe he was a prospect they were testing. He pulled up his shirt to show me he was carrying, but I knew he wouldn't go for it. He'd just tell the crew watching him that he'd warned me off and I'd gotten the message.

I left him a good out on purpose. Inside, if you take a man's dignity in front of his own people, he *has* to go for you, right that second. He doesn't do that, he's got no backup, ever again.

But I also know what happens if you let anyone so much as *tap* your commissary, never mind turn it all over. So I tried to practice what Solly's always telling me: the older you get, the weaker your body, so the only way to balance out is to grow a stronger mind.

Giving that punk an out, it was the same as me driving weight. Building myself bigger. Adding to the armor.

This was my third time on the Rock. First time, it was short-stay before I went Upstate. The second was that ninety-day joke. This time, it was going to be just like my first.

Except for the testing. When I was a kid, my size—and I was real big, even then—that didn't mean anything. Plenty of big guys roll right over when they see steel.

But nobody ever really pushed that hard. I even knew a few guys I had been locked up with before. Maybe they spread the word a little, I don't know.

So buying that shank this time, it was more about the message. The guy I bought from, he was AB, so I knew *they'd* know. I hadn't dealt with coloreds; that was good. But I hadn't asked to join up, and that could mean anything.

I knew flashing it would be all wrong. That's a rookie move, not something a pro does. Besides, the guy I bought it from, he'd take care of letting the word get around.

My first time in happened because I made a *lot* of rookie mistakes. Me and a couple of older guys, we figured, how is a fence ever going to run to the cops? That was before I knew some of them stay in business by switch-hitting.

I was seventeen. I wanted to be a heist-man, not a mugger. The fence wasn't any big-time guy. He ran a garage over by Shea Stadium, under the bridge. The way it worked, you drove your swag over to him; he'd close the doors, look over what you had, and tell you what he'd pay.

We had a little panel truck one of the other guys took right out of a parking lot. He picked us up and we threw in a bunch of empty cartons. Big ones, like the kind TVs come in. I sat next to the driver, and the third guy was in the back. While the fence was waiting for the guy in the back to open the boxes, I just stepped out and yoked him until he went limp.

When he came to, he reached for the phone.

My Legal Aid said I was being charged with strong-arm robbery. All that means is nobody showed a weapon.

He kept talking about a YO—that's Youthful Offender—like it
was the greatest thing in the world. The way he ran it down, if the
judge would give me a YO, my record would be sealed. That way, it
couldn't be used against me if I ever got in trouble again.

He said "again" like it was a sure thing.

I already knew that sixteen was the cutoff. No more Family
Court for me. No more rehabilitation bullshit, no more counseling,
no more GED classes. Prison.

I knew I'd have to go sooner or later if I wanted the right people to see me, so I was just as glad to get it over with.

Back then, on the Rock, they'd separate the young guys from
the older ones. That was supposed to keep us safe from "preda-
tors." I wondered if anyone actually believed that stuff.

But it wasn't bad at all. Nobody was going to be there long
enough to worry about pulling me into their crew. And I had
enough juvie time to send out the right signal: I'm not going to
gorilla anybody into anything, and I don't have anything you want,
either. But if you come at me, it's going to cost you something.

I was there a few weeks. It wasn't until I got Upstate that I
found out how that Legal Aid had screwed me over.

"What was the big deal about getting a YO?" the writ-writer asked
me. I knew I couldn't appeal behind my guilty plea, but I really
wanted that YO, and I heard I could appeal not getting *that* part.

I was surprised when he said that. Everyone said he was smarter
than any lawyer. He was in for double-life, but he'd gotten all kinds
of other guys out, 'cause he knew the law so good. Spent every day
in the law library they had up there, like it was his office. Had guys
bringing him coffee, sandwiches, whatever he wanted.

He read the look on my face. "Don't you get it, son? Far as the
judge was concerned, you were a first offender, right?"

"I . . . guess so."

"What I'm saying, you had a long juvenile record, but this was your first adult bust, right?"

"Right."

"And every time you copped to one of those kiddie crimes, didn't your lawyer say a juvenile record doesn't mean anything, because it all gets sealed?"

"Yeah."

"Yeah? Do the math. The judge on your case, he knew all about your priors. As a juvie, I'm saying."

"But if they—"

"It's pure bullshit," the writ-writer told me. "'Sealed,' all that means is they can't put it in the newspapers. They even changed that law back in '78, but that's only for homicides. And you didn't have . . . ?"

"No."

"Yeah. So, like I said, the public can't see your record. But the cops can. And they can pass that along to the ADA. And the ADA can pass that along to the judge. Just *psst-psst*, see? Nothing on paper. That YO you want me to appeal for? Even if you won, it wouldn't be worth the paper it was typed on."

"It's three crates, right?"

"I just told you—"

"Three crates to talk to you, that's what they said."

"Yeah. That's my consultation fee."

"I'll have it for you as soon as—"

"Forget it," the old con said.

"I don't take favors," I told him.

He looked up at me. "You're just dumb about *some* things, huh?"

I didn't know what to say to that. But I paid him, just like I said I would.

I didn't just learn things that first time in; I *earned* some things, too. That's when people started calling me Sugar.

Inside, color counts, but it's not like one race against another. I mean, it is, but there's lots of splitting even *inside* the colors. Like Puerto Ricans and Cubans, they're both Spanish, right? But they didn't mix. The PRs were mostly born here, but all the Cubans I ever saw, they got shipped in. *Marielitos,* the PRs called them. I didn't know what that meant, but I knew it wasn't no compliment.

The yard was divided up into what they called "courts." You couldn't step onto any crew's court without their permission, and the strongest crews claimed the best spots.

I was raised in a city where just being caught in the wrong neighborhood could get you seriously fucked up, so it kind of made sense to me. Besides, there was what they called the DMZ, places where anyone could go.

But even there you had to be on the watch. Like the weights. They'd have them out in the yard for anyone to use, and no crew ever tried to claim them. But they claimed the *time* to use them. So it wasn't just the yard that was divided up, it was everything *in* the yard, too.

That was the part I didn't know. And that was how I got my name. I was doing one-handed curls when the Muslims sent some guys over to talk to me. I saw them coming, so I was already slugging by the time they landed.

Lucky for me, they weren't carrying. I think seeing me with the weights was such a surprise that they didn't plan anything, just rushed me.

Everybody saw it, but nobody did anything. They just watched. Even the guards.

When they finally broke it up, they could see nobody was cut, so everyone got tickets for fighting. I got thirty days; I don't know what the Muslims got.

I know they got visits, though. Even in the bing, if you had religion, you could always get to see someone. Like me, I was down as Catholic, so the guards asked me if I wanted to see a priest. The Muslims, they were a religion, so there was this—I don't know what to call him—he came around every day.

One day, he stopped by my cell. He was wearing one of those

little round hats. I went over to the bars, carrying a towel wrapped around my hand in case he was there to stick me. I *had* to come to the bars, or they'd think I was weak.

He had a strong, calm voice. Kind of talked all around what he had to say, but what it came down to was that the Muslims had no beef with me. They got it that I didn't know the rules about what times you could use the weights. And they also knew I'd told the DC—the Disciplinary Committee—that I couldn't tell them who else was in the fight. It all happened so sudden, I didn't even remember what color the other guys were.

It's kind of complicated, but it wasn't like the Muslims were giving me a pass if I ever did it again, just saying I didn't need to look over my shoulder when I unlocked.

I didn't believe him, but it turned out he was telling the truth.

A few months later, I still didn't have a crew, but there was some guys I was all right with. I hung with them when they lifted. We spotted for each other—and not just on the weights. I was on my way over to them one day, just passing by this little court, when I heard something in Spanish. I figured it was about me, but I didn't want to challenge anyone without making sure I had to.

One of the guys I worked out with, his girlfriend was Latina. The first time he told me that, I thought that was her name, Latina. But I'm never dumb on the same thing twice.

Eddie was a real short guy, but he had huge arms and a big chest from pumping every day. Sitting down, he looked bigger than me. When I first came in, he could out-bench me, too. Not by the time I left, though.

Everybody liked Eddie, even the guards. He was always joking around, playing cards, goofing off. Had a smile for everyone. And he could tell some *great* stories—he only took vacations from jail to get some new material, is what he said.

One of the things that made his stories so good was how he could make his voice sound like other people's. He used that trick even when he wasn't telling stories, just to stop other guys from getting . . . depressed, or whatever you want to call it.

I remember when Reno came over to talk to us. Well, to me,

really. Reno was deep into that White Power stuff, and Eddie had tipped me they'd be coming around. "You look like a recruiting poster for some Aryan army, kid. Blond/blue, big and buffed. All you need is some ink."

I'd told Eddie that I didn't want anything to do with that crew. All that political stuff sounded weird to me. "What does a thief need with politics?" I asked him.

"That's a good one," he said, like I just told a great joke.

I didn't try and find out what I'd said that was so funny; I was just happy that a guy like Eddie thought I could tell a good joke.

Anyway, when Reno kind of strolls over one day, Eddie heads him off: "Sir, you *do* realize you are entering New York's most exclusive men's club? Membership is restricted to those bearing a personal invitation from the Governor."

Reno gave him a look. Then he decided Eddie was joking around, so he laughed along with the rest of us.

Then him and Eddie took a little walk. Not far, but enough so I couldn't hear what they were saying. The way they said goodbye, Eddie tapped his own chest, right over his heart, and Reno did the same.

"No ink, kid. Understand me? No ink, not *ever*. You don't go along with that, you could get me killed."

"I don't have any—"

"Yeah," he cut me off. "I know. That's what I used to pull that fool's chain."

"But you've got . . . I mean . . ." I felt so bad. I knew Eddie was trying to look out for me, but I was too fucking stupid to even figure out how he was doing it. Eddie's whole body was so covered with tattoos that it looked like he was wearing a shirt even when he wasn't.

"Look close," Eddie said. He touched his chest with one finger.

"I don't see—"

"I said *close*, bro."

It was like trying to read one of those walls when one gang overtags another, and then the first one comes back. After a while, it just looks like a mess. But I kept trying. And then I saw it. One of those Nazi crosses, only it was made out of lightning bolts and arrows. You couldn't see all of it—a lot of it was buried under other tats. But it was there.

"Get it now?" Eddie asked me. "If they need to check, the AB can see they got my heart. You can see it yourself, right where it should be. Only, I had to get it covered up. Like camouflage, see?"

"So nobody could see—"

"So the fucking *cops* can't see it. That's what they do now: they read a man's ink, and it goes in their book. But they look at me, they just see this big mess. I got every kind of ink you could think of, so I get put down as a tattoo-freak."

"What's so good—?"

"What'd I just *tell* you, kid? Okay, one more time, real slow. That fool who came over before, what I told him was that the Brotherhood needs men who can slip under the radar. We don't go to meetings, we don't be going all 'Heil Hitler!' on the yard, nothing like that. The law's got undercovers; why shouldn't we?"

"But you told me to never get one."

"Ain't *that* undercover, too, bro?"

"*That's* why you said never get any ink at all."

"And that still goes. I just told that sucker I was getting you ready for this big mission. Feeding you one spoon at a time. So you can't be seen hanging with the Double-Eights."

"He bought that?"

Eddie grinned. "You know what he's in for? Cooking up some crank. And guess who he sold it to?"

It was like Eddie's smile made me smarter. I know that's crazy, but that's how it felt, me hitting the right answer on the nose. "An undercover cop?"

"Oh yeah!" Eddie said, holding up his palm for me to slap, laughing.

Eddie, he was welcome all over the place. So I was glad he was there that day—you couldn't want a better guy to ask.

"You know what *azúcar* means, Eddie?"

He was on the last rep of the set he was doing. I thought he'd let the bar down first, but he kept the weight up and answered me between nose-breaths. "Sure." "Means." "Sugar."

Soon as he said that, I turned around and looked over at the PRs, trying to find the one that had said that word. I let them see me staring. That way, whoever said that about me, he'd have to step out.

Eddie put the weight down so quick it was a good thing the spotters saw it coming. He hopped off the bench and stood next to me.

"Hey! Don't chump yourself off, kid. You want to be like every other paranoid peckerwood in this joint? Just 'cause guys're talking a different language don't mean they're talking about *you*."

"Yeah, but—"

"Take a deep breath; you're gonna feel like a blockhead in about a minute. Listen: You know there's still Spanish guys in here for blowing up buildings and stuff, years ago? Older guys. Not gang-bangers—like political prisoners, okay? *Los Macheteros,* they call themselves. That comes from slaves who had to spend all day in the cane fields. What they wanted was to cut Puerto Rico loose from America, be its own country."

"What's that got to do with me?"

"I'm pretty tight with some of them," Eddie kept going, like he never heard me. "Good men, you get to know them. Smart as hell, and stand-up, too. You with me? Okay, now, some of them were watching that day you got jumped by those Muslims. The way they told it, you went through those fools like you was working in the cane fields. Chopping 'em down like you had a machete."

"I still don't see—"

"That's your last name, right? Caine?"

"Yeah . . ."

"I know you spell it different, but it sounds the same. Cane fields, they're talking about *sugar*cane, get it?

"Nobody was downing you, kid. *Azúcar,* it's all in how you say it. Like when people say a boxer's 'pretty,' you heard that, right? 'Pretty' don't mean he's a punk; it means he's slick and smooth."

Eddie reached up high, then brought his hand down into a fist. Held it in front of his mouth, like it was a microphone.

"Ladies, gentlemen, and those who have yet to decide," he boomed out. "Tonight we bring you fifteen rounds of boxing for the heavyweight championship of the world! In this corner, weighing in at a ready two hundred and eighty pounds, sporting a perfect record of twenty-six wins, twenty-four by knockout, two by fix . . . the challenger: Timmy 'Sugar' *Caaaiinne*!"

Everybody standing around the weight stack clapped, like I really was going to go against someone. One guy even yelled out that he had major money on me.

"You like it *now*, kid?"

I sure did. Beat the hell out of people calling me "Tiny." You know, "Tiny Tim." Big fucking joke.

After a while, everybody started calling me Sugar. When I gated, I took it with me.

That was a long time ago. I hadn't taken a felony fall since I wrapped up that first bit. Seven arrests, one misdemeanor conviction. The other cases all got dropped, one way or another.

My fall partners on that first one, the two older guys, they never did anything for me while I was Inside. Well, maybe one thing: they got the word around. I was taking the weight, like you're supposed to. If I'd "cooperated"—I don't know why I fucking *hate* that word, but I do—the Legal Aid had told me, I could probably get probation.

What was I going to do with probation, go to college?

But being known as stand-up so young, that gave me a head start. I was only on the bricks for a few weeks when a guy I didn't know asked me if I was interested in doing a job. A job with him and a few other men.

I didn't know that guy, but I'd sure *heard* of him. I felt proud he asked me.

I wished Eddie could have seen me then. But I knew he'd see the money orders I got this girl to send him. Not the money orders themselves, but he'd see the jumps in his account. I had the girl write him one time, to tell him money would be coming. It was a short letter, but starting it off with "Hey, Sugar!" would be all he needed to make the connect.

It wasn't really a girl sending the money. What I did, I picked a name. Conchita. Then I got about a hundred sheets of notepaper, and I paid this hooker a buck a page for her to sign at the bottom. All different ways, like:

Love, Conchita

Always yours, Conchita

I love you forever, Conchita

Except for those words at the bottom, the notes were all typed. I did that. The envelopes, too. After a while, I got pretty good at it.

I kept sending the money orders every few months or so for about ten years. Then the girl got a letter at the PO box I was using. One of those form letters. It was a whole page, but all I remember is: "Inmate Deceased."

In my head, I could see Eddie. Back to the wall, facing slicers and stabbers with his bare hands. Grinning like it was all a big joke.

I learned a lot. Every job, I learned more.

It's no different from those guys who work high steel. They know they *could* fall, but the more time they spend up there, the less they expect to. Still, they never forget it could happen.

Even though I didn't expect to take this fall, I knew *how* to take it. So, when they put me in a double, I knew what that was all about.

My cellie turned out to be a white guy; skinny, eyes still yellow from whatever he'd been using before they snapped him up. He was probably around my age, but he looked way older than me. Covered in cheap tats, kind of a hillbilly sound in his voice.

"You got a preference?" he said. "To me, they're all the same."

He meant the bunks. Me, I always like the top one. Figured the guy was saving face by claiming he didn't care.

He was good at the game. Pretty much kept to himself. Told me his name was Sandy, touching his hair when he said it, to tell me where the name came from. "Farin," I said, like I was giving my name, too.

"Like Faron Young? Damn, you don't look like—"

"I'm not. Born and raised right here. It's 'Farin,'" I said, spelling it for him.

"Never heard that one before."

"It's a nickname. Short for 'Warfarin.'"

"Viking name?" he said, pretending he was asking if I was a White Power guy. But he'd already seen me with my shirt off, so I was even surer I was right about him.

"No. See, warfarin is a chemical. They use it in rat poison."

I'd been waiting over ten years to use that line, ever since I first heard Eddie tell the story. Now I could tell it, too.

He tried to bluster up. "You trying to tell me something?"

"Yeah. Yeah, I am. I know why they put you in here. Take as much time as you think you can get away with; that's fine with me. But you're not cutting a deal for yourself off anything *I* tell you . . . because I'm not telling you nothing. And I don't talk in my sleep."

"You got me all—"

"Try and work me, you won't like what happens next," I cut him short. "No matter where they put you."

I learn from my mistakes. I got it down to such a science, I could be one of those counselors' wet dreams. Learning from your bad choices, they *love* that stuff.

That's why I never showed anyone my new shank. I know—I know *now*, I mean—that you never show a guy who might be a problem for you that you've got something for him. If he's not bluffing, that won't back him off, just make him bring something himself for next time. And if he was bluffing, showing him steel might just turn him serious. You can buy anything Inside. Even guys to do your work for you.

Whoever wants you, if he knows you're carrying, he's going to come in careful. Maybe even bring along some backup. And you never want that.

A guy who's gunning for you should never know you're carrying steel, until he feels it go in.

After a few weeks, I started to get steady mail from a woman. The letters sounded like we'd been together for a long time. And she always put in a little note, telling me she'd just put more money on the books for me.

This woman, she was always promising to wait for me, no matter how long that turned out to be. Solly, paying the premiums on his insurance policy.

I knew that much just from the woman's name. Marcy. That's what they call the loony bin—where they put you if they decide you're "criminally insane." Solly telling me, maybe I wanted to go the NGI route, say I got hit on the head and I couldn't remember anything, crap like that.

He was just reminding me that I could take a plea to the rape, and nobody would think it was for real. Wouldn't hurt my rep when I got out.

You pull off a job, every man gets his share. The planner, he's supposed to take care of anyone who gets caught, make sure they stay quiet. That's one of the reasons he gets half of the whole haul.

So, yeah, I got the messages. Both of them. I was being railroaded on the rape charge, but there was no point in me taking passengers along on the ride. And my money would still be there when I finally got off the train.

I wondered when that would be.

It took over a month for that slick Puerto Rican lawyer to come by and answer my question. Under his charcoal suit, he was wearing a dark-purple shirt with a white collar and cuffs, silk tie same color as the shirt. On the left cuff, "HSR," embroidered in thread the same color as the shirt, too. Some woman was dressing him, all right.

"If they max you on the rape, you're looking at half of twenty-five before you even see the Board."

The first time up's an automatic hit, so I had to figure on at least thirteen and a half. That's a tattoo you see a lot on old-time cons: "13½." Means twelve jurors, one judge, half a chance.

I shook my head. Not saying no, just . . . tired, I guess.

"I don't want to take this to trial," the lawyer said.

"I'm not gonna—"

"I know," he said. "But here's something else I know—*they* don't want to try it, either."

"You said the lineup—"

"I also said the lineup was *all* they had," he said, tapping a yellow legal pad with a fancy-looking pen—black enamel, with a touch of gold around the point. "And that's weak as water."

"But it's still a dice roll, right?"

"Right. And they don't like playing unless it's *their* dice."

"That much I know. But I got nothing to trade. And I wouldn't if I did. Only thing is . . ."

"What?"

"How come *you* don't like it?" I asked him. Not only did I know 18-B lawyers get paid by the hour, I could tell this guy wasn't scared of trials.

He waited until he was sure he had my eyes. Then he said, "There's one kind of client no defense attorney *ever* wants. You know what kind that is?"

"The kind that can't pay the freight."

"Sure," he said. Meaning, What else?

"I give up," I told him.

"An *innocent* one. That's every defense attorney's nightmare."

"So you believe me, too?"

"I talked to the cops who interrogated you. One of them, he as much as said it, flat out. You wouldn't even need that polygraph."

"The older guy, right?"

"I don't know. I didn't see the other one. Detective Woods, that's all I can tell you."

"Yeah. Well, if he told you he knows I didn't do that rape, he must've also told you *why*, too."

The lawyer nodded.

"So what's the difference? Time is time. Maybe I can't beat the rape case, but it's no slam dunk for them, either. I don't know why that girl picked me out of the lineup, but—"

"She's already been in the Grand Jury," the lawyer said, making sure I understood what he was telling me. Which was, if anything happened to her before the trial, the prosecutor could use her Grand Jury testimony . . . and that would be a lot worse for me. The jury might do the math, figure I had the woman hit. And even if they didn't, how was my lawyer going to cross-examine a transcript?

"I get it," I said. "I was just saying, maybe when she sees me in the courtroom, looks at me real close, she'll see something she didn't see when . . . it happened to her."

"Just any little thing, I don't know. She ID'ed me off a photo— at first, I mean—but she'd already told them *something*. And my eyes, they would have been in the book.

"Only what if she never saw the guy's eyes? Any little thing could do it. Maybe she just said the guy was big because he was like . . . large, you know. A fat guy, even. At least it's a chance."

"That's a double-edged razor, that chance," he said. "Could even be worth taking . . . if it wasn't for the gun."

"That's a pound, tops. I could do that stand—"

"Sure. Unless the judge decides you're a menace to society, and consecs you. Not taking a plea deal, that's enough to turn you into that kind of menace real quick. And they've got leverage on their deal, too. That gun again. If they were to call in the *federales* . . ."

He just let those words trail off, like making me look down into this pit so deep I couldn't even see the bottom.

"You came all the way out here just to tell me I'm fucked? Next time, send a postcard," I told him.

"They put an offer on the table. Not a bargaining chip. One time only. You want to hear it?"

"Sure," I said. What else?

"Five years on the rape charge. They knock it down to some kind of sex assault, make it a D felony. You're a predicate, so you're looking at two-and-a-half to five. And they forget about the gun. They never found one."

"Why couldn't they give me the five on the gun, and forget about the—?"

"And have picket lines all around the DA's Office? Sure, that miserable relic's finally stepping down, but he wants to name his own successor. Preserve his 'legacy.' Get a building named after him before he checks out. So anyone who wants to move up in *that* office has to be aces at getting the victim to go along with a deal— make her afraid of being cross-examined, you know how it works. Remember, the Mayor and the old DA, they weren't exactly pals, so there's serious pressure to *keep* getting those convictions, be tough on crime for the media. You do the math."

"If I take the rape—"

"Everything else goes away."

"Not everything," I reminded him.

"What do you want, immunity? Look, that's the deal. Take it or leave it. But if you take it, and one of your crime partners gets nabbed for something else . . ."

He looked at me close when he paused. But if he expected me to show him a new face, he'd grow old waiting on it.

"If that happens, you better hope he holds it together like you did," the lawyer said. "Because, if they can tie you to *that* job, they will."

"So I could end up doing time for the one I . . . for the one they *think* I did, plus the one they *know* I didn't."

"Exactly."

"Wait!" I remembered something. At least I thought I did. "What's the statute of limitations on . . . whatever they think I was really doing when that girl was raped?"

"Five years," he said. "Of course, if they could prove you eluded prosecution, left the jurisdiction, anything like that, they could get the time extended."

"But if I'm in their custody for the whole five, *they're* the ones who're fucked."

"Exactly." He leaned back in his chair, smiling like a guard dog giving you fair warning. Waiting.

"Tell them they just bought themselves a rapist," I said.

It was all supposed to go down quick-and-dirty, but the only thing that fucking judge got right was the dirty part. The fat-faced pig started off asking me simple questions, playing his role like he was supposed to. But then he switched up and started playing it for the papers. Made a big speech about how *he,* personally, didn't like the deal, but he was going to respect the wishes of the victim, especially because her therapist's report said that the stress of a trial might be too much for her.

I just looked straight ahead. He wanted to pose, what did I care? But then he goes and wrecks the train.

"Mr. Caine," he says, "I want you to tell the court *exactly* what happened on the night of July 3, 2005."

I didn't fucking *know* what happened.

My lawyer and the DA rushed the bench together. I couldn't hear what they were saying, but it looked bad—the judge was getting all red in the face.

When my lawyer came back, he whispered to me, "The deal was, no allocution. We'll have to straighten him out in chambers."

They called a recess. I went back to the holding cell. They probably had a long lunch.

When they brought me back in, my lawyer told me, "Just say 'yes' every time they ask you a question."

After that, it didn't take long. Then they were all finished with me.

The papers said I got five years. They always report the max, never the minimum.

But, this time, they weren't lying. I knew the Board was never going to cut me loose early. It's easier to do time when you don't get yourself all fucked up hoping for something. Hoping for anything, that's a mistake.

I didn't last long in the Sex Offender Treatment Unit. Once they finally figured out I was never going to talk about some rape I never did, they kicked me out. That's when I knew I wasn't getting any of that "good time" off my sentence for sure.

If you wanted to be in treatment, you had to talk about what you did. They called it "owning your behavior." I thought that was pretty funny, considering that the only reason you were there was that the State owned your body.

Some stooge—greasy little slob, a real veteran of what they called "group"—he decided to confront me.

"Confront" is what they call it when you get to spit on a guy and he can't make you pay for doing it. Like calling a man a pussy from the other side of the bars.

"You have to take responsibility, Tim," he said. "That's when the healing can begin."

"The assholes of those little kids you fucked, think *they* healed up by now, ChiMo?"

"We're not talking about me."

"Who's 'we,' ChiMo? *I'm* talking about you. What's *your* problem? Too much fucking 'stress'? You don't like it, go back to your cell and jack off some more, you baby-raping sack of puke."

"No personal attacks," the whiny little shrink who came in twice a week to run the group said, not looking at me. "And we don't use terms like 'ChiMo' in here."

"Look in one of those books of yours," I told the shrink. "See if it tells you what it means, you call a guy 'ChiMo' like it's his name."

"I know what it means," he told me, all snotty and superior.

"No, you don't. You think all it means is 'child molester'?

Maybe in this room. But outside this little 'group' of yours, it's another world. And it's got different rules."

"We all agreed—"

"'All'? Me, I didn't agree to shit."

I turned in my chair so I could look at all of them, one at a time. "How many of you skinners walk the yard? You, the greasy punk with the beard, you think fucking your own kid makes you special? Yeah, I know, you're *all* special, right?"

None of them said a word.

"What's *that* tell you?" I asked the shrink.

He looked everywhere but my eyes, rubbed the patch on the elbow of his sport jacket, like it would give him strength. "Societal attitudes—"

"Man, I can see why they all love you. Gonna write a lot of sweet letters to the Parole Board for them, huh? You fucking chump—all that college and you still get played for a retard? Or maybe you just get your rocks off listening to their stories, is that it?"

I crossed my arms. Not to make the biceps pop, the way some of those iron freaks do. Just to wall me off from them . . . and make them see it. "Me, I'm not in PC," I said. "I can walk the yard." I turned to look at the shrink. "You think that's because of your faggot 'societal attitudes,' you don't know shit. I can walk the yard because the people out there don't care about what you did to someone else—they only care about what you can do to *them.*"

When I got back from Yard later, I found the paper in my cell. I knew it had to be from the people who run the place—who else's got enough juice to get a kite put right on your bunk?

It said I was "found to be a poor candidate for treatment" because . . . ah, the rest was a bunch of words I didn't give a damn about. Just another reason for the Parole Board to hit me when I came up. Like they needed *another* one.

You never count the days unless your sentence is *in* days, like that county-jail slap I got before. Ninety days, that's a number you can count. Felony time, the faster you move, the slower it goes.

They sent me to the joint I wanted. Not because I asked or anything. Probably because they figured it would be the last place I'd want.

Dannemora. "Little Siberia" is what everybody called it. Just a few miles from the Canadian border. Nobody wants to jail there, because it means your family has to travel a whole day just to get a visit. Most of them, they come up the day before, stay at some motel. So it's really a three-day trip. That all costs money, makes it even harder.

Black guys *really* hate the place. They're all city boys. Not only do their people have to come all that distance to see them, but the town where they have to stay, everyone knows why they're there. The Latinos don't like it much, either.

But it's a good place for a guy like me. Everyone wants to transfer out, so the race-war thing is dialed way down. And if you don't try to go into business for yourself—like getting your girlfriend to mule in some dope, or opening a gambling book—you don't make anybody mad at you, either.

Lots of notorious guys were there when I was. I mean, guys you would have read about in the paper. Like that "Preppie Killer." When the jury hung on his first murder trial, they let him plead to manslaughter, and threw in a bunch of burglaries, no charge. Another one had killed hookers. Lots of them.

For most cons, the more of those kind, the better. They were always getting money sent in, and you could usually muscle them off a piece of their haul when they drew commissary.

I never did that. The best way to do your own time is to stay out of the rackets—even the little ones, like trading your phone time.

You never take favors. Like when a con offers to get a girl to visit you. His girlfriend, she's got a friend. All it's supposed to cost you is a slice of whatever you manage to work the girl for.

No use telling the other guy you've already got a girl, since anyone can see you're not getting visits. So you have to say no and make sure he never asks you again.

The first time I hit the yard, I was a little surprised that I didn't know one single guy out there. Eddie was gone, but I figured, my life, the odds were pretty good I'd know *someone.* I guess any decent outlaw would have managed to work himself into a joint where there was more action.

Action was what you needed if you were pulling a long piece of time. Me, I was probably the shortest guy in the whole pen. They used to keep this place reserved for the hardcores: double-lifers, cons who had stuck a guard, top-shelf gangsters. Then the dumb fucks who run the system figured out that a joint full of men with nothing to lose wasn't such a bright idea. I think it might have been the guards' union that tipped them off.

My account was always kept full, so I could get what I needed without going on the arm, or putting in work for one of the crews.

I *paid* for smokes, never borrowed any. After a while, I just quit. Whole goddamned place was supposed to be smoke-free, so you couldn't walk around with a pack, much less a crate. You had to do one at a time, and you'd catch a ticket if you got caught, too. Fuck all that.

You'd think prison, it'd be the last place to change. From the outside, it might look that way, but things had really shifted since I'd been away the last time. Even what the cons called the guards: it was "hacks" my first time, now it was "COs" or "cops."

Changing what you call things doesn't make them different.

There's two kinds of contraband: the kind that gives you power inside the prison, and the kind that you could use to get out.

The first kind mostly comes from drugs. Which means they have to be muled in. The gang that has the best traffic system could buy a lot more power with the profits. More fancy sneakers, more color TVs—stuff you could buy, that was how you showed off.

My first time, everyone knew the mob guys didn't use mules. They got their supply direct from the prison pharmacy. It was the best connection of all, until the blacks started jumping them, right out in the open. That wasn't about black against white; it was about gang against gang. The black gang might have been nothing on the street, but Inside, they way outnumbered the mob guys.

Some of the blacks ended up binged for life. Only too many of the mob guys ended up dead, so the blacks took over the drug trade anyway.

That was a long time ago, but I could see it was still that way. Only now, the Spanish guys had their own operation, too.

What did change was that other kind of contraband. On my first bit, if you got caught holding soft money, they'd lock you down tight. And if you got caught with a pistol—not a zip, the real thing—you'd probably never see daylight.

Only reason to have soft money was if you were planning to slip out. If you go without a dime in your pocket, you're as good as caught. Plenty of guys plan how to get out, but don't have a clue on what they're going to do once they clear the wall.

You can't make a life-without sentence longer, but you can sure make it harder. Anyone who ever got brought back after making an escape could tell you that.

A zip gun, that's for settling an individual beef, not for trying to bust out. Even a real pistol's no good for that—you can threaten to kill a guard all day and they're not going to open the gates. But it's great for taking hostages, and getting a lot of cells opened. Which means a riot.

Nobody could mule a pistol in. But a couple of gang bosses were known to have access to one. There *had* to be guards in on a deal like that.

That's the first thing that hit me. I hadn't been away that long, but now it seemed like nobody cared about going for the Wall anymore. The guys with real juice, they could get anything they wanted right there. They didn't care about soft money. Or even pistols. What they really wanted was cell phones.

A cell phone, that's super-bling. The ultimate. Perfect for a shot-caller who's never getting out of Ad-Seg. That's what they call the hole they dump you in for heavy violence now. Stands for "Administrative Segregation."

With a cell, the shot-caller can reach out anytime he wants. And touch somebody, too.

I thought that was amazing, but a guy who'd done time in

Mexico told me the narco kingpins *always* had cell phones there. Carried them around, nobody said a thing.

Some of the shot-callers spent too much time in Ad-Seg. Once they snapped that it was really going to be forever, it drove them nuts. They used those cell phones all the time, texting members outside about who needed to be hit.

If you're in *that* guy's crew, there's no way out. If you say out loud that he's having people hit for no reason, you'll be the next to go. And even if you keep quiet, you could end up on that same list anyway.

Yeah, that was the real difference. Instead of scheming to get out, everyone was scheming how to make their life better right where they were. You can't even *plan* an escape without some help. My last time up, the gangs trusted each other a lot more, too. Now being crewed up didn't mean you were safe. Not even from your own guys.

Outside, I never went near dope. In my line of work, nobody trusts a junkie. You get a rep for that, you're done.

For sex fiends, it's even worse. A junkie *might* kick his habit. An alkie *might* get off the booze. But no sex fiend ever gets off *his* train. Everybody knows that. Except maybe the people who run those bullshit "programs."

Or maybe they *do* know. It's a pretty good hustle. The State pays you to do something that can't be done, so you don't get blamed when one of them goes right back to doing what he likes to do after he's been cut loose.

There's another part about that "treatment" thing—it probably makes them harder to catch the next time. Those slimy fucks may call it "group," but all they're doing is passing around trade secrets. How this one slipped up with something on his computer, or this one took pictures with his phone and never deleted them. I guess you go through enough of those programs, you learn a bunch of new tricks.

So, yeah, probably it *does* look like the treatment works. I mean, how are they going to "relapse"—that's what they call it, when a sex sicko gets caught the next time, "relapse"—when they spend years learning how not to get caught the time?

What I did was: watch a lot of TV, read some books, work out every damn day. I even answered some of "Marcy's" letters, just to make sure Solly knew I was holding tight.

When I wrote Marcy that we'd pick up right where we left off, Solly'd understand that meant I'd be looking for my money.

Before I knew it, I'd already done the minimum.

The two weasels they sent up to decide what they'd "recommend" to the whole Board came with pages of reasons to deny me. I gave them a couple more. The man asked me, "Have you attempted to make any sort of restitution to your victim?"

"I don't have a victim," I told him.

"You're saying you're innocent."

"Bring in a polygraph, you'll see it for yourself."

"It's common knowledge that sociopaths are immune to polygraph examinations," the woman said. "A polygraph doesn't detect lies, it measures consciousness of guilt. And it's clear from your record that you qualify."

"Qualify as what?"

"A sociopath," she said, real fussy-like. "You exhibit a pervasive pattern of conduct which—"

"Sure. I get it. Look, you're not going to stamp my ticket no matter what, so just call it off, okay? I'm missing a show I always watch."

"What show is that?" the woman asked, like she really was curious.

"This whole place," I told her.

People on the other side of the law from me, I never tell them the truth. By now, it's more than just a habit; it's who I am. So, even when I did what they *wanted* me to do, I kept it to myself.

Like how they were always saying I should be "reflecting" on my crime. I actually did that.

I spent a *lot* of time thinking about the crime.

A lot of time hating.

Not the girl. It wasn't her fault I was in there. If she picked me, she must have believed I was the guy who did it. Or else she got pressured into it. That happens, too.

I didn't hate her—I hated the rapist. *He fucked us both,* I thought to myself. But I felt dirty just thinking of it like that, so I changed it. He *hurt* us both. That was better.

I'm not a killer by nature, the way some guys are. I don't go looking for it; I don't get a kick out of it, nothing like that. But, for this guy, I'd make an exception. I'd really like killing him. Specially if I could tell him why first.

It'd be extra great if the girl he raped got to watch.

I thought about that all the time. I even dreamed about the guy who did it. But I could never see his face.

I didn't think the girl had seen it, either. But maybe she knew *something*. Something the cops never connected to anything. Or even asked her about.

What I couldn't figure out was, how was *I* going to ask her?

The one good thing about maxing out is you're off paper the minute they close the gate behind you.

After that, they don't give a fuck. Why should they? Some cons are psycho mad dogs who'd tear a hole in your throat with their teeth for looking at them wrong. But the ones the guards in Ad-Seg really hated were the gassers—the ones who were so mental that they'd save up their own shit just so they could throw it at anyone passing by.

Too dangerous to be in Population, but they're fine for the street. Like doing time cures people or something.

You just walk through the gate, get on the bus. They've got one going downstate every day. Costs more than a plane ride, but they can charge whatever they want—there's no competition. Like with the collect calls. You can only call collect if the person you're calling agrees to accept it . . . and that means they pay through the nose for every minute. The phone company splits the take with the prison. They got guys in here for working that same kind of racket on the street.

I'd X'ed out my old apartment the minute they'd clamped the cuffs on. I wouldn't ask anyone to go back there for me; anything of mine was long gone by now. The super wouldn't know nothing. The landlord was some company name. And the cops weren't running a storage facility.

I didn't have much in there, anyway.

They'd vouchered what I had on me when I was picked up. Only the three grand and change got turned into six C-notes.

I wondered what they'd done with the pistol, but I wasn't worried about trace evidence on any of my clothes. After the job, we'd all gone back to this place Solly had rented. Left every stitch of clothes in these plastic bags he'd left behind. Took a good, long hot shower. Rubbed ourselves down with alcohol. Nails, hair, everything.

Then we each put on the stuff we'd been wearing when we first met up there.

"A good thief takes money, not chances," Solly said. He was always saying it.

He believed it, too. Solly never went along on any job he put together.

I had a phone number for him. I knew it was just a pay phone, someplace in Manhattan. Indoors, so nobody could try and set up shop with it.

But first I had things to do.

I had almost seven hundred left over—what I had on the books and my gate money. Not enough. I wasn't going anywhere near my share until I was carrying more than high hopes.

The money was enough for a prepaid cell and a night at this hotel every loser in the city knows about. One step above a flophouse, and they still charge over a hundred a night. Taxes, you know.

I didn't even bother to undress. The room made my cell look ritzy. The lock wouldn't stop a drunk who forgot his room number, never mind a guy who knew where to kick. No phone.

I could smell the disinfectant they probably hosed down the dump with every day. Didn't see any roaches, but I wasn't going to take a chance on bedbugs—or worse—in that foul-looking pad they called a mattress.

After I fixed the place so I'd get some warning if anyone tried to visit me, I rolled up my jacket on the floor and closed my eyes.

The next morning, I found a pay phone.

"What?" is all the guy at the other end said.

"I'm an old pal of Solly's," I said. "Haven't seen him for quite a while. About five years."

"Ain't no Solly here, friend."

"Let me leave you my number, just in case he walks by."

When he didn't hang up, I knew I was connected.

I went back to that fleabag. They kick you out at eleven-thirty in the morning, pounding on the doors like they had search warrants. When I hadn't heard anything by noon, I checked in for another night, just to be off the street.

The same desk clerk took my money. If he remembered me from the night before, you couldn't tell. I signed the register with a different name. He didn't look at it, just gave me the key and the usual speech about how I'd be held responsible if . . . It was a long list; I walked off while he was still talking.

My new cell rang a little after dark. I pushed the button, heard: "Don't say my name." Solly's voice.

"Okay."

"Say something that'll show me you're who I think you are. Nothing stupid, understand?"

I knew then that Solly had already recognized my voice from the "Okay." Solly liked me. He knew I was certified stand-up. Hell, he knew I'd just finished proving it all over again. But he never had too high an opinion of my IQ.

"Thanks for the warning," I said.

I could hear him chuckling before he said, "You got a place?"

"No."

"Good. Why don't you drop by? We'll talk over old times."

"When?"

"I'll keep a light on for you."

The light was at the back of an old apartment building, hanging over the stone steps down to the basement. It sat inside a little cage of wire mesh. You couldn't break the light by accident, and if you tried to poke something through the wire, a pair of giant navigation lights like they use on fishing boats would blast off right in your eyes.

There was a camera mounted behind the door. The lens was like the peephole for an apartment door, and the camera's motor drive would start firing as soon as the lights went on. A cable ran from the camera to some kind of computer. Solly once told me that even if someone used a battering ram on the door, their pictures would be in a safe place before they could get to the computer, so I guessed the computer automatically sent the pictures someplace else.

I didn't know all this because Solly trusted me. I know why he told me. Me and anyone else who knew where to find him. That's why I called and got the okay from him first.

Even so, I stood under the light long enough for him to see whatever he needed. Then I rapped two knuckles on the door. Three times, tap-tap-tap. I waited a couple of seconds, then I did it again. Seven, that time. Another wait before I slapped my palm against the panel. You had three shots to hit blackjack, and a flat palm counted as an ace.

I heard the metal-against-metal sound of a deadbolt being thrown open. Heavy metal. I didn't wait after that. Just turned the knob and stepped inside, pulling the door shut behind me.

The room was so dark all I could make out was the shape of a man behind a desk.

"What more do you need?" I said.

"I didn't get to be this old taking chances," Solly said. Not from behind the desk. That shape was a dummy. If you walked in shooting, you'd be punching holes in some plastic thing with clothes on it. Solly would be off to the side, one of those old Jew submachine guns in his lap. One long burp, everything on the wrong side of the barrel is dead.

And if more men were waiting outside, Solly still had an out. There was a second room behind the first one. Nothing in there but a giant freezer and piles of old books. And a door that would take him out to the hall. By the time anyone got a flashlight working, he'd be upstairs, in the apartment he lived in.

I'd never been in that apartment. Couldn't even tell you what floor it was on. Or even if Solly was telling the truth about it. What he told me was all I knew. I never asked him any questions.

"So?" Solly says. "Come on over and sit with an old friend."

A soft light showed me Solly's chair and another one, empty. One, only. Solly never let more than one person at a time in his basement.

That's what he told me, anyway.

I sat down. The chair looked old. It was comfortable, though. And soft, real soft. You sank deep down into it. Like sitting in quicksand.

There was some kind of little table to my right. Fresh ashtray, little box of matches.

"Go ahead," Solly told me. "Don't worry about the windows. I got a machine, filters out the smoke."

What he meant was, the basement windows had all been bricked up.

"I gave it up."

"Yeah? Good for you, kid. You want something to drink, maybe?"

"No thanks."

"Relax, okay? I was gonna do anything, I could have done it already."

"I know."

"You got the money, right?"

"The money you sent me Upstate? Yeah. I appreciate that. Made the time a lot easier. Those magazines, too. I never heard of cons subscribing to magazines before."

"Depends on the joint," Solly said. "Some, you can mail in just about anything. Others, you'd be lucky to get even a letter from your own lawyer."

"Yeah. Well, like I said, Solly, I'm grateful and all, but—"

"—where's the rest of your money, huh?"

"I don't care *where* it is."

"You didn't use to be this cute, Sugar. What'd you do, take one of those college courses while you were away?"

"I'm not the one being cute here, Solly. Everyone else got their money. Me, I waited a long time for mine. I don't even know how much there is, but we had to have cleared enough to give me a vacation. A long vacation."

"You don't want to work anymore?"

"Fuck, what *is* this? I don't know how big a pie there is to slice, but I know it won't be enough for me to live on the rest of my life, okay? So, yeah, I'm going back to work. But not for a while. There's something I've got to do first."

"What are you—?"

"Just give me my fucking money, Solly."

"Ah. Now, *that's* the Sugar I know. You want the numbers; I got the numbers. The stones came out to around five mil, retail. Even when loose stones are GIA-registered, you can still usually get about half for them. Overseas, I mean."

When Solly said "overseas," I knew he meant Asia. Just something I found out on my own. Solly never tells people anything, except what to do.

"So," he said, "figure around two-point-five. Take off expenses, came out to a little more than two. You, Big Matt, and Jessop did the job, so it's a three-way split."

He didn't bother to say that it was a three-way split of *half*. That's always Solly's deal. He sets up the job, does all the planning, deals with disposing of whatever the team he puts together takes, turns it into cash. For that, his piece is 50 percent.

One time, Solly even had to turn cash into cash. The thick stack of bills we found in one of the safe-deposit boxes I pried open sure looked used, but Solly said the consecutive serial numbers meant it couldn't be spent here. "Overseas," again.

I figured that box belonged to a bent cop. That's what some of them do—take cash out of the buy-money bin and replace it with their own stuff. The count comes out right, so nobody catches wise. Maybe that blows a buy-and-bust for the narco boys somewhere down the line, but a cop on the take wouldn't care about that. What he'd want was a way to track down his *own* money, in case some guy like me got his hands on it.

"So I've got about three-fifty coming."

"Not quite. Pretty close, though."

"You didn't send me *that* much money while I was—"

"You think I'd take off for that?" He sounded insulted.

I just shrugged.

"Big Matt and Jessop each anted up five. Me, I put up ten. Only fair, am I right? In fact, I didn't send even that much. You end up with a salary of about seventy-five K a year, Sugar. Three sixty-nine, total."

"Fair enough."

"Yeah, it *is*. And it might even be that you come out ahead."

"Yeah? *You* do a pound for that much money?"

"I don't mean that," he said, waving his hand like he was brushing away a pesky fly. "The statute of limitations—"

"It's up."

"It's up for *you*, Sugar. Big Matt and Jessop, they both took off right after they got paid. Me, I spent some time down in Florida. Couple of years, in fact.

"The only thing keeping the heat off is that this was just money. No big-deal 'cold case,' like an unsolved murder. Nobody's gonna do a TV show about some drill-through heist. But if either of the others got popped for something *else* . . . who knows?"

"Big Matt wouldn't give us up."

"I agree," he said, real solemn.

"And you put this Jessop guy in yourself."

"That I could have been wrong about."

"What!?"

"Jessop has been . . . hard to reach lately."

"Maybe somebody took him off the count," I said. That happens to men like us more than usual, I'm pretty sure. You steal for a living, you're going to make people mad. You pull off a big job and start living too large, you call attention to yourself.

And it doesn't matter *who* notices. Not too many people are real thieves anymore. Some punks, they think you're holding heavy cash, they might come in shooting. That's not a win-or-lose for you; it's just three different ways to lose.

You win a gunfight in your own place, the cops still aren't going away. Self-defense isn't worth much if you can't explain how you got your hands on all that cash the dead guys had been trying to jack you for.

You take a homicide fall, anyone you ever worked with is going to wonder how you'll stand up. Specially if you're looking at the needle.

Your partners wonder too much, you lose again. Someone you never heard of puts up your bail, that tells you you're on the spot. Sure, you can refuse the bail; stay right where you are. But where you are, there's no place to hide.

"Maybe," Solly said.

"You got his for-real name?"

"You think I'm stupid? I had that, I could find out what I need in an hour. I got *a* name, just like you did."

"The guy who sent him to you . . . ?"

"Gone. Not even two weeks ago, you believe that? Albie had a bum ticker. The fat fuck's idea of exercise was chewing."

"So . . . ?"

"So—*Albie,* I trusted. Known him for more years than you've been alive. Jessop . . . Ah, I'm getting too old for this stuff. I never even asked Albie for his vitals, just his credentials, you understand what I'm saying?"

"Yeah."

"I don't like loose strings, Sugar."

"What're you saying?"

"I . . . I don't know. There's guys in this business, nobody ever works for them twice. That's not me. Who's got a more solid rep? You don't get that for nothing. It's like everything else—you pay for it. I make my payments on the installment plan, understand?"

"No. Solly, if—"

"Look, kid. All I'm saying is, I always play it *careful,* okay? Careful, that's not something you are; it's something you *do.* Every job, every time. That's how come I'm . . . trusted, okay?"

"Sure. But I already—"

"Will you fucking let me *talk?* Just listen, for a damn minute. I got no reason to think this Jessop is . . . a problem. But I don't like not knowing where to find him."

"If he knew your pal, he's in the business. How hard could it be?"

"What, you think we're like some fraternity or something? Get together once a year, tell stories about the good old days? I know a few people, sure. But every phone call, that's somebody *else* I owe. Besides, this ain't phone work, understand?"

"Yeah. What I don't understand is why you're telling me all this. Tell Big Matt—he's the one with something to lose."

"He's out, Sugar."

"Somebody took him—"

"No," he cut me off. "The opposite. He's gone total Square John. Married, kid on the way."

"How could he just . . . ?" I couldn't finish the sentence; I didn't know what words to use.

"Oh, he told me in front," Solly said. "That last job, it was gonna be *his* last job, no matter what. We score, he's got enough to get a house, all the stuff you need to go straight. That's what he said. I remember it real clear. 'When this is over, so am I. No more stealing diamonds for me; I'm going to be buying them. Buying *one,* anyway.' His girl, she's not in The Life. Didn't have a clue what Big Matt did for a living. His real living, I mean."

"What did she think he—?"

"He buys houses. Real wrecks. Somewhere way out west, where you can buy them for next to nothing. Then he fixes them up and sells them. Lives in the house while he's doing the repairs."

"Pretty smart."

"It is," Solly said. "Big Matt, he's a thinker."

Meaning, I'm not, I thought, but I kept that to myself. Just sat and waited.

"Prices have gone through the fucking roof since you've been away, Sugar. Actually, more of a spike. So the co-ops are down from what they were asking a few years ago, but rentals, they *never* go back. You'd be lucky to find a decent apartment for under two grand. And that wouldn't even be the city—probably have to go out to Brooklyn or something."

"I'm not broke," I reminded him.

"No, you're not. But you're going to have to go back to work sooner or later."

"Sure."

"Aah!" he said, like he was throwing the word out of the room. "If Albie said this Jessop was stand-up, that should be good enough for me, right?"

"I didn't know him."

"It's . . . it's a respect thing, Sugar. I can't just go out and cut my losses. I got no feeling from this guy. Nothing. Probably solid as a stone. But . . ."

I kept quiet. Still couldn't figure out what all this blah-blah was about. Solly was a talker, I knew. I mean, he *liked* talking. I guess there weren't too many people he could talk to anymore.

"How about if you nose around a little? Find the guy, talk to him, see if he's righteous?"

"What do I care? You said it yourself—I'm in the clear. Even if he walked into a police station somewhere and started running his mouth, how's that my problem?"

"I got a responsibility."

"To who? Everyone who sits in takes their chances; that's the way it is."

"I got a responsibility to *Albie,* okay?" The old man was really getting worked up; I never heard him sound angry, like that. "I can't just . . . you know. It'd be like one of those preemptive strikes. Tap the guy, and we can all rest easy. But that wouldn't be fair to Albie. It'd be like I didn't trust his judgment.

"That happens, you know. Man gets old, he should get respect. Not for being old, but for the *wisdom* he has. Albie wasn't soft in the head. Not fucking *senile,* okay? He still had it up here," Solly said, tapping his temple.

"That's good enough for me."

"For you, sure. For me, it can't be. A man gets old, he wants to leave a will, make sure he takes care of everyone who he should be taking care of. But you know what nobody should ever leave, Sugar? Loose threads, that's what."

"I'm not going around playing private eye, Solly."

"I wasn't asking for a favor."

"What? You want to *pay* me, to do this thing?"

"Absolutely."

"Solly, I'm not exactly broke. I don't live big. It could be a real long time before I have to make another move. Anyway, you know I'm not a contract man."

"You got a car?"

"Where would I get a car?"

"You could've rented one, maybe."

"With what? My credit card?"

"Never mind. I got you a car. You'll love it. Papered to the max, full-cover insurance and all. Let's go and get your money."

"Solly . . ."

"What?"

"I got to get a place. Some clothes. Set up right, before I do anything. I can't walk around with a duffel bag stuffed with cash. What's your damn problem? I held up my end, didn't I?"

"Sure. Sure, you did, Sugar. You went first; now it's my turn. And that's—what?—finding you a place to stay, fixing you up with ID, all that?"

"It always *has* been," I said, letting him hear I didn't like what he was talking about.

"And, like I told you before, things have changed since you been away."

"I did five fucking years alone. Like I'm supposed to. *That* didn't change."

He nodded his head slowly, like a bunch of thoughts were bouncing around inside. "You're right, kid. Come on. Let's take that ride."

I followed him through the back exit. We walked down a cement hall. At least it looked like cement—the only light was Solly's flash, and he just sprayed it around a little. I guess he did that for me—no way Solly needed it after all these years.

We came to another door. When I followed Solly through it, I saw he had a lot of choices from there: take the stairs to his right, walk straight out the front door, or open another door.

He played the flash over that other door. "This one, it only opens from the inside. It's about a foot or so drop from there. Not so much, but you could break your ankle, you're not expecting it."

The old man jumped down. I followed him. The door closed itself behind us. Solly lit it up for a second—it looked like part of the wall. I knew he wasn't bragging, just showing me he still had things under control.

The alley wasn't even wide enough to get a car through, so it was pretty clean. No Dumpsters, so no homeless guys camped out waiting for a refill. And no rats to fight them for the kind of garbage you can eat.

At the end of the alley, there was this high chain-link gate. It wouldn't keep anyone out if they wanted to climb, but who does that just to go dice-rolling on a blanket?

Not a good shortcut, either.

Solly opened the lock with a key he had. He pointed a finger at the place where the wall ended, just inside the gate. I looked where he was pointing. I couldn't see anything for a few seconds. Then there was a long, thin flash of light. When it went away, I could see what Solly meant: slivers of mirror glass up there, set at an angle. If you looked at the left one, you could see what was coming up the sidewalk on the right. Same for the other side.

"You watch this one," he said.

When we each had a "clear," I went out first. I walked to my right. Not fast, but not so slow you'd notice. Solly caught up to me before we got to the corner.

We just walked along, side by side. It probably looked like we both knew where we were going, but only Solly did.

A few blocks from Solly's dump, there was this classy-looking high-rise, all glass and chrome. That's how this city is. There's no such thing as neighborhoods, like you have in Brooklyn or Queens. In Manhattan, you could have ten-million-dollar houses on one block and crumbling old slums on the next. It's split up so tight that they've even got special names for every few blocks.

I don't think any of that crap really sticks. Guys who came up in Hell's Kitchen would be, I don't know, proud of it, I guess. There was this Irish guy I used to know, Ken. "Catch me telling folks I was born in fucking 'Clinton,'" I heard him say one time.

On the rich blocks, there wouldn't be any alleys—the buildings are stacked together so tight not even light could shine through. But on the other blocks, they have backyards. Little ones, sure. And all fenced off and everything. But you could still go through a whole block without stepping on the sidewalk if you had to.

Solly walked right in the front door. There was a guy at a curved desk made out of some kind of dark marble. He was wearing a blue jacket with "WynterGreene" embroidered in gold letters on the pocket over his heart.

"Mr. Vizner," he said, smiling.

"Anthony, meet my nephew. Jerome, this is Anthony. He's in charge of making sure everything around here works the way it's supposed to."

The guy in the jacket got a little red in the face, Solly giving him a compliment like that.

"I'm pleased to meet you," I said, holding out my hand.

The guy in the jacket seemed a little confused, but he finally shook hands with me.

"Gets those manners from his mother," Solly said, like I'd done something weird.

We walked over to the elevator cars. Three of them were already standing open. Solly made a move with his hand. I got in; he was right behind me.

"This time of night, you want an attended car, you have to signal for one," he said.

The car stopped on 13. I followed Solly out. We walked on a thick dark carpet until we got to a door with "13F" on a little panel next to it. Solly opened the door with a key.

Inside, it was like a showroom, all brand-new stuff.

"Have a seat," Solly told me.

I found a chair—I guess it was a chair, because it was only big enough for one person. Solly sat on this little couch-thing.

"Solomon Vizner, that's me. They know I travel a lot. I tip good. Always pay the maintenance on time; they take it right out of my bank account."

"What's maintenance?"

"To keep the place up. The concierge—the guy at the front desk. The guy who shovels the sidewalk, the guy who takes out the garbage, the guy who vacuums the hallways . . . there's the taxes, too. Naturally. And if something breaks, they have to fix it."

"The landlord—"

"I'm the landlord, Sugar. Kind of, anyway. See, I own this unit. That's what they call them in this place, units."

"Damn."

"Yeah, it's a pretty good place. I got in when it first opened, almost fifteen years ago. Could've sold it for double that a little while back. Now . . . it's still worth more than I paid, but that ride's probably over. Not that I care—I got no reason to sell."

"But you don't really live here?"

"Nah. Who could do business in a place like this? They got cameras all around, and if you don't live here, you have to sign this guest book. Can you see anyone coming to visit me doing that?"

He was right. I couldn't even see *Solly* in this place, never mind some of the guys he puts jobs together for. I felt like he wasn't just showing the place to me, he was showing me respect, too.

"Anyone takes a look in here, it's like some maid just got finished, right?" he said. "But so what? The building, they give you that service. For extra, of course. That's a racket. I hire my own. You remember Ken?"

"Yeah," I said. He was that Irish guy I used to know. Well, maybe not *know*, exactly. But I looked up to him. Everybody did.

"He's gone on, God rest the crazy mick bastard's soul. Ken, he was a good man. Once did a longer stretch than you just wrapped up, never even nibbled at the cheese."

"He wouldn't."

"No. Ken, he was a piece of rebar."

"You mean tough?"

"Sure, tough. But that's not what I mean. You pour too much concrete without you got rebar in it, it won't hold together. That was Ken, see? You have him in on a job, he's the one who holds it together, even when things go bad. He was doing that, doing *just* that, when he cashed out."

I didn't say anything.

"Armored car. You don't see much of those anymore, except when there's an inside man. But this was a straight takedown. Perfect timing. Like a Swiss watch. Only, a squad car just stumbles across it. Shouldn't've happened—we had their patrol route down to the minute. But there they were.

"We had two getaway cars. One was okay, on the far side of the money truck. The other one—the one Ken was supposed to take—it was on the wrong side. The cop car was already past it when they spotted the play. Probably went right to the radio. If Ken ran to the car he was supposed to take, they'd know the guy sitting behind the wheel was in on it, too."

"I know the guy?"

"I already said—Oh, you mean the wheelman? Yeah. Sure. Everybody knows Buddha."

"He'd wait."

"Exactly! That's what Ken knew. So he opened up on the squad car. By the time they had him down, probably twenty slugs in him, everybody else was long gone."

"That's a man."

"You think everyone don't know that? His daughter, she got his share. To this day, she's got no idea where it came from. Ken didn't leave a will. He didn't have a straight-life cover like me; he was outlaw all the way. So, the way she got paid, different guys, they'd drop around, leave me the money they owed Ken. Just paying off a loan. They knew I'd take care of it.

"Must have been hard for the girl at first. She was still in high school. Private school, no less. But nobody could come around and explain until after the cops stopped nosing into the kid's life. They must've thought Ken was as dumb as they are—like he was ever gonna leave his work stuff where he lived!

"Ken had a little house. Out on the Island, I think. Or close to it, anyway. The cops practically tore it apart, but there was nothing for them to find. His daughter, Grace, that *is* her name, she never knew a thing about her father's business . . . and he never brought any of it home."

"She got his whole share, though, right?"

"Of course," he said, giving me one of those "What are you, stupid?" looks. "But not all at once. I mean, it had to be in cash;

what was she going to do, throw it all into a bank somewhere? I handled it for her.

"Anyway, she's in college now. Or maybe she's already finished—I don't know how long it takes to be one of those social workers."

"Me, either."

"That's okay. See, Grace, she's my maid. Comes in once a week. I never stay here, so there's really nothing for her to do. Plus, this is a quiet place to study, right?"

"Sure."

"Only, being Ken's daughter, she *has* to vacuum the place, do some dusting. I told her, by me, I don't care—all I want is that cover story. I have a maid in once a week, why *wouldn't* the place look all neat and perfect if anyone took a look? She says, sure, she understands. But she doesn't actually listen to a damn word I say. When I come back here—I try to do that, every couple, three weeks—the envelopes I leave for her are gone. And there's always new stuff in the refrigerator.

"See how smart this girl is? It's always this health-food crap. That's what *she* eats, not me. So she can have her meals in here, and, anyone looks, it's like I'm living here, get it?"

"Yeah, I get it. But you'd do it anyway, right?"

"What are you talking about?"

"Take care of the girl. Even if the job went bad. Even if there *was* no share to hold for him."

"Oh. Well, see, that was always part of Ken's deal. Anything happens to him, I do that, sure."

"He trusted you."

"Ken? Hard to tell with a man like him. He just . . . believed in things. Catholic, he was. Wouldn't spit on a priest, fucking *hated* nuns, but . . . Ah, who knows? Maybe he thought he could come back and haunt me or something."

"Like a ghost?"

"A golem, more likely. But what am I, a mind reader now?"

I wasn't going to ask Solly what a golem is—the last thing I wanted was for him to start going sideways before I got my money. "I was just . . . okay, why do *you* think she takes the money, Solly?"

"You mean, being Ken's daughter? Oh, I told her a *good* story about that, believe me. I leave her five hundred a week. Paying off a loan. With what I told her I owed her father, I'll be dead ten years and it still won't be paid off. Grace, she knows: first week there's no envelope, that means I'm not coming back. Then she won't, either. But she knows where her bank account is, see?"

"That's slick."

"That's me, kid. Mr. Angles. Now let's go get your money."

Solly hit "PG" on the elevator pad. When it stopped, it opened into an underground garage. A young black guy in some kind of uniform was waiting. Soon as he saw Solly, he stepped back.

"Mistah Vee!" a much older black man called out from the beat-up old easy chair he was sitting in, a few feet away. "Rex have your car ready for you in a snap."

A monster black car rolled up. I never saw anything like it. Only had two doors, but it was bigger than any limo. More like a freight car than something you drive.

The black guy in the uniform hopped out, and went back to his post. The old guy held the door open for Solly. "The boy ain't got a clue, do he, suh?"

"Which one, Lester?"

"Oh. Oh, I didn't mean nothin', Mistah Vee. I wasn't saying nothin' about your young man." Meaning me, I guessed. "I was talking about Rex over there. He my sister's youngest boy. Ain't too swift, but the building, all they just wanted was someone stay down here, make sure it's safe for the residents."

"How many years we know each other?" Solly said.

"More than I likes to remember, suh."

"Me, too. So why're you still running that plantation game on me?"

The old black guy lowered his voice. "Been playing it safe so long, it's all I know, I guess," he said.

"Yeah," Solly told him. "Guys like us, we got no choice, do we?"

He slipped the old guy a bill.

"Get in," he told me.

There was no door handle, so I pushed the button where it should have been, and the door opened. From the outside, the car gleamed like it had been dipped in a pool of black ink. Inside, it looked new. Solly pulled away, slow and smooth. I couldn't hear the engine.

"What the hell *is* this?" I couldn't help asking him.

"Putz," he said. "You never heard of the Lincoln Continental?"

"Sure. But . . ."

"Not *a* Lincoln Continental, Sugar; *the* Lincoln Continental. You know how they have them all with numbers, like the Mark III or the Mark IV, like that?"

"I guess so."

"This one's got no number. Know why? Because this is the first of the line. If they had a Mark I, that's what this would be. Back when this was new, they built cars to last, not like the crap they make today."

"They were all like this?"

"Don't be a clown, kiddo. A Chevy's always been a Chevy; a Ford's always been a Ford. But this baby never saw an assembly line; it was hand-built. Not just top-of-the-line, top of them *all*."

"I'm not surprised it lasted this long—feels like we're in a damn tank."

"A tank with plenty of pep. Not that you want to go racing around in a car like this. That would be . . . Well, it would just be wrong."

"I don't get it. The whole car thing, I don't get any of that."

"It's not the car; it's what it means. Me, I wanted one of these from the minute I first saw one, a couple of years after the war. A car like this, it sets you apart."

"From who?"

"From *everyone*. I don't care if you're a young *shvartser* in Harlem or an *alter kocker* in Miami, your idea of heaven is still a Cadillac. But next to *this* beauty, a Caddy's a piece of shit. Back when we were kicking the crap out of the krauts, this was the best car on the planet."

"You were in that?"

"You think I'm, what, a Zen Buddhist? Back then, a Jewish boy, he couldn't walk the streets unless he was home on leave. Better be in uniform, too. Otherwise, the old ladies, they'd spit on you. And the young ones—forget it.

"Don't get me wrong, that was one job I couldn't *wait* to get in on. Look at me now, you wouldn't believe it, but back then I was a lion. The only thing I ever worried about was getting sent to the Pacific Theater."

"That was extra bad?"

"It was all bad, kid. But how was I gonna get to kill any Nazis over there?"

"You wanted to kill them?"

"I wanted to kill *all* of them. I just wish the assholes who ran the government had dropped that big one on Berlin, too."

"The atom bomb, right? You mean, they only had the one?"

Solly slapped himself on his forehead. "Who am I talking to? We had *lots* of them, Sugar. You think we only hit Japan one time?"

"Well, if they had so many—"

"They weren't gonna drop nukes on white people, kid. Simple as that. I don't know how it was out west back then. But here, the Germans had their own part of town. First Avenue in the low nineties. They even called it 'Germantown.' Before the war, they had a lot of pull in this city, so you have to figure, they had it other places, too. But it still comes down to the same thing. You can't tell a German from a Swede just by looking at them, but you can spot a Jap at a hundred yards."

"Yeah, I get it."

"Nah. It's a lot more complicated than that. But let me ask *you* a question, okay? Tell the truth: you really give a rat's ass about anything that happened way before you were born?"

"I guess not."

I watched him drive, working the column shifter like one of those guys who can type with their eyes closed. It was all so smooth. Not just the ride, with the big car swallowing all the bumps in the road; Solly, he was smooth, too.

"Isn't this thing a little—?"

"What? Distinctive? Sure it is! What, I'm gonna use it on a bank job? Besides, people need to see what *real* class is every once in a while."

"It's . . . really something."

"Just like new," Solly said. "Better, actually. Things like tires, they don't make 'em like they used to . . . and that's a *good* thing."

Nearly five o'clock in the morning, and people were still staring at the car every time we stopped at a light. One time, it was a big black one like Solly's, only it was one of those SUVs. It was painted a different kind of black from Solly's. Even the windows were black.

Somebody stuck a cell phone out the window. It was on Solly's side, so I slumped in the seat, looked down. The SUV was playing some noise, sounded like an elephant stampede. Same stuff they play over the speakers at Rikers. That was another good thing about being sent way Upstate.

Neon ribbons inside the SUV kept changing colors. The wheels were black, but the centers were gold; they kept spinning even with the wheels stopped.

"Solly . . ."

"I see him, kid. Just taking pictures with his cell phone. Every place I go with this car, they do that."

"What about your license plate?"

"I should care?" Solly said. "This beauty, she's as legit as it gets. Those kind"—tilting his head in the direction of the fancy black SUV—"they don't know how to act."

We just kept driving. A long loop around the city, like old men taking a stroll in the park. Solly stayed in the right-hand lane on First, timing it so we rolled through on green. Way downtown, he caught a yellow light. Solly eased the big car to a stop, being real careful.

Looking straight ahead, he asked me, "Is that place still open?"

I didn't know what place he meant, but as I turned to look out my window, a flash went off. By the time I got done blinking, Solly had the green and we took off.

"I saw it," he said, like he knew what I was thinking. "Just one of those 'artiste' dipshits running around with a camera. Probably wants to catch the sun coming up over the East River or something like that."

"You sure?"

"How'm I gonna be 'sure,' Sugar? I'm saying, those kind, they're all over the city now. Besides, this guy, he had a girl with him. Probably his fucking 'assistant.' Like an assistant you fuck, get it?"

"Yeah."

"Get over yourself, kid. Who'd want a picture of *you*? Some CIA surveillance team? Come on."

We just kept driving. When we got near Canal, Solly pulled to the curb.

"In the back, there's a suitcase. See it? Everything you need's in there."

"I'm not—"

"Get out, walk back the way we came. A little over two blocks. Then turn left. Maybe ten, twelve doors down, you'll see a sign: 'Voodoo Veils.' It's one of those art places. Above it, there's a loft. This key"—he handed me a key attached to a little red tube by a short chain—"it opens the door *next* to that sign. You walk up two flights, you're in your own place."

"What about—?"

"It's all in there," Solly said. "Now get outta here before we start attracting attention. There's a cell phone in the suitcase. Call me when you want to work."

"Who owns the—?"

"Later," he said.

I knew I wasn't getting anything else out of Solly, so I grabbed the suitcase out of the back, stepped out, and closed the door. I did it soft, out of respect for the car. Then I started walking.

I only had a short distance to cover, but I was still glad it was already starting to get light out. I wasn't worried about muggers—they stop working in the early morning, and I don't look like a good target, anyway. But the cops, they do whatever they want.

If a prowl car called me over, I'd have to go. Show them ID. They wouldn't like the suitcase. Ask me if I minded if they looked inside. I'd have to say I *did* mind. Then they'd say they saw a gun in my belt, or make up anything they felt like. Once they looked inside that suitcase, I'd be cooked.

But I made it okay.

The little door was painted in slanted black-and-white stripes. Looked more like a pole than a door, especially being so narrow and all.

The key Solly gave me worked. I stepped inside, closed the door behind me. The stairs didn't have any lights. I stood there a second, getting my eyes used to the dark. I ran my hands over the key. The little red tube attached to it was metal—it felt cold in my hand. *Why would Solly give me—?* I twirled the little tube around a couple of times. It felt smooth except for a tiny little part near the far end. I ran my thumbnail around it, slow and careful. That part near the end was notched. I turned it and a little circle of light came out.

I hadn't ever seen such a tiny flashlight, but it sure threw enough light for me to climb the stairs. *This'd be a good thing for a man to carry around,* I thought.

Two flights, like Solly said. There wasn't any door—the whole floor was open space. I played the flash around. The beam was powerful, but real narrow, so it was slow work.

Finally, I found a lamp. At least, I thought it was a lamp—looked like an upside-down cone on a long piece of metal. I couldn't see how to turn it on, but I found the wire and felt around. There was a big flat thing in the wire. I pushed on it and the light came on. I guessed you were supposed to step on that flat thing to turn on the lamp.

It didn't throw much light, and all of it was pointed down. But it was enough for me to get a picture of the place.

There wasn't much up there. Mostly empty space. A thick pad on the floor had a pillow, so I guessed it was supposed to be the bed. One of those refrigerator cubes, looked new. The sink looked like it had come with the building. In a corner, toilet and shower stall.

Kind of like a convict's dream cell. But I didn't see a TV or a radio, so I guess it really wasn't, even with all that space.

I wanted to look around the place some more. I wanted to open the suitcase. Not just to count the money, to see what else Solly put in there.

But it was still too dark. And I was bone-tired. *Solly already knows where I am,* is what I was thinking.

Besides, if Solly was going to do something to me, it would only be to get the money. And if he wanted the money, he'd already had a dozen chances to take me out.

I know what to do when there's rules. I just follow them. I guess I was supposed to wait for Solly to call. No. That's wrong. He said to call him if I wanted to work. No, wait. *When* I wanted to work, is what he said.

Why would I want to work anytime soon? I had money. It was all in this suitcase, right?

My head hurt from all that. I flopped down on the pad, faceup, one hand on the suitcase. I don't remember closing my eyes.

When I came around, I could see the whole place. A kind of dirty light came down over everything. I looked up. It was a skylight. One of those old ones, kind of looks like a tent if you're on the roof. Probably came with the building, and hadn't been cleaned since.

I used to be good at time. I mean, I could kind of feel what time it was. But the last five years changed that. Bells and sirens. Hacks running their clubs over the bars, like an iron piano that only played one song. Inside, it isn't light that tells you what time it is. You might never see the sky at night. Or see it at all, depending on how tight they had you locked down.

Same thing for chow: In some parts of the place, they'd bring the food to you, shove it through a slot. Other parts, you had to be outside your cell for the count, then march down to eat. After a while, I couldn't *feel* the time anymore.

I looked at my watch. It was the same one I had been wearing when they took me. Cheap plastic thing, with a rubber strap.

It had been good for the job I was on—no tick-tick, you could press a little button and it would light up. And it was always on the nose.

But it was blank now. I guess the battery had run dead. The prison's supposed to give you back whatever you had on you when you checked in. It'd never be that much. Anything like a pistol or a knife, that'd be in some evidence bin. Personal stuff, you could sign and get someone to come and pick it up for you. Nobody in my line of work would ever do that.

But if you're holding a pile of garbage when they take you down, the prison makes sure to keep it for you. It's their last chance to remind you where you came from.

My watch was like that. If it had been a Rolex, it would have been lost somewhere along the line.

Lots of guys, they'd never stop bitching about all the jewelry that got taken off them. Gold chains, rings . . . stuff like that. You'd never know if they even had all that in the first place. You listen to them, you'd think they were all big-time. And if anyone *saw* you listening, they'd know you weren't.

The only reason I took the watch, it was mine. I didn't strap it on, just signed for it. They make you do that. My first night out, I put it on my wrist. Don't know why I hadn't just thrown it away.

When I got done with the toilet, I finally opened the suitcase. On top, new stuff, still in the wrapping. Three of everything: briefs, undershirts, pairs of socks. The bills were underneath, in those plastic bags you can seal up just by pushing the top pieces together. Thirty-six of them, all the same—two stacks of hundreds, side by side. Ten K in each one. Three hundred and sixty thou.

A towel, also in plastic. Toothpaste, toothbrush, mouthwash, shampoo. Comb, soap, nail file. Pack of three disposable razors, shaving cream.

Then another towel. Loose cash, mostly twenties. Two cell phones: the prepaid one Solly had told me about, and another one—a real one. Half a dozen envelopes, address and stamps already on them.

There was also a gym bag with a shoulder strap, the kind a

serious bodybuilder would carry. I opened it. In one of the inside pockets, a driver's license with my picture on it. Visa card. Registration for a 2007 Mustang. Insurance, paid through the end of the year. Scotch-taped to the registration was "Home Depot parking lot," and an address.

Business cards. A bank statement. Stack of checks. An ATM card, with one of those little sticky papers on it. "PIN number," it said. And a single key, stamped "303."

I figured the address on the business cards was one of those private-mailbox places, and the phone number would be that second cell.

Stanley Jay Wilson, personal trainer, had a little more than two grand in checking, another eleven in savings.

And three names that could be either first or last ones.

Everything I needed to find a place to live. Plus the message Solly didn't need to write out: find one *quick*.

That bank account was in Queens. Forest Hills. I took the subway.

The bank manager was a guy about my age, but nothing fit him right. Too loose, all around. Even the skin on his face.

He tapped keys, looked at a computer screen on his desk. "I hope you're going to get a good deal this time, Mr. Wilson."

"Me, too," I said. I didn't know what else to say.

"That is, if you're about to do what I think you're going to be doing."

"I just came here to—"

"You were such a *steady* saver," he said, like I'd done something to let him down. "Two hundred dollars a week, like clockwork. You had quite a fine balance built up. Money that could have been *working* for you. I understand how you would need a car for your line of work, especially if you have clients out on the Island."

"That's true."

"And I know it's a buyer's market now, so you can probably get into a new car really cheap. But you finished paying off your car loan a couple of months ago. That was . . . just about eight hundred dollars a month. Imagine if you put that money into savings instead of starting a new loan."

"Well, I—"

"Yes, I know. Some of the dealers are offering these 'no interest' loans, but you're an intelligent man, so I don't have to explain that they make that up in the price of the car, *especially* on a trade-in."

"Hmmm . . ."

A little color came into his face. "You take the car as a business expense, don't you?"

"Uh . . . sure."

"All right, look at it this way: the mileage allowance has gone up *considerably*. Your car certainly isn't *that* old. And, with your loan paid off, you don't have to carry the mandatory collision insurance, either."

"I never thought of that."

"How would you like to *triple* what your money is earning, starting today?"

"Sure I would. Only . . ."

"Instead of taking ten thousand out of your savings account to add to your car as a trade-in, you could turn that money into a CD. As you know, with the prime rate so low today, we're forced to pay a really low interest rate on savings. But we have a dynamite promotional offer, starting this week. If you're willing to purchase a thirteen-month CD with that ten thousand, we can give you a *guaranteed* two-point-two-five-percent return. Plus the safety and security of true FDIC insurance coverage. How does that sound?"

"It actually sounds pretty good," I told him.

"And if you continue to do all your banking online, we can also give you *free* ATM usage. We have branches all over New York. I see you've only used your card . . . *very* rarely. One, two, three . . . eleven times in five years. So I guess that privilege wouldn't be so valuable to you. Still, you never know when you're going to need cash, anytime, day or night."

"That's true."

"Well, we could offer you a choice of premiums, actually. Here, look this over while I print out your statement as of this morning."

He handed me a strip of heavy, slick paper, with the bank's name at the top. I could get a tote bag, an emergency road kit, a free safe-deposit box . . .

"This looks pretty good to me," I said, handing it back to him, with my finger pointing out what I meant.

"Oh, it *is*. Everyone should have a safe-deposit box, for valuable papers, or bonds, or . . . well, anything you want to make sure is always protected, no matter where you live."

"Sold," I said, holding out my hand.

He shook it like he'd just closed a million-dollar deal.

When I left the bank, I left a lot of money behind. I don't mean that CD—I mean three hundred K in the little safe-deposit box. I really had to pack it in careful; the "box" was more like a long, hollow metal slot.

The bank manager warned me not to lose the key to that box. If I lost it, they'd have to change the lock, and the charge for that was a hundred and fifty. He looked a little ashamed of himself for waiting to tell me that until after I bought the CD. I guess that's why he waited to tell me the box was only free for a year. After that, it'd cost me twenty-five a month. I signed another card so they could automatically take that out of my checking account when the time came. I saw from the printout he handed me that they were already doing that with the bill for the cell-phone number on my business cards.

I got back on the subway, a local headed toward Manhattan. But I got off after only a few stops. After that, I walked.

If it wasn't for the license number, I couldn't have found the Mustang. It wasn't even one o'clock in the afternoon, but the lot had a whole bunch of them. I knew mine was green, but even that didn't narrow it down enough.

When I found mine, I pushed a button on the key holder. The car beeped once, like telling me I'd been right.

I got behind the wheel and headed back the way I'd just walked.

It was righteous of Solly to set me up with all the ID. That was way past what the rule called for: if you ride the whole beef for everyone in on the job, all that means is your share has to be there when you make the door.

Sometimes, it could be more than one guy going down, but the rules don't change. You hold up your end, the other guys hold up theirs. Five men on the job, four get popped, that fifth man better be holding four shares. That's why it's better to have a planner—lots of things could happen to that fifth man over a few years.

If you fall, it's okay to do something for yourself. You don't have to plead not guilty and take your chances. You can take a deal. If you can clear up a whole lot of cases for the cops, you might score a pretty decent offer. Doesn't matter if you did them or not. Nobody cares. Solved is solved.

That doesn't happen too often to guys who do my kind of work. Those deals, they're usually for killers. Not hit men, sickos who get off on doing it. Those kind, they *want* to talk about what they did, unless they're holding out for a book-and-movie deal.

The cops, most of the time, they'll respect you being a professional. It takes a long time for them to do that, though. My first time down, the cops told me, if I wouldn't help myself, I'd be doing everyone else's time for them. They also said I wouldn't get any play from the DA unless they cleared it first.

That's all a lie. NYPD Special. The truth is, they *always* want a plea. Unless the case makes the papers, that is. Once the media gets hold of a case, then the DA's Office has to play hardball. Otherwise, unless they've got you dead to rights, they don't want a trial.

Even the Legal Aid guys know this. They'll sit down with you and tell you what they think the case is worth. *Any* armed robbery can land you with a quarter to do before your max-out date. Twenty-five years. It doesn't matter whether you're a first offender or a working pro, the top can't be more than that. For one job, I mean. If you've been down before, every year you can cut from the top is worth a lot, because then your minimum is half your max. There's always a going rate for pleas. Even for a guy like me.

Sure, the cops'll look me over, tell me, "You've got enough sheets for a king-sized bed." Meaning, so many priors they wouldn't fit on one piece of paper. Actually, what I've got is a lot of arrests. Only two convictions, and one of them a misdemeanor. Until I took the last one, I mean.

But that's just cop-talk. They know it's not up to them. If some ADA wants to cut a few years off your time, there's nothing they can say about it.

It's funny. The kind of work I do, the smoother the job goes, the more slack they can cut me if I get dropped. Armed robbery, that's one thing. Armed robbery where you have to *use* the weapons, that's another.

There's all these fine little edges. You break into a warehouse, cart away a truckload of loot, that's something you can deal on. But if you break into a house, not so easy. Those cat-burglar guys, you never know what they were really after, see? But with guys like me, the cops know it's always money. *Only* money.

The law makes you aim high. Take down a bank or stick up a liquor store, it's still an armed robbery. If they're going to lump it all in that same bag, why take a ten-year risk for cigarette money?

Must be the way those black-glove guys start thinking after a while. Once they've got the girl captured, they know what's next. Even if they let her go, they're *still* going down forever—that kind of thing, it's probably got twenty different crimes tied up in it. Murder, that's Life, too. So why let her go, maybe have her testify against you?

But on a professional piece of work, the cops usually know where to look. And they're not the only ones.

It was Ken that changed that, a long time ago. Solly told me Ken was the first heister who wouldn't pay tax on his work. Used to be, you pulled a job in anyone's territory, you had to let them slice a little off the top. Probably started back when the families were only taking Sicilians. I even heard you had to ask their *permission* first.

Solly really admired Ken. He never got tired of telling stories about him. Not what you might think, though. What he liked about Ken the best was the way the man stuck pins in so many balloons.

"You go up to some poor bastard, working his ass off to support his family, and you sell him fucking 'protection,' yeah? He don't pay, you bust his place up, then you go back and tell him, 'See? The cops can't protect you, but we can.' That's not a man's work. Me, I do a man's work.

"So—you gonna protect me? You got cops that'll look the other way, judges on your payroll? That's some insurance I wouldn't mind buying.

"That's what Ken told them at the sit-down," Solly told me. "And when they said, yeah, they *did* have that kind of juice but they couldn't put their *names* on the table—could they?—Ken, he says:

"Why is that, then? 'Cause you'd be giving me info on dirty cops and crooked judges, yeah? And maybe I could trade that, if I got in a jam, is that about right?

"So the dagos, they all nod, like the fucking movies, you know? And Kenny says:

"That door swings both ways, doesn't it? If I come to you about a job of work I'm going to do, or even if I pay your tax after the work is done, and you get jammed, what's to stop you from trading that?

"I thought it was gonna be the O.K. Corral right there," Solly said. "But Kenny sliced into them first. Had a whole list of family men who'd turned rat. And the big shots at that table, they couldn't deny it. So Kenny says,

"Tell me a guy who'll give up a boss wouldn't give me up. Can you do that?

"It was quiet for a minute. Then one of the older guys—a real survivor, he must have been—he says, 'We let *you* slide on the tax, word gets around, then *nobody* pays.' But Kenny, he's ready for that one.

"'Only way word gets around is if one of you spreads it.'

"The man had steel balls," Solly said to me. "But it wasn't just that. Ken made *sense*. He had a rep. Not just for being crazy—

which he was, I grant you—but for keeping it low-key. No flashy suits. No diamond rings. No nightclubs. You see what I'm saying?

"The man was a master. No trademarks, no patterns. It could be a bank one time, a truckload of furs—only way you could tell it was Ken's work was by how smooth it went.

"So what would be in it for Ken to brag about not having to pay tax? Nothing. He'd be killing his own golden goose. His game was no-ego, see? The family guys knew he was telling the truth: if they made a deal with Ken, nobody was gonna hear about it from him."

Only Ken wasn't around anymore. Which gave me a real problem with Solly being so generous.

He'd gone to a lot of trouble, setting me up like he had. The cops didn't know Stanley Jay Wilson, but Solly knew him. Knew him real well. Where he banked, what car he was driving . . . even the business he was supposed to be in.

I didn't like that last part. I'd been using that "personal trainer" tag for a while before I did my last bit. But, truth is, I don't know the first damn thing about how to do it. I picked up some lingo from magazines, and I guess I look like someone who *should* know that stuff. It wasn't like I actually had to convince anyone.

But I'd never mentioned this to any of the guys I ever worked with. It isn't the kind of thing you talk about.

So how did Solly know?

And how come he told me so much stuff about himself? It was like he wanted us to be even up on info about each other.

I knew this much: Solly never did anything just to be doing it. "It's all investment," he once told me. "Risk against gain. Everything in life always comes down to that."

That's why my first stop was this Verizon store. The kid in the red shirt called up my account on his screen, said they were really sorry about my phone getting smashed on the subway platform, and sold me a new one.

The place was kind of frantic, people running in and out, arguing about credit, getting their friends to cosign for them, trading up to a fancier model . . . so the kid I got just told me to pick out whatever I wanted—it'd go on my next bill.

I told him I didn't want my wife to know I'd broken another phone, so I wanted to pay cash.

That got his attention. "So I'm guessing, maybe your new phone wouldn't need a GPS . . . ?"

I threw him an extra twenty for being so considerate. And put a fifty on top of that to get a new number right away. He didn't act surprised.

It took one of those instaprint joints only a few minutes to make me some new business cards.

Still not enough. I drove over to a Toyota dealer closer to the city but still in Queens. Traded the Mustang in on a used—they called it "pre-owned"—2004 Camry.

That bank manager had been right. The salesman hardly listened to me tell him my kids were too big for car seats now, so the Mustang wouldn't work. We went back and forth a couple of times, but I wasn't going to spend the whole day there, and I made sure he'd see that.

"My car's only got thirteen thousand miles on it," I told him. "Yours has got almost seventy-five. And it's three years older, too. I told my wife I was taking the day off, and I'd be driving a different car home tonight. So I'm gonna do that. Started first thing this morning. So far, I've been to five dealers. I want a Camry. I'm taking the best offer. So tell me yours. Then I can say yes or no and be done with it."

"We'll beat any—"

"Jesus Christ. All you guys say the same thing. Fine. Never mind the 'check with my manager' routine, either, okay? You take my Mustang, I take the Camry. I'm not asking you for cash back. Which I *should*. So—what's it gonna be?"

The Camry felt solid. I don't know much about cars, but I knew this beige one I was driving looked like a million other cars on the road.

Sure, I traded the Mustang away, even though I knew Solly could trace it easy enough if he wanted to.

There was still another reason to get rid of the Mustang, a more important one. Say a guy wants to sell you a really top-shelf piece. Only half-price. Looks brand-new, sure. But you never know where that gun's been. Or what it was used for.

That Mustang had been bought new, while I was still locked up. With thirteen thousand–plus miles on the odometer, it still *looked* new. But I hadn't put those miles on myself.

I figured they'd detail the Mustang before they put it out on the lot, so if I duct-taped that GPS'ed phone Solly gave me under the front fender, they'd find it. I had to wait until I could find a better place.

I was just ahead of the outbound traffic by the time all the paperwork was done. I knew it would be smooth sailing to just past the outer edge of Queens, which is where I wanted to go.

First, I stopped at a cemetery. The thing was huge. Almost empty that time of day. I paid my respects to some guy who cashed in thirty years ago. Then I scooped up enough sod to slip Solly's phone under it, with the ringer turned off.

Soon as I saw the place, I knew it had been what I thought it was when I read the ad: "One bedroom, furnished, immaculate. No smoking, no pets. Quiet neighborhood. Must pass credit check. Rent includes all utilities."

The woman who answered the door took a little step back when she saw me. I was neat and clean, but I couldn't do anything about my size and that scar.

"You're so . . . big," the woman said, like she was answering just what I'd been thinking.

"Yes, ma'am. I guess it comes with the territory."

"Are you some kind of . . . bouncer or something?"

"Oh no, ma'am. I'm a personal trainer. I also sell fitness equipment. So I'm always in one gym or another, it seems."

"Well . . . come in," she said. Still a little flustered, but calming down quick. I wondered if her husband had a problem with bookies.

After I told her that I never smoked—"How would *that* look, in my business?"—and I didn't have a pet, she got right down to it. Eleven hundred a month, plus one month's rent and one month's security. "You couldn't come *close* to a place for that much in the city."

The apartment was over the garage. Looked fresh-painted. Press-on fake-wood paneling. The furniture was all cheap stuff, but it looked new. The only reason I bothered to look around is, if you don't do that, it makes landlords suspicious.

"It looks perfect to me," I said. "Except for one thing."

"What's that?" she said, hands on her hips like I'd just said she was putting on weight.

"Where would I be able to park my car? The last thing I need is another damn ticket."

"Oh! That's easy. Come on downstairs and I'll show you."

I thought she'd head for the side door. That was the one we came in by—the front was just a couple of windows. But there was a back door, too, right off the downstairs kitchen. "See?" she said, pointing at a blacktop slab laid down in their backyard. "It's not indoor parking, I know. But you never have to worry about getting a ticket."

"I'm sold," I told her.

"You don't have . . . ?"

"Loud parties?"

She smiled.

"Ma'am, by the time I'm done working, all I want is a hot shower and plenty of sleep. A lot of my work is at night. Some of it, it's even out of town. If that carpet you put down is as good as it looks, you'll probably never even know when I'm here and when I'm not."

"Well, that seems fine."

"I hope so. Could I leave you a deposit while you're waiting for the credit check to come back?"

"Why, certainly, Mr. . . ."

"Wilson, ma'am. Stanley Wilson. My friends call me Stan," I said, taking out my driver's license while I was talking. I took something else out, too: thirty-three hundred-dollar bills. "If this is okay, I'll just leave it with you. If you're not satisfied with the credit check, just give me a call and I'll come back to pick it up."

She fingered the money. The tip of her tongue shot out of her lips for just a split second.

"This is . . . unusual, isn't it?"

"Ma'am?"

"To pay in cash, I mean?"

"It's what I prefer, actually. I mean, I'll be happy to write a check instead if you—"

"No. No, that's all right. I guess I . . ."

"Most of my clients pay *me* in cash," I said, like we were sharing a secret.

"You mean, you'd *always* be paying your rent that way?"

"Yes, ma'am. You did say utilities were included, didn't you?"

"Of course. I mean . . . Oh, I see. You wouldn't have to write checks to Con Edison, either. But the phone would be your—"

I held up my cell phone, smiled at her again. "The bank automatically deducts every month's bill out of my account. If you wanted, I could have them do the same thing with—"

"Oh no. No, that's all right. Why go to all that trouble?"

"Yes, ma'am."

"You have very good manners."

"My mother thanks you," I said, remembering how Solly had handled that back in his fancy building.

She gave me a full smile at that, but she didn't say anything.

"Would you be able to tell me when you expect the credit check to be completed?" I asked her. "I don't want to be stuck—"

"Oh, you won't be," she said. "This is Monday. Thursday's the fifteenth. If you moved in on Saturday, the rent would have to run from the fifteenth to the fifteenth instead of from the first every month. Would that be all right?"

"Sure. But would you mind calling me as soon as you're sure, either way, so I can make my plans?"

"I'm sure you'll pass the credit check, Mr. Wilson. My name is McGrew, by the way. Mary Margaret McGrew, if you can believe *that*. My friends call me Margo."

"I hope we can be friends, then."

I wasn't exactly knocked off my pins when she called my new cell early Wednesday morning and told me I had passed the credit check. I knew I'd done that the second she saw all that cash. She said I could move in Thursday if I wanted—the rent was going to start on the fifteenth, anyway.

There's no way that apartment was legit; the city makes you get a Certificate of Occupancy for any rental unit, but a lot of folks convert a basement or put something up over their garage. They're not going to report the income, so the last thing they need is a paper trail. If they get caught, it's heavy fines. The tell is "utilities included"—they can't have two different names on bills going to the same address.

The fines aren't even the worst part of renting an illegal apartment. There's no way to evict tenants, even if they don't pay rent. You take a deadbeat to court, you'd just be pulling the covers off yourself.

I'd spent Tuesday buying things. Enough to fill two good-sized suitcases and the shoulder duffel.

I was the tenant from Heaven, she'd tell her husband. Paid cash, and I hadn't even asked for a receipt, never mind a lease.

She was the only one around when I came Thursday morning. Told me about ten times that I must be very strong to carry all that stuff upstairs in one trip.

After she handed over the key, she gave me a little speech about not "changing" anything. Meaning the lock, I think she was saying.

I was patient while she gave me another little speech: how the microwave worked, how it was better to leave the air-conditioning off when I wasn't actually there, all this fussy stuff. She saved what I guess she thought was the big finish for last: the apartment not only had a flat-screen TV, it came with free cable.

The only way to get her out of the place was to check my watch, grab my cell phone, and punch in some numbers.

"I'll let myself out," she said.

Probably let yourself back in soon as you're sure I'll be gone for a while, too, I thought, but I just gave her a little salute and went back to the conversation I was having with myself.

You'd think a man with as much prison behind him as me would be an ace at killing time. And I guess I am, in some ways.

As long as I know how to act, I can do it. In prison, it's as clear as if they painted it on the walls. There's only so many things you can do in there, make the time go by. So what you do is, you pick one, and get as deep as you can into it.

Some guys, it's the weights. They do it in groups, spot for each other, talk about "reps" and "delts" and stuff like it's a secret code. There's steroids for sale Inside, and they were gold to the body-boys. Mostly pills, but there was even needle stuff around. The trick was getting clean needles.

Steroids aren't much of a racket—you need tranqs to really bring the cash. You don't have to risk a smuggle to do that. A lot of the loons on scrip, they're happy to sell their meds. They don't even want them in the first place . . . unless they're saving them up until they get enough to check out. Some of them, you could see they'd already left. Locked up, sure, but not on *this* planet.

Some cons work on schemes. Letter-writing, that was always a good one. You just had to be careful. The real pros, they kept charts and everything, so they never got the women they were working mixed up. Once they got three, four of them on the string, just keeping up with the letters would take all day, every day. That's why some cons have really fine handwriting, all that practice.

There're guys who can play cards. Or dominoes. Chess guys,

they could even play by mail, have a couple of dozen games going on at the same time, all around the world.

But if you run a racket, there's no such thing as part-time. You have something going for you, there's always going to be people who want it going to them.

Gang guys, they always had business. Meetings, karate practice, praying, plotting . . . it all eats time.

For some guys, doing time was no different from hanging out on the corner. Same routine: play the dozens, tell lies, brag about what they had going for them. Prison's perfect for that. It's a lot easier to lie about what *was* than what *is*.

Only thing missing was the girls walking by. Nobody ever complained about that—you could be walking into a shark tank if the wrong guy took it the wrong way.

Religion, that's always big. No matter where they lock you, there'll always be some "fellowship" or "ministry" or whatever. If you're Christian, I mean. The Muslims have their own thing. A few Indians, they would get together, too. I hadn't seen that before, but I guess there's more of them Upstate than in the city.

I remember asking Eddie how come there's no Jews in there. "Oh, they got 'em," Eddie had told me. "But not enough to form no crew. So they find their own ways to get by."

That's also when Eddie told me about Reno, that Nazi guy. He was one of them. A Jew, I mean. I don't know how Eddie found out, but when he told me, I got the joke. That's what Eddie called it when you understood something—that you got the joke. See, when Eddie told Reno about me working undercover, he was telling him something else at the same time.

Some guys had a whole library of paperback books. They put them all on the juggle, rent them out. It doesn't matter what you lend—in prison, you borrow two, you pay back three.

The tattoo artists always have plenty of business. Even guys who come in covered in ink, they always want more. Like Eddie told me, the cops keep a record of all your tats. You can change your hair, grow a beard, stuff like that. But ink, especially just past the knuckles—like LOVE on one hand and HATE on the other—that's forever. You can walk around in a long-sleeved shirt even in the summer, but you can't wear a pair of gloves.

A good thief would be hard to pick out of a lineup; the *best* thief would be invisible. I already had my size going against me, never mind the scar and the different-colored eyes. I sure didn't need more.

Doing time, there's really a lot of choices. And even when all you can do is try and stay alive, that's still something to do. As long as you don't spend too much time thinking about it.

But once you get out, there's no rules—only laws. So you have to find something with rules. Like a job, maybe. It doesn't matter if it's working an assembly line or collecting debts, every job has its own rules. Always things you're supposed to do and things you're not.

If your whole life is outside the law, the rules are much tighter. Say you're a thief—you never want to take a muscle job. A loan shark pays you to break a guy's arm; you do it even once, it's like diving off a cliff. Once you break enough bones, they expect you to step up to doing hits. Or maybe one of the guys that owes, you end up totaling him, even when you didn't mean to. I remember something Ken once said: *I'm not a hired hand, pal. I'm what you call self-employed, get it?*

In prison, that's the way you want it. It's okay to be friendly to different guys, but you don't ever want to be *with* them.

See, if you're with a prison crew, that's got rules, too. You follow them too close, you're never getting out.

That's why I always do the same things. I live good. Not for show, for real. I eat good, have decent clothes, a good car, that kind of thing. I keep case money, so I always have enough to get by even if there's no good job coming for a while. That lets me pass up the shaky-looking stuff. A true pro, he never lets himself get desperate.

So I still had about eighty grand stashed from before I went in, but I'd picked the wrong spot for it. I'd been staying with this girl for a while. You move in with a girl, you never know when you'll be leaving, and you can't be sure you'll ever be back. So I never bring anything with me that I can't walk away from, and I always keep a place I can walk back to.

You have to expect a girl to go through your stuff. Every girl I ever moved in with did that.

I hate handcuffs. Always dangling open, ready to snap closed. I'm not putting myself where I'd always be one dime-drop away from going back to prison.

So, when I move in with a girl, I always bring enough stuff over so she thinks she's got a hold on me. Stuff too big to just carry out, like a TV. Or even a lot of clothes I don't care about. They're always sure you'll *have* to come back, even if it's only to pick up your stuff.

I heard stories about girls pouring bleach on a guy's clothes when they got mad. That's why I'd never let a girl buy me anything I'm not ready to throw away. Or lend me money. Or put me on her cell-phone plan.

This last girl, she told me she was a student. I told her I hung drywall—what other kind of job could an ex-con expect to get if he was trying to go straight? Interior work; I was on the night shift. She lived on Central Park West, in the nineties. Three bedrooms. A huge place for just one person. It used to be her mother's.

I figured the girl would still be there—nobody gives up a rent-controlled apartment in this city. So my money would probably still be where I'd hid it, in a hole I made in the top of one of the closets. She was always saying the plaster was moldy, made her clothes smell. So, when she had to go someplace for a weekend, I emptied all the closets and rough-sanded the insides. Then I painted them, fresh, bright white.

I mixed a little lemon juice in with the paint; that's a trick I learned from an old guy who hired me to lift heavy stuff for him. I was supposed to be learning how to paint, but it never happened. This guy did tile, too, but he told me I didn't have the hands for that.

When she came back, I showed her my surprise. She loved it. I told her she couldn't put her stuff back in the closets for another couple of days. I had laid it all out on the beds in two of the rooms. She didn't care, she was so happy to see the closets looking so good.

And they did, for real. With the plaster re-covered, the primer, and the three coats of paint, you couldn't even see where I had planted the cash.

I hadn't planned on leaving it there long. But then I got popped for that rape I never did.

When you have money, you don't get all crazy about needing some more. Gives you time to think. Which is what I did, my first night in that over-the-garage apartment.

Maybe Francine—that was the girl's name—maybe she had a guy living there, like I had been. Or got married, even.

Or maybe she turned the place into a moneymaker, subletting it out for ten times the rent *she* had to pay. A lot of people do that. It's a risk, because the building owners are always watching for those kind of moves.

Maybe the building had gone co-op. Francine might still be there, but probably she would have sold the apartment a couple of years back—Solly had said something about real estate going way up then.

The real problem was the five years. More than that, actually. I'd never expected to be gone more than a few days, so what could I tell Francine that wouldn't sound like complete bullshit? And it wasn't like she was, you know, *crazy* about me or anything.

I balanced it out. Breaking into the place wouldn't be a hard job—they didn't have a doorman, at least when Francine lived there. But I'd have to do a lot of scoping it out first, and even then I'd *still* need a lot of luck.

And if I pulled it off, what would I have? Eighty grand . . . and maybe Francine telling the cops about an ex-boyfriend who had painted those same closets where there was a chunk missing now.

I made the decision before I fell asleep. I was going to take a pass. I remember thinking how Solly would have been proud of me, just before I went out.

It's supposed to be tradition that the first thing a man does when he makes the gate is get himself some pussy. For sure, it's what everyone who's about to go *says* they're going to do.

I think that's probably more about what's waiting for you than anything else. If you've got a wife, or a girlfriend—or even some woman you've been pen pals with, then probably it's true. Or if you're with a crew, they're supposed to have that all lined up and waiting for you. Throw you a party.

There's other ways. One old guy—hell, he was probably younger than I am now, but this was during my first bit—he told me the only difference between getting married and picking up a hooker is that, one you buy, the other you rent. But he was in there for killing his wife, so even I could figure out that he probably wasn't wrapped too tight.

Finding a hooker used to be easy. Almost no-risk. At least not for me. Guys who worked the badger game, they'd tell their girls never to pick up anyone who looked like he could do damage. Plus, they'd want a guy in a suit if they could find one. A suit and one of those little briefcases.

There's a different play on that game, but it only works if the john is looking for underage. The girl has to look real young, and they work it like a shakedown, not a rough-off. I wouldn't be a good mark for that one, either.

But everything's so . . . extreme now. Either you pick a girl up off a stroll, or you use one of the out-call services. A stroller could be underage. Carrying anything from a disease to a straight razor. And you'd have to get it on in the car, real quick. An escort could be an undercover. Or a psycho who kept souvenirs.

Most of the strip clubs, they had private rooms where you could get whatever you were willing to pay for. But there's always some Law sniffing around those places. Not for the sex, for the skim. So the undercovers spent their time in the upscale places. The more the joints charged, the more likely there was Law around somewhere.

On top of all that, I knew the owner of that jewelry store we'd hit was still trying to collect on the insurance. He had to sue to get that, which is how I knew about it, from the papers.

All the insurance company had was suspicion. Nobody had ever been bagged for the crime, and real thieves *had* done the work— even the cops told the papers that it had been a professional job.

I admit, reading that made me feel good. Respected. I can translate cop-talk, so I knew what they were saying: "Either we find ourselves an informant, or this case is going to the North Pole."

I knew something else: even if the cops quit trying to solve that one, it was a sure bet that the insurance company wouldn't. And some of their guys were supposed to be *real* good. I don't mean any ex-cop with a few pals still on the job. I mean one of those serious, fuck-the-rules spooks. The kind who get fired for going over the line once too often.

It had to be the cops who told this guy that they knew I'd been in on that jewelry-store job, but that they could never prove it in court. That's why I got a visit, the only one I got all the time I was away.

Now, you can refuse a visit. Even if it's the cops, you can still say no. Or at least you could have your lawyer there. I didn't recognize the name the CO told me, but I . . . ah, I guess I was just bored. Or maybe curious.

My visitor didn't look like an ex-cop to me. More like an accountant. He was maybe in his fifties, in good shape, but everything about him was a kind of gray. I don't mean he looked blurry or anything. And it wasn't his suit, or even his skin color. It was like he was part of a dark cloud.

Sure enough, he started raining. "We know you were one of several individuals involved in that jewelry-store robbery," he said, flat out.

I almost told him it wasn't a robbery, it was a burglary, but I didn't. I still can't figure out *why* I'd want to tell him that.

"We don't care about the people who did the grunt work," he went on. "What we want is the man who planned it. And we know who that was, too."

Maybe he'd been a soldier once, because when he said "grunt work," he was watching my eyes. I don't know what he was looking for, but I know it wasn't there.

"What are you telling *me* all this for?" I asked him.

"Mr. Caine, I'm telling you 'all this' because you're doing a prison sentence. When you come out, you'll be broke. And the owner of that jewelry store will be rolling in money. That doesn't seem quite fair to me. We thought it might not seem fair to you, either."

"I'm not in here for no robbery."

"Yes, you are," he said. That's when I knew for sure that the big cop had talked to him, face-to-face. Woods was too smart to put my real alibi on paper, or talk about it on the phone. So, even if this guy had connections strong enough so they'd open the whole file on that jewelry job for him, my name wouldn't be in it.

Who has that kind of connections? I thought. Not the feds; everyone knows they don't get along with NYPD. This guy looked like a private contractor, but he had to be working for some . . . company. A big company. Sure! The insurance company. Their investigators kept on going long after the cops quit. I heard of them staying on death cases for twenty years, trying to get their money back. Sent a lot of people to prison doing that. Same with fires. Your business is going belly-up, so you move all your stock out, then hire a torch. Might get by the arson squad, but the insurance guys were like the pit bulls of detective work.

Insurance companies. Yeah. They had the edge over the cops— a pile of cash outweighs a badge, every time. You can buy more than info with cash, you can buy people. That's why the DA's Office spends most of its budget on white-collar crime—mugging victims don't make campaign contributions.

What I said about a sex jones? A little while back, the Governor lost it all. He started out being the Attorney General—that's where he made his rep. The guy was no Eliot Ness; he got his name from going after investment bankers, not for racket-busting.

But he was running the biggest racket of them all. Everybody loved it when he made those places cough up zillions. The papers made him out to be this big hero, fighting for the little guy. Most of that money went to the State . . . and nobody went to jail. Solly told me it was one of the sweetest scams he ever saw.

So this guy had all the momentum behind him when he ran for Governor. Nobody even wanted to run against him. He won in a landslide. Everyone said he'd be the next President.

Then he got caught up in one of those escort deals, and lost it all.

That's why you stay away from a guy with a sex habit. If it's only a matter of time for them, it's a sure bet you'll be doing some yourself.

The gray-cloud man leaned in a little closer. "You wouldn't have to give up anyone who was in on it with you," he said. "Nobody on *your* side at all. Just the owner. He's the one we want. He's *all* we want."

I just looked at him.

"You pleaded guilty to a crime you didn't commit. We know why you did that."

I blank-faced him.

"How would you like to have that rape conviction vacated? Wiped off the books. *And* full immunity for the jewelry-store robbery."

"I'd like that fine," I told him. "The first part, I mean. The other part, I don't need that."

"Because you're going to let the statute run, I know. But a *rape* charge? A man like you, he wouldn't want something like that on his record."

"That's true, I don't."

"What's the problem, then? You think the locals haven't already done a KA on you?"

I knew they must have. Too bad for them—I didn't *have* any "known associates." I always wanted to be one of Ken's, and I was getting pretty close, but I don't think I ever really made the cut while he was still alive. Now, every fucking punk whose idea of a classy job was a smash-and-grab claimed they'd been with Ken. Me, I would never disrespect him like that.

So I answered the visitor's question: "What's the problem? The problem is that I can't tell you what I don't know."

"You don't know if the owner was in on the job? You just did it as piecework? Hired labor? Please don't tell me you weren't even in on the shares."

Ex-FBI? I asked myself. This guy knew his way around a pro thief's mind. At least enough to know I'd take the idea of being hired to carry bags as an insult. Giving me the chance to say something stupid, that was a pro move from *his* side, I had to give him that.

But "I don't even know what 'job' you're talking about" is all I said.

"Sure. That's what I expected. And, between us, I respect you for it. That's your reputation, Mr. Caine."

"Is that right?"

"Yes, that's right. And even if it wasn't, you've only got a couple more years to go, so I won't waste your time telling you the men who pulled that drill-through left a lot of evidence behind. . . ."

He let his words just kind of hang there, watching my eyes again.

It was too weak to even count as a bluff, and he knew it. So he finished up with: "But you're a pro, and a pro only plays for money."

"I don't get what you're saying."

"No? Then let me spell it out for you, *very* clearly: you tell us what we want to know, you walk right out of here. And if what you have to say stands up in court—we're talking *civil* court now, none of this 'beyond a reasonable doubt' stuff—two hundred and fifty thousand. Cold cash, in your hand."

"The IRS would love that."

"If we were to pay a witness a contingency fee for his testimony, that would be a very serious crime, Mr. Caine. One single conviction for that sort of activity would topple even the most reputable company. A huge backlog of cases the company had won could be reopened. Nobody wants that kind of disaster, rest assured. *Nobody.*"

"Fuck!"

"What?"

"Mr. . . . Johnson," I said, reading it off the business card he'd handed to me, "this is the first time in my whole life that I wish I *had* done the crime."

He looked at me for a long minute. Looked hard. The gray got deeper. Darker.

"We're not paying off on that jeweler's policy. He's got to sue us to get paid, and *that* case will still be open long after you walk out of here. On the back of the card I gave you is a number. Call it and you'll reach me. Me, personally. Anytime, day or night."

Then he got up and walked away.

So I was right—that guy *was* an insurance investigator, with plenty of clout behind him. I didn't know if he had enough to pull tax records. On me, I'm talking about. But one thing I was sure of: "Robert Johnson" might not be his real name, but him being the kind of man to take a job all the way, *that* was real. I was glad it wasn't me he wanted.

That jewelry-store owner, I wonder if he knew about the gray cloud yet. What I knew for sure was that he had nothing to trade. He wouldn't have Solly's name, much less me or Big Matt's.

Solly was a master storyteller. Like that wild card, Jessop. I didn't even know if there *was* any Albie who'd vouched for him. But when I thought about that gray man, I could see a lot more reasons why Solly would want to be sure of this Jessop guy. Even dead sure.

The best time to find what I wanted was mid-afternoon. The best place was outside Manhattan.

The club's parking lot was nearly empty. Inside, a single dancer phoned it in on the pole. Half a dozen guys were watching, none of them sitting together. The whole joint was about as sexy as a morgue.

When the waitress came over, I told her what I wanted. She answered on autopilot: "Got anybody special in mind, big boy?"

"If I had my choice, it'd be you."

"For real?"

"You're the best-looking thing in this place, by far."

"Once, maybe. But I'm not a dancer, not anymore. We're not supposed to . . . Oh, fuck it. What can he do, fire me? But could you go another fifty, hon? If I don't give the girl who's up there now something, she'll tell the boss."

"A buck and a half?"

"I know," she said, kind of sad. "For that kind of money, you could get—"

"A bargain," I told her.

She leaned all over me, whispered, "You won't be sorry, I swear."

Then she told me to give her a few minutes, and how to find the room in the back.

They had a guy posted on the other side of the curtains—maybe to make the girls feel safer. Long hair, cowboy mustache, dungaree vest. I guess he was supposed to be some kind of biker. Looked like a guy who threw weights every day when he was Inside, then stopped the minute he got out. From the size of his gut, I figured he must have been out for years.

He eye-fucked me just to play the role, but his heart wasn't in it—if he still had any left. I figured the girl had tipped him, too. Not to get me past Fatso, just so she could show off a little.

And she was right. I wasn't sorry at all.

"So? You find everything you needed? At that loft, I'm talking about."

"Yeah," I told Solly. "Thanks. You had it set up real slick."

He looked at me funny. Just for a second, but I caught it.

"You don't mind Ken's daughter getting a look at you, right? I mean, we went over this. You might need to stay here sometime. Who knows how things are gonna go?"

"Nobody," I said. "Nobody knows."

"You believe that?"

"Huh?"

"By me, 'nobody,' that's people. Not . . ." He pointed at the ceiling.

"You mean, like God or something?"

"There's no God 'or something.' Either there is or there isn't. A God, I'm saying."

"Okay."

"You got one?"

"One what?"

He took a deep breath. Let it out slow. "All I'm asking, it's a simple question, Sugar. I'm not trying to get into your business. Some people, they get raised a certain way, it stays with them forever. Some trace of it, anyway. I knew a guy, Rico. He did contract hits. I even saw one go down."

I gave him my listening face. You can't trip yourself up if all you do is listen.

"Only reason I was there," Solly told me, "it had to be out in public. No other way anyone was gonna get to the man who was on the spot. He lived in a fortress. Never went out without body-guards. But, see, he *had* to go out. If he couldn't show his face, the up-for-grabs stuff was all going over to the other guy.

"Certain rackets, you'd think they're all . . . *transactions,* okay? Like a whorehouse. You pay the money, you buy some broad's time. Then you're done. That's all the customer ever sees. But what you need isn't just customers, it's the license to operate."

"You mean the cops?" I asked him.

"Depends on how high-class the operation is. But that's not what I'm trying to explain. If you want to open a house, you got to pay. Not some cop on the pad, that's pennies. The big money goes to whoever owns the territory."

"Like that tax thing you were saying? Like with Ken?"

"Yeah, like that, only this is *regular* money. Every week, every month, every year. The collectors aren't leg-breakers. They're just like the paperboys out in the suburbs. Toss the paper on your porch every day, come and collect once a week. But the paperboy doesn't set the price for the paper, see? That all gets negotiated. And it's never a percentage. It's not like these places keep receipt books.

"Now, this time I was telling you about, the time I saw a con-tract kill up close, it was over that kind of thing. Guy's running a whorehouse, he knows he's gonna have to pay *someone.* But he's not gonna pay more than one."

I moved my head and shoulders a little, so Solly could see I was paying attention, but maybe not getting everything he was saying.

"Look at it this way, Sugar. Paperboy knocks on the door. Woman opens it. He says he's there to collect for last week. The woman says, 'My husband already paid you for last week.' What's the kid gonna do?"

"I don't know."

"That doesn't matter. Here's what matters: that woman's not going to be paying that paperboy. See?"

"Yeah. Two big players were in a war over who gets some territory. Maybe even new territory . . . ?"

"Right! Okay, now I'm on this bench in Central Park. Just an old man, reading his paper, taking the sun. At an angle across from me, there's Rico. Him and this broad; you couldn't really see her face, what with her hair being so long and those big round sunglasses.

"Not that anyone'd be looking at her face. Whatever those implant things cost, this broad, she'd paid double. Probably why she couldn't afford a bra.

"The mark, he's strolling down the path, big slabs of beef on each side of him. Going for an outdoor meet with a guy who's supposed to be like a go-between.

"The woman yells something at Rico in Spanish. Rico gets to his feet, like 'I don't fucking need *this,*' you know what I mean? He turns like he's gonna walk off, but then I see him cross himself, the way you see some fighters do just before the bell.

"Before you could blink, Rico spins around and puts one in the boss's head, drops one of the bodyguards, and he's still spinning, like, when the other bodyguard opens up on him. Bang-bang-bang.

"Close-range, but the last bodyguard, he's—I don't know—scared, maybe. Anyway, he misses. Rico, he don't. Even runs over and blasts the boss a couple more times in the face, probably in case the guy was wrapped.

"Everybody's screaming, ducking for cover. A kid on a bicycle swoops in, takes the handoff from Rico, and keeps rolling.

"I look up, the girl is gone. Disappeared. It was a beautiful piece of work."

"Expensive, right?"

"Had to be. But what I'm trying to tell you about Rico: how's a guy, does what he does for a living, think he's not going straight to Hell when his time comes?"

"You mean, being a Catholic and all?"

"He's no more Catholic than I am," Solly said. "But he was

raised Catholic—see what I'm telling you? That crossing himself, it's just a habit. But one he can't break."

"Maybe he thinks it'll bring him luck."

"Sure. Maybe he throws a wad in the collection plate once in a while, too. It don't matter what Rico believes. What matters, you see Rico cross himself, you better start shooting."

"I don't have those."

"Those . . . ?"

"What you're talking about, it's not a religious thing, right? It's a tell."

"You got it," Solly said. Smiling at me like he was a teacher giving me an A. "Habits, they'll kill you. Like smoking. I don't mean that lung-cancer bullshit, I mean, say, if you're holed up in a little town. People looking for you. They know you got to be close, but that's all they got. Okay, so they figure Sugar, he's too smart to be going out shopping himself. Must have someone doing it for him. Probably a broad. If they know you smoke a certain brand, that could be enough, right there."

"I . . . guess so. Maybe. But it seems like a—"

"That's just an example. Say you light up while you're waiting to do a job. With what they got today, just the butt can put you right at the scene.

"That's what you got going for you, kid. All anyone knows is that you're reliable. You'll do the work. And if you get caught, you'll take whatever weight they drop on you.

"That scar"—Solly touched his own eyebrow—"you could make it disappear with stuff you could buy in a drugstore. Yeah, you're a big guy, got a body on you. But there's a million guys fit that description, no offense. And sure, you got those two different eyes, but that's an ID thing. You don't have a *trademark*. No way the cops look over a crime scene and say, 'Yeah, this had to be Sugar's work.'"

"This is about Jessop, huh?"

Solly was just starting to open his mouth when Ken's daughter walked in.

"Oh, Mr. Vizner! I didn't expect to see you here."

"Well, my nephew just came in from out of town."

I stood up. The girl looked at me, but she didn't jump back or anything. Her face was . . . I don't know what you call it, but you could see she was one of those kids. When she smiled, it was like the whole room got brighter. Then I remembered. Down syndrome, I think they call it. I knew about it from a TV show this girl I used to stay with watched all the time. The boy on that show, he wasn't a baby—like a teenager, I think. He had that, too. And he was an actor.

"My name is Jerome," I said, and held out my hand.

"I'm Grace," she said. Even her voice was like that kid's on TV. "Did you know my dad, too?"

"Yes, I did. Not as well as . . . my uncle here, but we worked together a few times. He was a . . ." I was stumped for the right word, but she just waited, like she knew I'd get it, sooner or later.

Then it came to me. "Your father was a truly honorable man," I told her. "Everybody had respect for him."

"Thank you," she said. "I miss him a lot. But I know he'll be waiting for me. In Heaven, I mean."

"I'm sure that's true."

"Mr. Vizner, do you want me to—?"

"What's with all this 'Mr. Vizner' stuff? What happened to 'Uncle Solly'?"

"You said not in front of other people," the girl said. She wasn't mad, just saying it.

"I *did* say that," Solly told her. "I'm a stupid old man."

"Don't you say that!" Her big eyes filled up.

"Ah, Grace. What I meant to say is, it's my fault, that's all. I thought, with my nephew here, you'd know it was okay."

"But he's not your nephew, is he?"

"Why would you say that, child?"

"I guess because he doesn't look a bit like you, does he?"

"Don't you remember, that time we had dinner? You, me, and your dad? Remember what he said? 'Who'd ever think an ugly mug like me could have such a beautiful daughter?'"

"Oh, Dad always said stuff like that. But he was just teasing. He was *very* handsome." She turned to me: "Don't you think he was?"

"A very handsome man," I said.

"See, there!"

"I give up," Solly said. "I know when I'm beat."

The girl smiled again. That smile, I never saw one like it before. It was like a . . . blessing.

She kind of floated out of where we were sitting. I could hear her in the kitchen, putting things in the refrigerator.

I waited until I heard the girl go into one of the other rooms and close the door behind her. I guess she was going to study, like Solly said.

"I'm not a hit man," I told him.

"This I asked for?"

"I been thinking. About the way you broke it down and all. Something's not right."

"What do you know, something's not right?"

"Solly, I have to be a fucking genius to see through glass? The five years are up. For me, I know. And for you, too, never mind that fairy tale about being down in Florida. Maybe you went, maybe you didn't . . . but you didn't stay. And, knowing you, I don't think anyone could prove you even left the state at all."

"Okay," he said.

That surprised me, him giving it up so easy. I expected more, but I could tell—if I wanted more, I was going to have to ask for it.

"Okay, what?" I said to him.

"Okay, you're right. So here's what you're thinking: even if this Jessop got popped tomorrow, and even if he wanted to roll, he's got nobody to roll *on*. Except Big Matt, I suppose . . . but that's *his* problem, not mine. Tell me if I'm wrong."

"You're not wrong."

"Good. Then just listen for a minute. Listen good, Sugar. I'm not . . . I'm not responsible for this Jessop. Just for you and Big

Matt. The guys *I* brought in. That's the way it's supposed to be. Now, Albie, *he's* responsible for Jessop. Only, Albie, he's not around."

"So tell Big Matt—"

"Tell him fucking *what*? There's a guy named Jessop who could maybe blow up his whole life? Tell him this guy could reach out from his past and destroy his future? I should tell him, maybe that baby he's waiting on, that kid's fifteen years old before he ever sees his father, except maybe on Visiting Day?

"I should tell him his wife's gotta put the kid in some day-care place, go out, and get a job herself? 'Cause you *know* the law's going to be sitting on her forever, waiting to see some sign of the money. Want me to go on?"

"No. No, I get it."

"If you 'got' it, you wouldn't be telling me you're not a hit man. A hit man, that's a guy who kills for money. Plenty of them around. But it wouldn't cost me a cent, I wanted this guy done. One call to Big Matt and . . ."

"I know."

"But it's not that simple. This Jessop, he's probably rock-solid. Wouldn't even think about giving anyone up. No way he even knows where Big Matt is, anyway."

"So why don't you just let it go?"

"You wouldn't understand."

"I'm smart enough to follow orders, but not smart enough to understand them?"

He looked at me. Straight and hard, like he was boiling-over mad, but keeping a lid on it.

"Let's look at it the way Albie would have. Can we do that? Yeah? All right. Try this: Albie doesn't know you. Not even your name. So, if *his* guy, this Jessop, if he comes back, says it went fine, Albie wouldn't expect him to hang around. But he'd know where to find him, he had to.

"Next thing would be, Albie gives me a call. Only, this time, there's no answer. Then he gets the word. I'm dead. Not killed— that would be different—just, you know, dead. Natural causes. You with me?"

"Yeah," I said, even though I wasn't sure I was.

"Okay, so what does Albie do *then*?"

"I don't— Ah, wait a second. You're saying Albie, he'd have to go and find *me*. And Big Matt, too?"

"At last!" Solly said, just short of ranking me.

"Not find us to . . . do anything. Just to be sure *we* hadn't done anything."

"Now you've got it, Sugar."

"So you, like, owe your friend?"

"My brother, more like. That's how close we were. And I owe him the same as he would owe me, it went the other way."

The girl came in so quiet I didn't realize she was there until she said, "Uncle Solly, would you and Jerome, would you like some apple juice? You know it's good for you, and—"

"That would be lovely, sweetheart," Solly told her.

Ken's daughter. I never thought of him having a kid. A house. Stuff like that.

Solly, he never *stops* thinking.

Only Solly, maybe he was more than just a thinker. If he hadn't been lying about that war, he'd killed a lot more guys than any hit man I ever heard of. And not for money.

It was what he *didn't* say that I heard the clearest. Some things, they just have to be done. Taking out this Jessop, that wouldn't make me a hit man. It would make me what I always wanted to be: a good thief. And a good thief always cleans up after himself.

"I'll do it," I said.

"I knew you were the real thing," the old man said, showing me teeth.

I was working on getting back to things everybody does, like getting up when the alarm went off. What I mean is, the alarm *I* set, not those damn prison gongs.

But I hadn't even bothered to set the alarm last night; I knew I couldn't do any of the things I wanted to do until the afternoon, so I just slept in.

I'd filled the refrigerator with protein shakes and power bars, stuff like that. I'd picked up a lot of vitamins, too. I don't really know much about them. A young guy in the health store, he picked most of the stuff out for me.

He didn't know he was doing that, I don't think; just assumed he knew what I'd want. Which was a good thing, since I didn't want to be asking a lot of questions. You do that, people remember you. I even let him sell me a set of dumbbells for traveling . . . the kind you fill with water.

I didn't really have any special taste for that powdered stuff, but it was what guys who power-lifted were always talking about. And I figured that woman downstairs, she'd be nosing around, sooner or later. I wanted it to look like I really was what it said I was on those business cards.

"It's always better you don't try looking like something you couldn't be," Solly said. "Nobody's gonna buy you're an accountant, but you don't have to look like a thug, either.

"So forget the fancy suits. Get a nice leather jacket—a *nice* one, I'm saying. Go to Bally on Madison, spend some money. Clean pair of jeans, good sneakers. Not like the kids wear, like . . . you know, athletic shoes? Simple black ones. There's a store a few blocks from Bally. Mephisto. All they sell is shoes, and they'll have what you need.

"And a white shirt. Not a stiff one, like mine," he said, holding out his hand so I could feel his cuff—it was like a smooth-faced brick. "Silk is best. No custom-made stuff, just off the rack. A *good* rack, though. You wear a shirt like that, no tie, under that leather jacket, you're good to go."

"Okay," I said. I'd lived a lot of years without stuff like that, but Solly, he was setting up jobs before I was born.

"Next, you get yourself *another* leather jacket. Heavier one. Pair of work boots, steel toes. Scuff 'em up so they don't look new. Lose the good shirt, wear a pullover. Now you're a guy who works with his hands for a living. Between those two looks, that's all you'll ever need."

"You said there was something I could do about—"

"Way ahead of you, kid." He handed me something that looked like a skinny tube of lipstick. "Just fill in the scar with this. Not too much; you want it to look natural. The scar's so white you really can't see it until you're up close. Unless you get a flashbulb exploding in your face, nobody'll even notice. I even got you a present."

He handed me a long, narrow little box. Inside, a pair of glasses. I put them on. But I didn't see anything different.

"'What're these for?' is what you're thinking, am I right?"

"Yeah. I mean, it's not a . . . disguise or anything."

"No? That's *exactly* what it is. These glasses, they got no prescription. Just plain glass. With a tiny little bit of tint, like the ones they make for indoor-outdoor. You know, the brighter it gets, the darker they get? Go look at yourself in the mirror over there."

That's when I saw what Solly meant. The glasses didn't change my face or anything, but you couldn't see my eyes through them. I mean, you could see them, but not good enough to see the colors.

"Get used to them," Solly told me. "I got three more for you, exactly the same. Wear them all the time. After a while, it'll be just like brushing your teeth in the morning."

"Thanks, Solly," I said. And I meant it—compared to Solly, I was still an amateur.

I was unlocking my car when the woman came out.

"Those look good on you," she said.

"What?"

"The glasses. When did you start—?"

"Oh. No, I always wear these," I told her, "they're prescription." *This one doesn't miss much.* "But it takes a while to make them up in the flexible frames I like. I just got these back."

"You work some strange hours," she said.

"Yeah, I do." *Nosy, too.* "But that's what this business is. The people I train, they've got important stuff to do. If I want to make a living, I need to understand that their schedule's more important than mine."

"I guess that pays pretty good."

"Better than you might think," I told her. I had a decent bit of cash upstairs. Not hidden, like I had done with that closet years ago, just stuck in different places, like one of my jackets and my gym bag. I figured she'd find it anyway. I was worried about snooping, not stealing, and I figured *not* having loose cash around would only make her suspicious.

"It sounds like you never have too much time for yourself."

"Sure, I do. See, I work whatever hours the clients want, but that's only when they're here. In New York, I mean. They go away, I do, too. Like a long vacation. One time, I was gone almost three months."

"Wow!"

"Well, like I said, they pay good. And I'm careful with my money; I don't throw it around. If you don't waste money on . . . *things,* you know, then you can pretty much travel anywhere you want."

"That sounds—Ah, I'm holding you up, aren't I?"

"A little," I said, looking at my new watch. It gets a signal from some atomic station, and it's always on the nose. It wasn't flash, either.

"Well, nice talking with you."

"Me, too," I said. Then I got behind the wheel and turned the key. She walked back into the house like she was sure I'd be watching.

"Do you have an appointment?" the girl behind the glass-top desk asked me. She was slim, dark-skinned, with shiny black hair. She wore it pulled up, held with a little heart-shaped diamond clip.

"No, I'm sorry. A friend of mine told me about Mr. Ramirez, and I thought I'd ask him about this . . . thing. I guess I should have called."

"Well . . . he *is* working on a very important case. A brief to the United States Court of Appeals. But let me just try. . . ."

She punched a number. Talked in Spanish. So fast that I couldn't even make out a single word. I only know a couple of words, anyway—everyone who's done time knows those.

The conversation went on too long. By the time she said it was okay to go on back, I figured out that she was the lawyer's girl, not just some secretary.

He stood up when he saw me come in. Reached out his hand. I shook it. He made a little move, telling me to sit down across from him.

First thing I did was slide one of my business cards across to him. He glanced at it. Nodded to tell me he got the message—he'd never seen me before.

It was a seriously upscale office. Thick carpet on the floor, real wood on the walls, big window behind him. My money was on one-way glass.

"Look at the door behind you," he said.

I turned, saw it had some kind of thick padding on it.

"Soundproof," he said.

"Nice." I doubled my bet on the one-way glass in his window.

"Gloriana said you wanted to see me?"

"Yeah. I want to do something, but I can't do it myself. It's completely legit, only I'm not the kind of guy who can go around doing it without taking a chance."

"So mysterious?"

"Nah. I'm just . . . I don't always know how to make things sound the way I want them to come out."

"Ah?"

"I need to hire a private eye. A good one. Probably the kind a high-class lawyer like you would use on a big case."

"You want this private eye to do . . . what?"

"I just want him to find somebody."

"Somebody around here?"

"I don't think so. I really don't have very much to go on."

"Tell me what you have."

I did that. Gave him all the scraps Solly had, plus a description. I'm good at stuff like that. I see something once, and I've got it for-ever.

Jessop was a little taller than me, probably six four or so. We'd both been wearing the same kind of work boots, so I figured the measurement was right. I was about two sixty-five then, and Jessop was maybe a hundred pounds short of that.

That job had been hard work. Hot as hell. After a while, we took our shirts off. Then I could gauge his body real easy. Skinny, but all muscle. Not pop-out muscle; all ropy, like.

I thought me and Big Matt were going to do all the heavy work, and they'd picked this guy because he was skinny enough to slip through places we couldn't fit. But he was seriously strong, pulled his weight. I guess Albie must have known that he could.

Jessop had some ink, but you couldn't tell much from it. Confederate flag on his chest, right over his heart, but no "88" or shamrock or other race stuff.

It looked professional, that tattoo. He had outdoor skin, too. If he'd ever been Inside, it was a while ago.

Dark-brown hair, cut pretty short, like a businessman. Dark eyes. Kind of a big nose, but nothing that'd make you look twice. The little finger on his right hand was crooked, like it was broken once and never set right. Long fingers, thin wrists. A rip scar on his left forearm—the kind you get from blocking a blade.

If I had to guess, I'd say he was somewhere around my age. No way this was his first job: he knew how to use tools, and he lifted with his back. Never tried to pick up something he didn't think he could handle.

Didn't talk much, but none of us did, so I didn't know if he was naturally closemouthed or just being a pro.

He wasn't from New York, that was for sure. I don't know how people talk in Florida—that was where Albie lived—so he could be from there, maybe.

He was the kind of guy, you walk in a poolroom, he's waiting for you. When I tried to picture what he did when he wasn't working, I could see him doing that. He didn't look like a gambler.

"Would this person know you?" the lawyer asked me.

"Yeah."

"Even in your new glasses?"

Showing off? I didn't know. I just said "Yeah," again. I figured that was smarter than telling him a story like I told the girl who owned the house I was staying in. On this slickster, it would never fly.

"So you'd know *him*?"

"No question."

"Say we could get a picture . . . ?"

"That would do it. For me, I mean."

"If he's got a record—and I'm thinking he probably does—shouldn't be that hard to find. Okay, so this person gets . . . located. What then?"

"Well, if your guy could find out some other stuff, that would be good, too."

"Such as?"

"Like you said, if he had a record. Or if he was a drunk. Or a junkie. Things like that."

The lawyer touched that pencil mustache of his. "Anything that might make him, should we say . . . unreliable?"

"Uh-huh." *Damn,* I remember thinking, *this one's got a fucking stiletto for a brain.*

"Mr. . . . Wilson, is it? Mr. Wilson, is it correct for me to assume that should he be located nothing is going to happen to this individual?"

"Absolutely."

"No . . . difficult questions you want to ask him?"

"Not a one."

"You understand, in such a situation, the investigator would be working for me, but *you* would be the client, yes?"

"Sure."

"And you understand there is no way *I* could claim I haven't met you before?"

"Yeah, I know."

"And the reason you want this person located?"

"An old friend of mine—I mean old-old, he was like eighty-something—he died. While I was Upstate. This guy, the one I want to find, I heard he and my friend were close. My friend, he wanted to be buried in Arlington. You know, the place where—"

"So he was a veteran, your friend?"

"Yes."

"So you're not certain his final wishes have been carried out? And you believe this gentleman might know?"

"Exactly," I said, trying to say it like Solly would.

"Very good," the lawyer said. "You understand that you've really provided very little by way of information, yes? So this could take a while."

"And time is money, I know. But this is real important to me."

I left my new cell-phone number with the lawyer. And ten large in hundreds.

I was in the middle of a workout the next morning when I heard someone coming up the back stairs. Before I could . . . I can't say what, exactly, because I wasn't ready for anyone knowing about the place.

Which makes me stupid.

Then I heard, "It's just me." The woman from downstairs.

"I'm sorry, Mr. Wilson," she said, when she was standing in the front room, where I'd been working out. "I wanted to ask you something, and I thought it would be silly to call, since I could see you were home. I mean, from your car and all."

I just looked at her.

"I didn't want to ring the bell, either. In case you were asleep. Or on the phone."

I put down the weights.

She ran her hands through her hair. Looked like she'd just washed it. She was wearing a white tank top and black stretch pants—I couldn't see her feet because she was still on the staircase.

"And . . . well, you know how people are. I wasn't going to use the outside steps. The old lady who lives right across the street, she's like Neighborhood Watch. Sits there all day, watching."

"You wanted to ask me something?"

She took that as inviting her to come the rest of the way up. I saw where her shoulder came to on the wall above the railing—she was maybe five two, at the most.

"More like a professional opinion," she said. "Now, I *know,* this must happen to you all the time. Like at parties: people find out a man's a doctor, they start asking him all their medical questions. I apologize if . . . if I'm doing that."

I stepped back, making it like I did that so I could sit on the couch, get some distance.

But she came closer.

"Could I ask you a personal question?"

"Uh . . . okay."

"How old are you?"

"Forty."

"Well, what it says on your license, you're only thirty-nine. I mean, you were born in 1970. December. This is still only July, so you're not forty *yet,* right?"

"On my next birthday."

"I know. I was just . . . I mean, I didn't believe you were that old when I first met you. But I guess, being a personal trainer and all . . ."

I didn't say anything. I wasn't trying to stare her down, or even make her uncomfortable, but I didn't want her coming up here all the time. I was glad I had the glasses on.

"I'll bet, if you asked a hundred people who were about to turn forty how old they were, ninety-nine of them would say thirty-nine. Maybe all one hundred."

I shrugged. That's what I do when I can't see where someone's going.

"It's not the age you are, it's the age you *look,* isn't that true?"

"On the outside, maybe."

"Well, I bet for the people you train *that's* what's important to them."

"Oh sure," I told her. I was a lot more comfortable now that I could see where she was going. "Yes, it would be. But there's a lot more to it than losing weight. Like cardio. And eating right. I guess it's more about being healthy than looking . . . younger, or whatever."

"Could you tell by just looking at a client what they'd need for a . . . a program, right? Isn't that what you call it?"

"Yes. A program, I mean. But you can't tell anything by looking at someone. You need a body-mass index for that," I told her.

I could feel the confidence in me, now that I knew she wasn't asking her questions to check my credentials. The more a person is paying attention to themselves, the less they pay to you.

"Are you saying you can't tell if someone is too fat?"

"That wouldn't be my decision."

"I don't understand." She walked over to where I was sitting, hesitated a second, then sat down in the armchair to my right. She crossed her legs. I could tell she was pressing down hard over her knee, because her thigh pulsed. She was barefoot. Small feet, high arch. Shoulders back, spine straight.

Posing.

If I didn't say anything, she'd think I was going along, looking her over. So I told her:

"If someone *thinks* they're too fat, that's what counts. Or too skinny. It doesn't matter what anyone else thinks; if someone's . . . dissatisfied with themselves, that's enough. But nobody should go into training because of what other people think."

"Really? Then how come so many movie stars have all kinds of plastic surgery?"

"I don't know any movie stars, so I'd be guessing, but I'd still come down on the same spot. Maybe, for them, it's still about what *other* people think, only there's a lot more of those people."

"But that's dangerous, isn't it? Botox in your face, collagen in your lips, that'll cost you in the end."

I could tell she wasn't asking a question, so I just nodded.

"Even liposuction, people *die* from it sometimes."

"I guess so. I don't know anything about stuff like that. My clients make their own goals—it's my job to make up a program so they can reach them."

"Well, my husband is always telling me I'm too fat."

I shrugged again. She was headed back to a place I didn't want to go.

"He thinks what I do is just sit on the couch all day and watch TV. You know what 'secretarial spread' is?"

I shook my head, hoping that wasn't some personal-trainer stuff I should have known about.

"It's what girls get from sitting all day. Kind of spreads them out, so they take up more room."

"Oh. Yeah, I . . . guess so."

"Well, see, that's what I was. A secretary, I mean. In fact, I worked for my husband. He wasn't complaining about my fat ass back then, believe me."

I made some sound, just enough to tell her I was listening. Anything I said out loud would be a mistake—I knew that much.

"I don't think he says it to be mean, but it kind of hurts my feelings, you know? And he . . . well, maybe he's thinking he didn't get what he paid for?"

"Paid for?"

"I just mean I'm not the same girl he married."

"How could you be?"

"What does *that* mean?"

"Nobody stays the same forever. Does he look just like he used to?"

"Charley? You must be joking. Oh, that's right; you've never even met him, have you?"

"No." I said it the same way you'd say a weather report. I didn't want her to think I *didn't* want to meet him, but I didn't want to talk to him, either.

"It's not the same for men," she said. "They can get fat and bald and . . . anything they want. It doesn't matter. That's if they've got money, I mean."

"I guess that's so."

"But I don't want to be unfair. Charley treats me like a princess. Anything I want. So, I was thinking, maybe he makes those cracks—you know, like I said before—maybe he's just trying to make sure I'm like you said. Healthy, right?"

"That's what I said, sure."

"But it would be a great present for him, too, don't you think?"

"That kind of thing never works," I said. Not a chance in the world I was going to let myself be played into training her husband—I'd end up having to move.

"But you just said—"

"Sure. But when you give someone a gift certificate for training, most times they kind of resent it. And even if they do show up, they're not really motivated. Once they see how hard it's going to be to really reshape themselves, they don't stay with it, anyway. So you'd just be wasting your money."

"Not for Charley, silly! I mean, yes, it'd be for Charley, but the present wouldn't be some gift certificate; it would be me."

Stepped right into that one, you fucking mope, I was thinking, but I didn't say anything, just tried to look surprised.

"You know what my measurements were when I first went to work for Charley? I was a C-cup thirty-seven, twenty-four, thirty-eight. . . . I guess I was always a little hippy. I weighed a hundred and nineteen pounds. That wasn't so long ago—our tenth anniversary is next year. You know how much I weigh now?"

"I couldn't even guess."

"You don't *want* to know, trust me. Don't you think it would be a wonderful surprise if I could squeeze myself into one of the outfits I wore back then? I'd probably give Charley a heart attack, I did that."

"You couldn't do that."

"What?! Why would you say such an awful—?"

"No, no. I don't mean you couldn't train to whatever shape you wanted. I just meant, something like that, it's gradual. So it wouldn't be a surprise, see?"

"Oh."

"It's not like you could wake up one morning and be all changed. That's the hardest thing for people to swallow, patience. They want to work out for a month and turn into something different."

"Well . . . it kind of depends on the person, doesn't it? I mean, I'm not exactly an elephant, right?"

"Of course not. But if you want to do it correctly, it *always* takes time to—"

"Fair enough. But that's not what I'm saying. I'm saying, it depends on how much you get *noticed*, right? For it to be a surprise, I mean."

"Like if someone hadn't seen you in a couple of years?"

"Or if someone hadn't *looked* at you in a couple of years."

"I . . . guess that's right."

She stood up. "I didn't mean to take up so much of your time. If you ever need—"

"No problem," I said. That's what people say when they want to get rid of you.

She walked over to the staircase. It was only a couple of seconds, but I could see she didn't walk like a woman who thinks she's too fat.

There were a few places I could walk in and some people there would know me. Buy me a drink, slap me on the back, tell me the last stretch must have been sweet, since I was looking so good.

Places I knew I couldn't go near. Maybe Solly thought I was already down in Florida. He gave me a list of all these people who Albie might talk to, but I knew that was a shuck—no way Solly hadn't already talked to those guys himself.

So, I could go down there, play a hunch that Jessop was a local.

But what I couldn't do was lie to Solly. If he ran across me still here, I could always tell him the truth about me hiring the PI through that lawyer. But it would be better if it didn't come to that.

The story Solly told me, on the surface it made sense. If he wanted Jessop canceled, he would have called Big Matt, like he said. I worked with Big Matt twice before. He was an angry guy. I don't mean he had a temper or anything like that. But he was so angry, you could feel it standing next to him. He walked around like that. I guess maybe he wasn't angry anymore, not with all Solly told me. But if Big Matt thought anyone might knock his new train off the rails, he'd kill them. Not a doubt in my mind.

I didn't know any way to reach him. I never did; that isn't the way it works. Guys like Solly, they're all over the country. They're the ones with the numbers. And even those numbers, they're just message drops.

So I was thinking two things: Big Matt had closed down his contact number. He was out of the business, what did he need it for? I was also thinking about that responsibility thing Solly went on and on about. If Jessop could give up Big Matt, why couldn't I? The way Solly put it, I had that statute-of-limitations thing going for me, so Big Matt wouldn't worry about me. Just Jessop.

I had to concentrate. That's a lot harder than pushing weight. When I concentrate, really, really hard, I can feel my brain—it burns just like muscles do when you work them to their limit.

But I did it. Some guys, they say it helps to write stuff down. Draw lines, make things connect. I could never do that—it always made me think of other things, instead of what I was trying to figure out.

If I'm Big Matt, I know there's a bunch of people who can put me in on that jewelry job. And not just Jessop. That statute-of-limitations thing, it was just . . . a misdirection. The kind of trick you pull on purpose. Like training yourself to drop your left shoulder and throw the right hand over at the same time. A guy sees your left shoulder drop, he thinks the hook is coming from that side. All you have to do is distract him for a little piece of a second.

The way Solly told it, if Jessop got caught, he was dead meat, because he couldn't use the statute-of-limitations thing. Okay, so that meant Big Matt wasn't safe, either. But Big Matt's not going to work anymore, so there's no chance *he'll* get dropped pulling a job. Jessop, why would he retire? Me, why would I?

Big Matt knew I could have dealt him on the jewelry job, and he'd know I hadn't done that. Jessop, he'd know that, too. But I was still just as dangerous to either of them if I ever got caught again. It was like I held this trump card, and I could play it anytime.

I'm not a killer. But when you do my kind of work, it can happen. Like with Ken. I'm still a pretty young guy. Looking at another bit wouldn't change my mind about who I was. Jessop, he was around my age. At least, I think he was.

But for Solly, even a nickel would be a death sentence. You can buy protection Inside. Buy almost anything you could imagine, if you've got the money. And Solly had the money. But, no matter how much money you have, you can't buy a decent hospital. Get serious-sick in prison, chances are you won't get better. Throw in Solly being such an old man, you know he'd never finish out the bit.

Solly knew me. He knew Big Matt. He knew neither of us would ever go outside the rules. Jessop, he didn't know. But Jessop, what did *he* know? Maybe, if he was close to Albie, he knew a lot.

Solly told me if he wanted Jessop gone he could have just hired a shooter. I went along like that made sense, but all the time, I was thinking, *That story Solly told me about this guy Rico, the contract man. Maybe he made that up?*

Why I thought that was I didn't believe Solly could find a shooter without going outside his safe zone. He put jobs together. Jobs, not hits.

If I started nosing around, this Jessop would know I was coming way before I got to him. How was that supposed to help Solly? He knew I was good at some stuff, but I wasn't any secret agent. Chances are, I go down to Florida, where this Albie used to live, Jessop makes *me* disappear.

Yeah. That was Solly, down pat. Let other guys bet on fights, Solly wouldn't care who won; he'd be the guy keeping the vig. Maybe Jessop fucks up. Gets me done, but not so smooth. A murder, he couldn't really say it was self-defense without bringing up the jewelry job. That'd probably only make it worse for him. Florida, it's not like New York. We got the death penalty, too, but down there, they *use* it.

Anyway, the only one Jessop could give up was me, and what could that be worth? He never laid eyes on Solly; and Albie was dead.

How come, all of a sudden, Solly was going to a lot of trouble to make sure I knew stuff? Much more than he ever did before. Was he trusting me or setting me up?

I remembered one thing Solly said to me, a long time ago. "It's not how much you take, kid, it's where you take it from. Me, I always take my half out of the middle."

Even with my head hurting, one thing came through clear: I go down to Florida looking for Jessop, the only sure winner would be Solly.

It was so cute: I find Jessop, only one of us walks away. Wouldn't matter which one; Solly could always find Big Matt. Tell him a story about whichever one of us was still alive.

Somewhere, way in the back of my mind, I thought Solly would be proud of me. For not trusting him, I mean.

Even without Solly's game, I had a stronger reason for not going to Florida right away.

"Woods," is the way he answered when he picked up the extension. I don't know how cops usually answer the phone, but that didn't sound like it.

"You were straight with me once," I said into the mouthpiece. "I never forgot that. And I figure now, maybe you and me, we want the same thing."

"Who the—? Wait! Are we talking about someone who went down for something he didn't do, and skated on one he did?"

"Just the first part is right," I said—who admits something over the phone? "I want the guy whose time I did. And you want him, too."

"You got *that* right," Woods said. Cold and serious.

"I'm not coming in," I told him.

"Say where and when."

"Now. There's a vitamin shop, northwest corner of Eighty-first and Broadway."

"I'm rolling."

I didn't bother telling the cop not to bring backup or wear a wire or any of that crap. I wasn't a wanted man. And Woods, he hadn't told me to call the Sex Crimes Unit. Which meant they'd never caught the real rapist. Probably never even looked for him.

Woods must have circled the block a couple of times, because I spotted him on the other side of Broadway, getting ready to cross at the light. I liked that. He didn't badge some guy to let him park at the curb, or leave his unmarked at a fireplug. He did what a regular person would do.

Hard for a guy as big as him to be low-key. Last thing he'd want, call attention to himself. And if you saw him once, you'd remember him.

"Did every day of it, huh?" was what he said. No "hello" or nothing. But he had his hand out, and I shook it.

"Let's take a walk," I said. "Riverside's not far, and it's a beautiful day."

He knew what I meant. We walked side by side a few blocks west until we came to Riverside, found an empty bench.

"Is it okay if I make sure of a couple of things, before I say anything?"

The cop opened his coat. "Got an ankle piece, too," he said, like that was what I wanted, check him for weapons. I couldn't figure out why he was playing it like that, but I let it go.

"You know I didn't rape that girl."

"Yeah. And *you* know why—"

"No, I mean, that was the question. Are you just going along, in case I got something else for you on that other thing, or are you saying you believe me?"

"I believe you," the cop said. "I did from the beginning."

"But she *was* raped?"

"No question."

"So, if she picked me out of a lineup, whoever did it, he must look *something* like me, right?"

"You'd think so," the cop said, leaning back and lighting a smoke. He didn't offer me one. That was a good sign.

"A lot of guys could look like me. That doesn't narrow it down much."

"Big guy, white . . . sure, that covers a lot of ground. Hair is something you can change easy enough. Beard, mustache . . . takes only a few minutes, make them go away. Except for this"—he touched his own right eyebrow—"nothing makes you stand out except your size." He gave me a close look, not making any secret out of what he was doing.

I stayed still.

"Your eyes. Your eyes, that'd set you off. *That's* what those glasses are about, huh?"

"Why are you playing me? I haven't done anything for you to treat me like this. You know damn well, anyone gets a look at my eyes, they'd remember."

"They would. And, yeah, I did."

"But she didn't?"

"Where's all this going, Caine?"

No more "Sugar." No more "have one on me" cigarette. Good. If he'd acted like we were pals, I wouldn't have bought it.

And he'd know that. So maybe it wasn't as good a sign as I thought.

Fuck it. I'm no good at this sideways stuff. I just went for it.

"You think I got off cheap, don't you?"

"Five years? Far as I'm concerned, you lucked out when that girl ID'ed you. Wasn't for that, you'd still be where you belong."

"Lucked out? Right. If that girl had never ID'ed me, you'd still have been waiting when I came back to my place, that's what you're selling?"

"One man's luck is another man's loss. And I *still* say you got off cheap."

"Let's say I did. But if the sex-crimes cops hadn't gotten her to ID me, you wouldn't be saying what you just said. That's true, too."

"Okay. But I'm still waiting for the punch line."

"I want to get off the RSO list."

"So you can sue the city? It's a little late for that now, don't you think?"

"Five years—"

"I'm not a lawyer," the cop said, like he was proud of it. "If some shyster told you there was money in this, you're brain-dead, Caine. You *pleaded* guilty. I don't care if they found enough of some other guy's DNA to fill every test tube in Quantico, it wouldn't do you any good."

"I don't have a lawyer. I'm not going to sue anybody. You know why I took that plea."

"So? What, then?"

"So that DNA, it *would* do me some good. A lot of good."

"You brought up the RSO, not me."

"Right. You know what that means, being a Registered Sex Offender? I maxed out, but I *still* got to keep an address, let them know when I move, stuff like that."

"Cramps your style, does it?"

"No, that's not it. They don't actually *do* anything. It's just a stupid Web site. And you know who uses it the most?"

"Uses what the most?"

"This 'registry' thing. The people who use it most are those . . . 'pedophiles,' they call them. See, what they do, when they're trying to worm their way in someplace, like with a single mother who's living with her little daughter, they tell her to check them out. On this Web site, I mean. When that comes up empty, it's like the government is saying, 'This guy, he's all right,' see?"

"How come you know this?" Woods asked me. He was way too casual—I could see he really wanted to know.

"When I first went in—on the last bit, I mean—they put me in this group for sex offenders. It was supposed to be voluntary, but all of them know, if they don't go, the Parole Board's gonna nail them."

"And you didn't want to call attention to yourself, so you played along?"

"On the nose. I didn't last long—they threw me out—but that was one of the things they talked about in 'group.'

"They talked about this registry a *lot*. Some of them, they were all . . . outraged, like. It was a violation of their rights, they were branded for life, blah-blah. But a couple of them said the truth: that was one scam they could never use *again*, which was a shame because it always worked. *That's* how I know about it."

Woods went back to looking bored. "So what d'you want, Caine? You think I'm going to sign an affidavit or something?"

"I *think* you want the same thing I do."

"What? Justice for the victim?" The cop took a drag of his smoke. For a second, I was sorry I quit—he sure made it look like it tasted good.

"Not for her. For him."

"Jesus. You did too many fucking crossword puzzles up there, Caine."

"What d'you get out of making fun of me, cop? I know I'm no Einstein, but I don't need to be one to add *this* up."

"Huh?"

"The guy who raped that girl, he owes you guys for doing it. But he also owes me, for doing the time."

"You want me to help you find him so you can shake him down?"

"You get a kick out of saying things like that? I thought you were a right guy. You fucking well know what I'm saying, but you're still just jerking my chain. So how's this? The guy who raped that girl, his life isn't worth five years of my time. But I can't find him without help, so I'll settle for him going down. And he'd go down *hard,* no matter where he's locked."

"And I care about that because . . . ?"

"I'm not asking you to tell me anything. Just listen. No way he was someone the girl knew, or you would have nailed him. He got away with that one, so he probably got away with a lot more. Maybe he still is."

"Or maybe he's already doing time on one of the others."

"If you *know* that, just tell me. What could it hurt? Hurt you, I mean."

"Oh, I know what you mean, pal. And even if I *did* know, I wouldn't tell you—I'm not playing bloodhound for a hit man."

"I'm not—"

"You've got no rep for that, I know. But for this guy, I'm betting you'd make an exception."

"Try me and see."

"Can't," the cop said. "Far as I know, nobody's ever been convicted of that rape. Besides you, that is."

"But he *could* be in the system, right? Those sex-crimes guys,
they 'solved' the case, so they're all done. But you might get a DNA
match off someone who's still locked up and—"

"If there *was* DNA, maybe. I never asked."

"There you go. That proves we could help each other. If you
want the help, that is."

He changed position on the bench. Dropped his cigarette to the
ground and stomped it *out*. "How come you didn't go to Sex
Crimes with this?"

"How come you knew I didn't do it?"

"What do you want, Caine? I'm not asking again."

"I want you to tell the girl I didn't do it. I want the chance to
talk to her. I don't think anybody ever really did. Nobody's looking
for this guy. But me, *I'd* look for him."

"You carrying?"

"No, sir." He had to be asking for some reason I didn't understand. Anything I got caught "carrying" would guarantee me
another few years inside a State box.

"You'd take a polygraph?"

"Right this minute."

"And that's the only crime you want to talk about?"

"Come on."

"Yeah. Yeah, I know."

"If you catch a terrorist from another country—catch him *here*,
I mean—how come you ship him back where he came from for
questioning?"

The cop didn't say anything.

"I could be that other country for you. I find this guy, he's
going to tell me everything. Not just about the rape I did his time
for, about every one he's ever done."

"Somehow, I can't see you wearing a wire."

"Wouldn't need one. On every rape this guy committed, they
found *something*. Maybe he's got a trophy case. Maybe he takes
pictures. Maybe he had a partner. I don't know. But, whatever I

get, add it to what you already got, wouldn't that be enough to nail him?"

The cop pinned me with his eyes. Wasting his time—I wasn't going anywhere.

"I'll get back to you," he finally said.

"How?"

"That's a good question."

"I'll call you, okay? Just say when."

The cop looked at his wristwatch. Maybe it had one of those calendar things in it.

"I got two years until I pull the pin," he said. "Retire. Me and the wife, we've already got a place picked out. Far from here."

"It was worth a shot," I said.

"I said two years, Caine, not two days. There's benches by the other river, too. You know the Hospital for Special Surgery?"

"I can find it."

"Just keep walking on Seventy-first; you'll find a little bridge, takes you up to where you can look at the river over the FDR. Next Friday, two o'clock, I'll be on that bridge."

"Me, too."

Walking around without a gun felt good. I never liked them—they always seemed to make things worse. But what I *really* didn't like was guys who liked guns. Some of them, when they handed over what they were carrying so I could see all the special stuff for myself, it made me feel . . . slimy, like.

Not the gun itself, the whole idea. Like the way those guys in the Sex Offender Treatment Unit would be talking about the stuff they did. Just listening, it was like some of their—I don't know what to call it—like some of what they were would rub off on you.

I don't like being around the iron jockeys, either. I never felt right listening to them talk. Maybe that's just me. Maybe I just don't like *most* people.

I got shot once, a long time ago. The slug went into my upper arm, never touched bone. The doc in the ER was an Indian. Not one of those guys you see in cowboy movies; from the country India. He said I must have done something very good in another life to have deserved such luck. I was a little fuzzy, but I could tell he believed what he was saying.

Turned out, the bullet just went in one side and out the other. A nick, they called it. That Indian doctor said the only danger would be infection. Not from the bullet, from not keeping it clean.

I remember asking him how come I couldn't get an infection from a bullet. In prison, some guys would dip the points of their shanks in their own shit, so you could die from the poison after you were stabbed. I didn't tell the doctor that, but I really did want to know.

"A projectile launched at supersonic speed would generate so much heat that it would be sterilized," he said.

"What's 'supersonic'?"

"Did you hear the shot?"

"Yeah. After I—"

"You heard the shot because it broke the sound barrier. That's what makes it supersonic."

"Thanks."

He gave me a confused kind of look. But maybe it was the drugs they were pumping into me that made me think that.

They didn't even keep me. Just gave me a couple of more shots, cleaned it all out, and packed stuff inside before they taped me up.

The cops came. I knew they would. The ERs, they're supposed to call in any gunshot wound, even if you tell them it was an accident. There's docs you can go to who won't call it in, but they charge an arm and a leg, even if they don't have to take one off.

And—who knows?—they could be on some cop's Rat Rolodex themselves. A doctor who gets nailed for writing scrips by the pound, he'd "cooperate" with the cops in a second—that prescription pad, that's his moneymaker.

So the rule is, if you got shot doing something that could drop you down a well, that's when you take the chance. Say you've got a cop's slug in you, no way you can let a hospital take *that* out.

But with the bullet I took, I knew I was on solid ground.

What I told the cops: I never saw the shooter. I got no beef going with anyone. Broad daylight, probably one of those punks trying out his new nine. Or maybe it came from inside one of the buildings I was walking past.

What they told me: They can't protect me if I don't come clean with them. Maybe the next time, the shooter won't miss.

They were as bored as I was. Without a slug to put under their microscopes, there was nothing they could do, and we all knew it.

Whatever they put in the wound finally dissolved, just like the doctor said. All it left was a little pucker mark, like a vaccination.

But when I went back to the gym, some of the guys looked at the arm and said it was ruined. They were really sorry for me. I didn't get it at first. I mean, soon I was back lifting the same weight I always had, so what was the big deal?

One of them explained. He said that bullet had spoiled my skin. You could hide some stuff, like the blackheads they were always getting all over their backs and shoulders, but what I had would never look right.

I asked him, look right for what?

"You don't compete?" He sounded kind of . . . disgusted, like I told him I didn't wash my hands after I used the toilet or something. This was the same guy who was always telling me I had great genetics but I'd need some help if I ever wanted to get *really* big.

I didn't go back to that gym.

Fuck it. Wasn't like I was friends with anyone there or anything. I like working out by myself more, anyway.

I guess it depends on what you want it for. These guys, they were more worried about how good a suit of armor looked than how good it worked. Not me.

People think the worst thing about being locked up is that you can't have the things you had on the outside. But that's not it. Plenty of guys who hit the joint never had anything on the outside. So what did they lose, really?

Freedom? How much of *that* do most people have, if you think about it? In prison, they tell you what to do. Outside, they do the same thing. Some people, they hate being told what to do so much that they end up Inside. Again and again. Time after time.

What you *really* lose are choices. I've seen men stabbed over which TV program to watch.

You get to make *some* choices, but those are only between bad and worse. One of the heavies asks you to do something. Say no, and somebody in there gets told to kill you. Or at least fuck you up so bad that you end up wearing a diaper or breathing through a tube in your throat.

You could ask for PC. Or you could do what you got told to do. Either way, you'd be alive. Protected, even.

You'd also be nothing.

So, if you have to kill somebody, you might as well start with the guy who started your problem.

Having to sit and wait until I could meet with the cop again, that was okay. Truth is, I didn't even want to go out—I wanted to be where it was safe. I had that apartment. With a TV where I could watch whatever channel I wanted to.

So I worked out. Watched TV. I didn't cook, just brought home takeout. There were like a hundred different places for that—I never even had to go to the same one twice.

I drank a lot of water. The kind that comes in bottles.

I tried to figure out what the cop would do. Maybe I would have been better off with his partner, the black guy. He was closer to my age, and you could see that the rape stuff had made him angry, like he took it personal.

But it hadn't been the black guy who'd figured out why my alibi for that rape was no good. That older cop, Tom—the other guy was Earl—Detective Tom Woods, he snapped it right away.

In my whole life, I never gave up a man I worked with. But the guy who owned that jewelry store, I didn't know him. Never even met him.

I kept thinking about whether that would be enough to make it right. It's hard when there's no rules for something you have to do, because you still have to do it.

He was already on the bridge when I showed. Even in the heat, he was wearing an old-style raincoat, had to weigh a few pounds. Probably miked to the max. Which meant I'd have to dance around with every word out of my mouth. Even if the big cop had done the right thing, I knew his kind; if anything happened to the guy who'd actually raped that girl, I'd be good for that one. *Extra* good.

While I was still deciding how to play it, he got off first: "It's no go."

"What d'you mean?"

"That girl, she may have been . . . say, unsure of herself before. Even after the plea. But now it *has* to be you. In her mind, I mean."

"But if I could just—"

"The court gave her a Permanent Order of Protection, okay? You go anywhere *near* her, and you're going back in."

"But if—"

"If you *contact* her, same thing. Or someone doing you a favor contacts her. She gets a letter, a phone call, a fucking e-mail . . . it's gonna be on you."

"But you *know* I didn't do it."

"And *I'm* going to tell her that?"

I looked at the river. People's boats were going by. Mine was sinking.

"What if I knew something?"

"About the—?"

"Yeah."

The big cop took a step back, like some invisible pair of hands had pushed him off.

"*Now* you're going to give up—?"

"Come on."

"Yeah. What would be the point? You were willing to do that, you could have skipped your last jolt altogether."

"The statute of limitations, it's run."

"Meaning the other guys with you on that job haven't, huh?

Could be true, for all I know. The owner, no way that little slime-ball's leaving town—they're going to keep his ass in court for years."

"How could they—?"

"Not for the crime. The lawsuit. The insurance company's not going down without a fight, not for that kind of scratch. That jeweler, he's been living small. Claims he can't make a living because that heist of yours wiped him out."

"You don't want him?"

"For what? Like *you* said, it's too late for us to charge him with anything."

"So why bother to talk to me at all?"

"You didn't plan that job, Caine. No offense, but I never liked you for *that* part either."

I looked out at the river.

"If we knew who put that one together, we could probably tie him to dozens of jobs."

I shrugged.

"We couldn't even arrest him. But we *could* put him out of business."

"You said, putting the job together, that wasn't me. You *that* sure?"

"Like I said, no offense, but . . . yeah, I'm that sure. Now, *that* guy's name, that would be worth something. Maybe even some-thing like me and my partner visiting that girl. . . ."

"Yeah. Only, not the same way you'd 'visit' the guy you *think* set up the job you *think* I was on."

"Who said anything about rough stuff? I just mean, we go over and have a talk with the man. We explain what we know. Tell him we've got all kinds of warrants. And all the time in the world. So we sit on him, see who comes and goes. He doesn't get hurt. But he does go out of business."

"I get it."

"So I talk to the girl, and you—"

"No."

"How bad do you want this guy, Caine? You did *his* time, remember?"

"Not that bad."

It was the cop's turn to look out at the river. After a minute or so, he turned around.

"Don't get me wrong on this, okay? I know who you are. You're one of the bad guys. No hard feelings. Nothing personal. I'm not talking about any particular crime, I'm talking about who you are. But, for what it's worth, I know you never raped that girl."

"It's worth a lot to me."

We looked at each other for a little while, like we had nothing else to do.

He put out his hand. I took it. More like a grip than shaking hands, but . . .

I couldn't be sure what he meant with that move. But I knew what it added up to: I shouldn't ever call him again.

What the fuck is wrong with you?

Like a tape playing in my head. A loop, going around and around, with no OFF switch.

I held on to the railing for a long time after the cop left. Something solid.

That was me, a few minutes ago. Solid. A man you could count on.

It was all I had, that . . . I don't know the word for it. More than a rep, it was who I was. Not a part of me, inside *all* of me. Something you couldn't separate out.

Years ago, I remember, I heard about this guy. He hated the government, blamed the government for everything that wasn't the way he thought it should be. I think his brother was on the run for blowing up abortion clinics or something like that.

This guy, he had one of those electric saws they use on lumber. Only, instead of a board, he put his arm down and pulled the saw right through it. Cut off his own hand. He even made a tape of himself doing it, so he could mail it to the FBI, show them how serious he was.

See? A piece of him got taken away, but he was still himself. More of himself, really.

He may have been a nutcase, but he didn't give up anything. Me, a couple of minutes ago, I almost had.

That guy, he gave up his *own* hand, not somebody else's.

And I'd just come so close to giving up somebody else's that it scared me.

I had to get away from there.

All the way back to my apartment, I blocked it off. I thought about all kinds of things: girlfriends I'd had, fights I'd been in, stories Eddie used to tell on the yard. Anything, so long as it wasn't about work. I didn't want to think about that until I was someplace I could sit for a while.

I even thought about the time I got tricked into an arm-wrestling match with a guy who'd hurt his good hand in a car wreck. It was still in a cast, so we went left-handed. I didn't find out until a couple of days later that the fucking hustler was a natural southpaw.

The guy who told me was Buddha, the wheelman. This place—just a dump of a bar where guys like me hung around when we weren't working—it was never loud, never any fights. The reason for that was the same reason that it wasn't a place where you'd bring a girl.

They had a table for arm-wrestling, with pegs and all. The guy who ran the place, Nathan, the deal was this: if you wanted to do something for money—they had darts, and a full-size pool table, even a place to play cards—Nathan was the ref. And you didn't argue with Nathan. Not because he was such a hard guy, because that was the rules. Anyone who could walk into that place knew the rules.

I never did stuff like that for money. It's just stupid. You win, then there'll always be some other guy who wants to try you. And then another one after that. And if you lose, what good comes out of that?

This guy, he outweighed me by seventy-five pounds, easy. I

don't make the same mistake about fat guys most people do. Some guys, they can power-lift like gorillas, they still stay fat. Fat-*looking*, I mean. No definition at all. Big round arms, thick around the gut. But strong. Real strong.

I'd never seen this guy before, and I could tell nobody else had, either. I could feel how bad people wanted me to take him on.

"How do you do it?" I asked.

That was fair—the table was there, all right, but nobody had ever seen me on it.

That's when Buddha tapped me on the shoulder. I turned around and followed him over to the table. Buddha showed me how it worked. When I thought I got it, I sat down.

"A little side-bet?" the fat guy asked.

"Not for me," I told him. "You look like a pro at this."

The fat guy grinned. One of his front teeth was chipped. He sat down across from me. Nathan came over and wrapped this strap around our wrists. My elbow was on some padded thing; the other guy's, too. Buddha told me my elbow had to *stay* on that pad or I'd lose.

"When I let go," Nathan said.

The fat guy jerked so hard I almost couldn't hold him. But I did. I just stayed like that, same way you pull against the bars in prison. You can't bend the bar, but it's a great isometric.

The fat guy's face got all red. A vein came out across his forehead. He called me some name, but I couldn't make it out, what with everybody yelling at the same time.

Butterfly, I thought to myself. In my mind, I was back in the gym, pulling the two pads together, over and over again. I'd gotten to the middle, where the pads meet, so I should release to set up another rep. But I couldn't do that, so I made like I was doing a shoulder cross, pulling my right hand against the peg and my left toward my right shoulder.

To the fat guy, *I* was the prison bar. Maybe he was gassed from struggling, maybe he saw it coming, I don't know. I just pulled. Smooth and slow, like you're supposed to do, not jerking the weight like the fat guy had tried to do to me.

Even after I felt him start to give, I didn't speed up, just pulled all the way through until I touched down.

The fat guy mumbled something, and we shook hands. Left hands, 'cause his other one was in that cast.

I could tell the people watching were happy, but nobody really said anything to me.

Except Buddha, later. That's when he told me what the fat guy's hustle was.

"How'd you know?"

"I've seen his act before. That other guy with him? He's the moneyman. Backs his boy against anyone who wants action. He's slick. Never does anything lame like *asking* for bets, but he'll cover anything you put down. If you ask him for odds, he'll give a little—three-to-one is about as far as he can go without tipping his play."

"Why didn't you tell—?"

"Like I said, I've seen his act before. The way they work it, they just pick a guy who looks like muscle. Every joint like this place, they always got guys look like you. Only, this time, *I* had the sleeve ace, not them. I know you don't have a power arm, Sugar. Lefty, righty, makes no difference to you."

"I guess not. But I still don't see why—"

Buddha put ten C-notes on the table between us. "Your cut," he told me. "I got the three-to-one, on a grand. The money guy, he saw me take the cash out of my shirt pocket, figured me for a degenerate gambler. You know, the kind who bets on any fucking thing, because they gotta have action going all the time."

"Huh!"

"He'll make it back by the end of the week. You didn't hurt his boy."

"How could I hurt a guy doing . . . that?"

"If he *resisted*, you could. But that's not the way he's got his man trained. He takes one real *blast*. If he can move the other guy, he reloads and fires again, until he breaks through. But if he can't move the first time, he won't fight too hard when the other guy comes back against him. He knows he could get his arm broken that way."

I put the thousand in my jacket. "What if I had lost?" I said.

"I would have taken the moneyman off to the side and asked him if he wanted me to cut the cast off his guy's hand. In front of everyone."

"That'd get him—"

"Sure would. But all he has to do is pay off *my* bet. He does that and he gets to walk out of here with all the other money he just banked. It's the perfect play, see?"

"Perfect for you."

"You just got your cut, didn't you?"

Buddha never even smiled. For him, it was business.

I started to think about how that was a side of him people didn't know. It was like he had some of Ken's guts, and some of Solly's brains. He didn't just know the rules, he knew how to make them work for him.

Lucky for me, I was only a couple of blocks from the apartment by then.

I wanted to be tired, not sleepy. So I lifted for an hour or so. Drank lots of Gatorade. Took a steamy shower.

Then I sat back and closed my eyes.

Buddha having a side hustle didn't mean he wasn't still Buddha. Anybody seeing him work that hustle wouldn't think, *Buddha, he's not the same man he was.* They wouldn't worry about him not waiting with the motor running, no matter how nasty things got on a job.

But what if anyone heard of me offering to give someone up? If it was some guy who knew me, I wouldn't be me anymore. Not to him, not to the other guys he'd tell. Not even to myself.

Like those prison choices.

I didn't know the rules for someone like the guy who owned that jewelry store. He wasn't one of us. So maybe I didn't owe him anything. But I didn't *know.*

Who could I ask? Solly, he'd know. But then he'd also know what I'd been ready to do. And Solly was the only one that store owner could roll on—he didn't know any of the men who'd actually pulled off the job.

Christ! How fucked in the head could I be? I met Woods thinking I could give up the jewelry-store guy without breaking the rules. But I didn't know anything about that guy, only Solly did. And if I even brought it up, Solly'd have questions about *me*.

I started shaking. Not like I was scared, more like I had this terrible fever.

If that cop hadn't turned me down . . .

When I woke up, I was on the bed, facedown. I must have . . . I don't know. Maybe I blacked out when I got to the part about why the whole thing mattered so much. Sure, I did that scumbag's time for him. But it wasn't that much time, and I slid out from under a lot of worse things when I took the deal. Plus, I still had the money.

And the cop had warned me about that Order of Protection thing. I couldn't go near that girl, even if I knew where she was. I didn't even know her name—it wasn't in the papers. And she hadn't been in court when I was sentenced—like to make one of those statement things.

I stopped myself, because I knew where I was going. In my head, I mean. There's things you don't think about. Not if you want to keep your mind right.

That's what rules are for. And that's one thing I *did* know, the rules. I was raised on them.

Not everyone knows the rules. Or maybe different kinds of people have different ones.

Not everybody's the same. For men like me, you can do all kinds of things as long as you stay inside the lines.

Some guys, they make a big score, they go through it all in a week. That's okay. Stupid, but okay.

Those guys, they always get caught. Either they splash so much money around that people can't help noticing, or they live straight, like they've got a job and all, but they pick too expensive a neighborhood.

Thing is, you want a rich-suburbs lifestyle, you have to *keep* working. No time off.

It doesn't matter if they blow a big score in two weeks or live on it for five years—soon as they need money, they go back to work. They can't be picky, so they take whatever's on the table.

You never want to work with guys like that. They get known. They know the rules, sure. But it's not that you're worried about them giving you up if the job goes bad, it's that any guy who *needs* the money, there's a lot of ways he can take everyone else down with him.

Like if the planner says we've got two hours between rotations for the security guards in some building. But it turns out that we're not getting into the safe in any two hours. The box man says there's some new stuff on it, going to take him a lot longer than we planned to be in there. Something like that happens on a job, what you're supposed to do is walk away.

But a guy who *needs* that money, he's not leaving. So he changes the plan. That's hosed right there—nobody can make up a good plan in a couple of minutes.

I know because it once happened to me, just like that. The guy who *needed* the money, he took over. "You," he said, pointing at me, "we need more time. We know the guard's rounds; he's on his way right now. All you have to do is go down the hall and wait for him to walk past you. Old guy like him, they wouldn't even trust him with a gun. Step out behind him, choke him out, and we've got *another* two hours to get this thing open."

"Not me," I said. I didn't say why. You never have to say why unless it's something that was in the plan from the beginning.

I picked up my bag. Two of the other guys got their gear together; one of them kept looking at his watch.

"Fuck it, then," the guy who needed the money said. He took out this little black gun from one pocket and a silencer from the other.

The three of us got out. The guy who needed money stayed. So did the box man and one other guy. I didn't know any of them, never worked with them before.

They stayed inside the lines, right to the end. The guy who

needed money, he stood up and said he was the one who'd killed the security guard. Said the whole job was his idea. He even said he made the other two guys stay—if they had tried to leave, he would have shot them, too.

It was worth a try, I guess. If the jury believed the other two hadn't known he was carrying, they might have cut them some slack.

But they put the killing on all three. It doesn't matter who pulls the trigger, everybody pays the same. I even heard of a getaway man who got life for killing a bank guard who went for his gun. The driver never even went inside the building, but it didn't make any difference.

There were a lot of good reasons for me not trying to choke out the guard. You hit a guy over the head with a pipe, you might knock him out . . . or you might kill him. I learned that from the doctor who closed up my face during my first bit.

"You know how people say, 'He's got a thick skull'?" that doctor said.

"Sure," I said. "They're always saying it about me."

"Well, in your case, it's not a pejorative."

"A what?"

"Derogatory. A put-down."

"But it means you're dumb, right?"

"Yes," the other doctor in the room said. "That's the way it's used. But in the medical sense, the human skull can vary in thickness. Here, look at this."

It was a pair of X-rays, side by side. "Yours is the one on the left. The one on the right is normal. Average. See how much more bone there is in yours?"

"Yeah. Is that why that hatchet didn't chop into my brain?"

"Exactly," the first one said. "Dr. Leong is a radiologist. He was the one to bring this to my attention."

"What are you, then?"

"What am . . . ? Oh, I see. I'm a dermatological surgeon. When you first came in, the ER triage team sent you up to the cranial unit. Head wounds bleed considerably, so it wasn't until the scans came back that you ended up in this wing."

"That's why my head's shaved?"

"Yes. The fracture of the skull was so mild it was barely discernible. It will heal on its own. It was my job to suture the wound."

"You are most fortunate," the X-ray doctor said. "Dr. Trotta is one of the finest plastic surgeons in the country, and he came right over from the university. The reason the prison transported you straight to this hospital was because a brain injury was assumed."

"Huh! You're right about that one, doc. If those guys in the prison infirmary had stitched me up, I'd probably be blind in that eye by now."

Neither of them said anything. For the first time, I felt scared. "The eye, it's okay, right?"

"Certainly," the first doctor said. "The weapon's major force was to the hairline. It cut all the way down to below the eye, but it didn't touch the eye itself. You have a heavy shelf of bone above the eyebrows. That's what saved the eye."

"Thick skulls, they're good for something, huh?"

Both doctors smiled. Even the nurse. She'd been over in the corner; I hadn't noticed her until I turned my head a little.

"Have we answered your questions, Mr. Caine?"

"Yeah," I told them. "And thanks for what you did."

"Could you perhaps answer a question for me?" the X-ray doctor said.

I figured he was going to ask me who did it, but I wasn't even close.

"How could someone get a *hatchet* inside a maximum-security prison?"

"Make it himself. Or buy it."

"That seems . . . bizarre."

"I don't get what you're saying."

"Lethal weapons *inside* a prison—it seems like an anomaly."

"If you're saying it doesn't add up, you're wrong," I told them. "If you were walking down a dark alley in the middle of the night, wouldn't you want to have some kind of weapon with you?"

"I . . . I suppose so. But how is that—?"

"Prison's like that, doc. Every day."

I hadn't heard about that thick-skull thing, but I'd never hit a guy in the head with a pipe unless I wanted to kill him. Same for choking him out. There's a little bone in the throat. You crush that, the guy dies. But I wasn't thinking about that. All I heard was *two hours* . . . playing like a song you couldn't get out of your head.

The three who went down never mentioned the three of us who left. If they'd gotten away with the job, none of us would have come around asking for a share.

That's the rules.

I was never going to put myself in a position like that: where I needed money so bad that I'd have to change a plan.

I knew I couldn't live on the money from the jewelry job forever. But I could be real careful about what jobs to take. That's the best any man who does what I do can hope for.

It's happened before. A guy looks like me, he can always find work. Not *score* work, regular work. Like collecting debts. But even that kind of work, there's risks.

I worked construction once in a while, but I didn't have an in, so I could never get on with the union. Mostly, I'd end up with lousy jobs, like being a bouncer in a club.

I never kept one of those jobs long. Usually, I'd get fired. Not for going too far; for not going far enough. If I couldn't scare a guy, or just wrap him up and carry him outside, I'd step off. Guys don't walk around with warning labels telling you if they had real thin skulls or a bad heart, stuff like that.

So I'd get fired for not doing my job. I'd listen to some greasy little puke in a suit tell me I was a punk—all show, no go. I was probably taking it up the ass, they'd say. Tell me to go work in a gay bar. That always got a laugh from the others in his office.

There's always other guys in the office. I just look at them, one at a time. They never say anything themselves.

That's why I only took cash jobs, the kind where you get paid after every shift.

Just let it go. That's what I kept telling myself.

"Go" was the word, not "no."

Go on down to Florida and see about this Jessop, like Solly wanted me to do. Don't say no to him.

"Buying time," those words go either way. Could mean you're playing it smart; could mean you're playing it stupid. I couldn't find this Jessop, but maybe the PI the lawyer used could.

I knew I didn't actually have to find the guy. But I had to be able to tell Solly I tried. And it had to be the truth.

Talking to that cop, that had been insane. Way too close to the edge. I should only talk to my own kind.

But I just couldn't get that girl out of my mind. Not her, the guy who raped her. The guy whose time I did.

Something else was off about the whole thing. But I could never get my mind to open up and show me, no matter how hard I tried.

So I just let it go.

"I'll take the bus," I told Solly.

He kind of smiled. "That's smart, Sugar. You don't need a credit card for the Greyhound. I'll set it up for Albie's niece to pick you up at the depot."

"Okay."

"By his neighbors, Albie was just another old retired guy, moved to Florida to get away from the cold. Tallahassee, it's not where you go if you like boats, stuff like that. The whole town's built around the college. Big-time sports school, that's about it.

"But it was perfect for Albie. Prices—for land, I mean—prices were real cheap, especially to a guy used to paying Miami scale. So Albie got himself, like, twenty acres. Had a house built. Then he could do what he's always wanted. Albie, he was a stamp collector. Talk your damn ear off about them, you gave him a chance.

"Albie made me executor of his will. That means I got to make sure everybody gets what's coming to them. The house, his cars, everything. Especially those damn stamps. Meant so much to him, ten-to-one whoever gets them sells them in a week.

"Ah, so what?" He looked sad for a second, then said, "You

know who wants to see that will? Rena, that's her name. She's down there now, living in the house. Driving the car, too, maybe—that I don't know. She'll do old Uncle Solly a favor, guaranteed. Just get yourself to the bus depot, and she'll meet you.

"That's the way we worked it out, Albie and me. If I went first, Grace—you see how she calls me Uncle Solly, too?—would get all my stuff.

"You understand, we're talking about *legit* stuff. House, car, bank-account stuff. For that, you need paper. Cash, that's something else. Grace knows where I keep my will; it would be up to Albie to what they call 'probate' it. In court, with a lawyer. But Albie's girl, she don't know where Albie kept *his* will except with me, understand?"

I could tell more was coming, so I just kept quiet.

"And there's one more thing," Solly said, "and, for that, this girl *won't* know where it is."

"The cash?"

"Forget cash. Albie's book, that's what she won't know about."

"Book?"

Solly took a little book out of his jacket. It was real old. You could tell because the leather covers were a faded-pale shade of blue, and it was all cracked, like a windshield gets if you hit it with a rock. Small, too. And thin. "Exactly like this one," he said. "There were two of these, a long time ago. Twins. The writing inside, it wouldn't make sense to anyone. It's in code. Albie and me, we're the only ones who could understand it, because we made it up between ourselves."

"*Exactly* like that one?"

"Yeah. And this is how you make sure," Solly told me. He opened the little blue book. On the first page, there was a thumbprint. Looked like it was once done in blood, now it looked more like a brownish color. "You don't see the same thing in Albie's book, it's not the one you want."

"What's that under the print? I can see—"

"Forget the *print*, Sugar. Just that there'll *be* one, you with me?"

I nodded, so he'd know I was. "This girl, the one in Florida, is she like . . . is she like Grace?"

"You mean . . . ? No, she's not. But Grace, don't underestimate her, kid. In her own way, that is one *sharp* young lady. And loyal? Forget it! She already knows what to do when I go. There's enough legit stuff, keep her safe the rest of her life. Only thing is, Albie went first. Now I've got to shlep down to the lawyer's and change my will, probably cost me an arm and a leg."

The old man looked at me for a long minute. Probably trying to figure out if I knew it wasn't this Jessop he was worried about; what he really needed was to get his hands on Albie's book. Wondering if he was making the same mistake about me he warned me against making about Grace.

"Solly, can I ask you a question?"

"Of course. Anything you—"

"You got a book. Albie's got a book. If you went first, Grace would give your book to Albie, right?"

"Absolutely."

"So she knows where your book is. But Albie's girl, she *doesn't*?"

"Yeah," he said, nodding his head like he was agreeing with himself. "Try it this way. Grace, she's like my niece for real. Just like I told you. But Rena, okay, she calls me 'Uncle Solly' same as Grace does, only she wouldn't ever be saying 'Uncle Albie.' She was . . . like his girlfriend, all right? Been with him a long, long time."

"So you're saying Albie, it was okay with him if his girlfriend gets all his stuff, like a house or whatever, right? But not the book?"

"I guess that's right. Albie must have . . . look, I don't know, okay? Grace, you could bet your life. Whatever she says she'll do, it's as good as done. Just like her father. But Rena, I don't know her like that.

"I don't know why Albie decided he couldn't trust her with that book, but that's what he must have decided. That book, it's *way* more important than any money, Sugar. And it could be bad—real, real bad—if Rena managed to get her hands on it."

"If you know where it is, why don't you just—?"

"Are you fucking *listening* to me? I *don't* know where it is. It was *supposed* to be like I said: Grace for me; Rena for Albie. But when Rena called me, not one single word about that book. Never said,

'Come down and get it.' Or even just FedEx'ed it. So either she doesn't know where it is, or she's got it and she wants to turn it into cash. That's why I never sent her Albie's will."

"So Albie never trusted her with that book—which means you can't trust her, either?"

"That's it," Solly said. He looked real old then. Like he could see the end of things. "Jessop, he's not a big deal, okay? But I've got to have that book. Me and Albie . . ."

I waited a long time, but Solly didn't say anything more. He just looked at me.

"I said I'd do it," I told him. I hoped I said it just like Ken would have.

"This is a lot of money," the woman who wanted me to call her Margo said.

"It's just three months' rent. I'll be away for a while. It could be just a couple of weeks, but it could just as easy be a couple of months. You know how those things are."

I said that last thing because people never want to admit they *don't* know how things are.

"So I guess, if I wanted to start . . . training, like we talked about, I'd have to wait until you come back, huh?"

"I'm sorry. This came up real sudden. If I had even a week or two, I could show you enough to keep you going until I got back. But, the way things are—"

"Oh, I *know*. Especially today. Nobody seems to have any money. You can't pass up a chance like this."

"Thanks for understanding," I told her.

I spent the night getting ready. I didn't like some parts of this bus thing. They don't let you take much luggage on board; they just check it for you. And *this* bus ride, it was like a day and a half long. The girl I spoke to at Greyhound looked it up for me, and said I'd have to change buses a couple of times.

The train would have been better, but the lady at Amtrak said it didn't stop in Tallahassee. Not even close.

Everything in the refrigerator I either finished off or poured out. A lot of my dry stuff, I could take with me.

It was pretty easy, stripping the place. All I left behind was some stuff in the closet. Way before my rent advance ran out, Margo would find some excuse to stick her nose in.

The weather report said tomorrow was going to be in the nineties. Swell time to be going to Florida.

I waited until the husband's car pulled off. He drove a big white Lexus, and he was real careful with it, always checking when he backed out of the driveway. I didn't want him to look up one day and see the shades move, so I just poked a tiny hole in one of them with an ice pick. I could see out fine.

When I was sure, I packed the trunk of my car like I was going away for a long time.

She came outside while I was stowing away the last of my stuff. Leaned over the rail and looked down, putting on a show.

"I think I'll start working out anyway. You think that's a good idea?"

"Like I said, the way you can tell, if it makes you feel better."

"And, like *I* said before, all that matters is that you *look* better, Stan. It's all right to call you that, isn't it? I mean, you don't look like a 'Stanley,' somehow."

"You don't look like a Mary Margaret," I said.

"Margo, remember?"

"Sure, I do. I was just saying . . . it's like we have something in common."

"Oh, I'm sure of that. Well, you have a good time, okay?"

"It's work."

"Some things are hard work and fun, too, aren't they?"

"I . . . I think that's right."

She turned and walked back inside.

I had already asked the guy who ran the gas station a few blocks from the railroad if I could rent a space for my car.

He was surprised at first. "You could just leave it over in the commuter lot. It's pretty safe around here."

"No, I mean for a couple, three months. You know how people are. They see a car sitting alone for more than a few days, they come back at night."

"Yeah, that's true," he said, like it made him sad. "So why don't you just leave it at home?"

"I don't have a house. Just an apartment. I have to park on the street. That's okay for overnight, but . . ."

"I get it. But I couldn't guarantee you indoor space. It just depends on whatever comes in, you know? I mean, I could park it out back; there's the chain-link, and the dogs, too. Anybody would have to want your car pretty bad to risk that."

I knew what he was saying: who'd want *my* car that bad?

"That sounds good enough. This way, I can catch the train, jump off in Queens, and I'll be at JFK pretty quick. You got any idea what those long-term lots at the airport are getting now?"

"Yeah. Everything in the city's gone through the goddamn roof. How about a hundred a month?"

"That's fair. For both of us, I think."

I gave him three months in front. Took my suitcases and the shoulder duffel out of the trunk, and gave him the keys—I had another set.

"I'd give you a lift to the station, but . . ."

"That's okay. I only need to catch the ten-fifty-five."

That's the train I caught. It didn't matter where I switched—I think every subway line stops somewhere near the Port Authority. Forty-second Street, Times Square, Grand Central—they're all close enough to walk.

There were a lot of kids on the subway for that time of day. All

different kinds; I guess with summer vacation, they didn't have anything to do. A couple of times, I wished I hadn't been hauling all
that baggage around. It made me uneasy, no matter what I did. If I
put down the suitcases, one of them could be snatched. If I didn't, I
wouldn't have my hands free.

A seat would be better, but I never saw an open one.

When the train finally stopped, I told myself I'd been worrying
about nothing.

I made it over to Port Authority with more than two hours to spare.
After I paid, I asked the tired-looking black girl on the other side of
the counter what platform my bus would be leaving from. She
pointed up at this huge monitor. Not real friendly, but I could see it
wasn't anything personal.

They told me I had to check the suitcases. One of the bus people said something about my duffel, too, but another one said the
bus was going to be half empty, so what was the big deal?

I was glad about that. You make a fuss, you draw attention to
yourself.

The guy in the uniform was right—there couldn't have been more
than a dozen people on the bus when we pulled out. I found a pair
of seats all the way at the back. Nobody would want those seats if
they had any other choice; the bathroom was just across from them.

I put the duffel on the seat next to me, all the outside pockets
facing me, with the strap looped around my wrist. Just habit—
who's going to snatch a bag on a bus?

Probably everybody on that bus had a different reason for going
wherever they were headed. I never try and figure out stuff like
that—there's no way to ever find out if I'd guessed right.

It was easier after it got dark. A few people put their lights on—to
read, I guess.

The bus smelled a lot like prison. People smells, I mean. Closed
in. That kind of smell, it gets into everything—you couldn't get it

out with a barrelful of bleach and a power-washer. The seat was a lot better than anything you could get in prison, but, even cranked way back, you still had to sleep kind of sitting up, so it was a push between that seat and a cell bunk.

When we stopped to change buses, some people bought stuff to eat or a book to read. A couple of them tried to smoke a whole pack of cigarettes while we were waiting.

They changed drivers, too. The bus filled up a little more, but it was still about half empty. Nobody even got close to sitting near me.

I heard people talking to each other. A real skinny girl walked past me to use the toilet. She saw me, ran her tongue around her mouth. I looked out the window.

She was in there a long time. I hoped she wasn't still poking herself, trying to find a vein. Or nodding out.

A guy walked back toward me. I could see him coming in the reflection from the window. He wanted the toilet, but he was out of luck. He shrugged, like he was used to it.

The skinny girl finally came out. She had to put her hand on the top of the seats to get down the aisle, but she made it.

I felt sorry for the next person to go in there.

Then I must have fallen asleep.

It was bright outside when I opened my eyes. The toilet was what I expected. When I came out, I poured some of this clear stuff over my hands, and rubbed until they were dry. Then I took out one of those tubes for keeping your lips from cracking and used it on each nostril.

I had two of the power bars and a whole bottle of water. I made them last a long time.

It was still light when the bus pulled into the last stop. There were a couple of cabs waiting, but I moved in the opposite direction.

One thing for sure, I didn't want to hang around the bus station. Places like that, they get bad at night, no matter where you are. And I knew I didn't look too good—a day and a half on a bus, nobody would. *Solly should have told me more about this,* I was saying to myself when a horn beeped. A little beep, like, polite, almost. A dark-blue car was at the curb. The window nearest me slid down. I didn't think that had anything to do with me, so I moved away a little bit . . . but the car followed along.

I looked in the open window. It was a woman—her face was shadowed, but I could see her legs.

"Get in," she said. "I'll take you where you're going."

I knew she had to be Rena. No woman goes to a bus station to pick up guys.

"You *are* a big boy."

"I'm not any kind of boy."

She blew smoke at the windshield. "See, that's one of the differences between us."

"You and me?"

"Men and women. Call a man a boy, he's all insulted. Call a woman a girl, she's all happy and sweet."

"I never thought about it."

"Men don't," she said, like she was done answering a lot of questions I never asked.

I didn't look at her real close, either—you don't do that. The windows of the big car were tinted, so you could look outside without sunglasses or anything. There wasn't all that much to see.

The car was like a room with the curtains pulled. Every time the woman finished with a cigarette, she pushed a button and her window went down so she could snap the butt out into the street. Like opening the curtains for a second.

All I could really tell about her was she had long hair. Some dark color, but not black. I couldn't see much of her upper body—she was wearing a light jacket and a dark blouse—but her right leg had a lot of definition around the calf. Dark nail polish, big flashy stone in a ring on her left hand—I saw it every time she made a right turn.

I didn't see how she could drive with such high heels. White ones, with red soles. I remembered what this one girl I stayed with for a while was always telling me about the tricks women used to look thinner. White made you look bigger, she always said. So either this girl had small feet or she didn't give a damn.

No way this one doesn't give a damn, I thought.

"You're Albie's niece, right?" I said, just to make certain-sure I was in the right car.

"His *what*?"

"Solly said—"

"Uh-huh," she half-laughed. Sounded like sandpaper on soft wood.

I just shut up.

The longer we drove, the less the place looked like a city . . . and it hadn't looked much like one when we started. It took about forty-five minutes before we came up on a pair of big stone piles, with a space between them just wide enough to let a car through. As we turned in, the girl reached into her purse. Her hand stayed there for a couple of seconds, came out empty.

We went down a long road. It was paved, but no wider than a driveway. Ran pretty straight, but sometimes it curved around a giant tree or some swampy-looking water.

She reached in her purse again just before we took a sharp right and then an even sharper left, like a zigzag. That's when I saw the house.

It was more like a warehouse than a place people lived. Not that it was a dump—you could see it cost a lot of money. But it was only one story, and everything around it was cement, like a parking lot.

A garage door lifted. She pulled the car inside. I got out and waited for her to pop the trunk. That's when I saw the car was one of those Lincoln Town Cars the limo companies buy.

"That one's mine," she said. I looked in the next bay. A little turquoise convertible, two-seater. "I thought you might have too much stuff to fit in it."

Yeah, that's why, all right, I thought to myself. The Lincoln was something you wouldn't look at twice—but a long-haired girl in a little convertible . . .

"Follow me," she said.

We went down a corridor. The carpet was so thick we didn't make a sound.

"Yours is there," she told me. I figured she meant where I was supposed to stay, so I dropped my bags.

It looked like a hotel suite. Not just a bedroom, but a living room, too. Lots of closets. A big chest of drawers, with the bottom drawer opened. No kitchen.

I wondered if that had been Albie's idea of a joke: every decent burglar knows you start with the bottom drawer, saves you a few seconds on each one, because you don't have to close it before you move up to the next.

"You can take off those glasses now." I did it. One glance at my eyes was all she needed.

"You need to unpack?"

"I guess so."

"So . . . ?"

She stood right there, watching me put the stuff from the suitcases in the closet and the drawers. I didn't open the duffel.

"Come on," she told me, turning around and moving off.

I followed her again. It wasn't just the heels that gave her the height—I put her at around five nine. I could see muscle flex all the way up to her lower thighs. From the way that little jacket bounced, I guessed the muscles didn't stop at her legs.

We ended up in a white room. Not just the paint; it had all white furniture, too. The floor was white glass tile—her heels started clicking as soon as she stepped on it—and even the walls looked like they were made of some kind of white stone.

She knew exactly where she wanted to sit. A white leather chair with padded arms. She crossed her legs, opened both hands, and made a "pick your own" gesture.

I did that. One whole wall looked like a monster fireplace. Who would build a fire in weather like this? But it looked like it had been used plenty.

A flat-panel TV was on the opposite wall—it kept showing different pictures of flowers, one after another. Pyramid speakers almost as tall as me in two far corners. I couldn't hear any hum, but I could feel the A/C.

No windows. None at all. But two doors. Besides the door we came through, there was one behind where she was sitting.

"You want anything?"

"Water would be great."

"Go through the door behind me. The kitchen's to the right."

Making sure I got the message: she wasn't the maid; she was the owner.

The kitchen was all stainless steel. I could see a side-by-side refrigerator-freezer, an oven, even a chrome microwave, but no stove. There was a long strip of something laid into the top of what had to be a fifteen-foot slab of ash-gray granite—maybe that's where they cooked.

The refrigerator had all kinds of drinks. I didn't want to go poking through all those stainless-steel cabinets looking for a glass, so I just took the biggest bottle of water I could find and went back inside.

"That's Containe," she told me, pointing at the bottle I was holding.

"Not water?"

"It's *fortified* water."

I uncapped the bottle and took a big swig. Tasted like water to me.

"You can't taste the difference," she said, like she was cutting me off before I could say it myself.

"It's fine the way it is."

"What it is, is *enhanced*," she said, shaking her head a little when she said that last word—her hair kind of breezed before it settled down. A dark shade of red, easy to see against all that white.

Her blouse was almost the same color as her hair. A couple of buttons were opened. I could see that what she meant by "enhanced" covered more than a dye job on her hair.

"I'm Rena."

"Stanley," I said. "Stanley Wilson."

"I like 'Wilson' better. You look like a guy who should have that one."

"I don't—"

"For your *first* name. So I'll do that. Call you 'Wilson,' if you don't mind."

"Me? No."

"It's not like it's your real name anyway," she said. Not asking a question; just saying it.

"Is 'Rena' yours?"

"It's what Albie liked."

"You're his . . . widow?"

"That's a sweet way to put it."

"Solly said—"

"Now, Solly, I *am* his niece."

"For real?"

"What's real? To me, he's Uncle Solly. To him, I'm Rena. That's the way I was introduced to him, understand?"

"Not really."

She took a deep breath. She was either getting annoyed or showing off.

"Albie and Solly were brothers. And do *not* ask 'For real?' again, okay? Solly comes down here, oh, maybe seven, eight years ago. Albie meets him at the airport. They walk in, and here I am. Albie says, 'Rena, this is your uncle Solly.' And that's the way it's been ever since."

"Okay."

"How old do you think I am?"

"I don't know. Twenty . . . seven?"

"I've been with Albie, it would have been exactly twenty years next month. What does that tell you?"

"Nothing."

"I'm thirty-nine."

"Okay," I said, flashing on what Margo had told me about that age being the one any woman would lie about.

"That's all?"

"Uh . . . you know why I'm here, right?"

I had to ask her like that. Fucking Solly never told me what to expect, so I didn't know what *she* was expecting, either.

"Jessop."

"That's it."

"Sure it is," she said, as she stretched her hands high, like it was some kind of exercise. When she brought them down, she had another cigarette in her hand.

"You lost me," I told her.

"Ssshhh," she said as she blew out a long stream of smoke. "Go take a shower. Shave. Change your clothes. Call Solly—there's some throwaway cells in the dresser. Take a nap. Whatever you have to do. I'll be back here by . . . eight. We'll have something to eat, okay?"

"Sure."

We looked at each other for a few minutes. When she blew a smoke ring at the ceiling, I got up.

I did most of what Rena said. But I didn't call Solly. I'm scared of cell phones. I know they can do all kinds of things with them. Anyway, Solly might still think I was carrying the one he gave me.

One good thing about prison, it teaches you what to do when you can't do anything.

That little suite was like upscale solitary. I remember wishing solitary could *be* solitary, but the noise in there never stopped. *Never.* And the smells, they never changed, either.

"Wake up."

I hadn't even heard her coming.

I opened my eyes. She was standing in the doorway. Either she was smart enough never to touch a sleeping convict or she just plain didn't want to get close to me, I couldn't tell.

"I'm not Room Service," she said.

"I fell asleep, okay? It's not like I disrespected you. Save the speeches."

"Then—"

"Then nothing. I'm not playing some guessing game. I came

here to do something. You met me at the bus station, brought me here. I appreciate you doing that. But that's enough."

"Enough work on my part, or enough of my big mouth?"

"Both."

She stood there for a few seconds. "You want the food, or what?"

We ate in that big kitchen, sitting on bar stools, chrome with thick black leather padding, using that slab of granite for a table. I still didn't know anything about the stove, because my dinner was a big wooden bowl of salad, with slices of onion, radishes, celery sticks, and chunks of white chicken mixed in. There was also a little plate of garlic breadsticks.

Hers was the same, but her bowl was a lot smaller.

I had a glass of that *enhanced* water. She left the bottle on the countertop. Whatever she was drinking was a dark-cherry color. I didn't think it could be wine, because she really slugged it down.

"Thank you," I said when I was done. "It tasted real good."

"No big deal; it's pretty much what I eat all the time. I just cut you a bigger piece off the same loaf."

I got up. Put my bowl and glass and the little plate in the sink, the bottle of water in the refrigerator.

"What about mine?" she said.

I closed my eyes for a second. Took a couple of quick-and-shallow breaths through my nose. "What's the game?" I asked her.

"Which game? There's always a game. Lots of them. Going on at the same time. Sometimes, one inside another."

"That's cute. You're cute. This is your house. I get all of that. What I don't get is why you keep trying to insult me."

"Insult you? Like *you* said, it's just a game, Wilson."

"How about if I don't like your games? I got to find this Jessop. So just tell me what you're going to do . . . what you're *willing* to do, okay?"

"What *could* I do?"

"Fair enough. Is it all right if I stay here while I'm looking for him?"

"Of course," she said.

"Uh-huh. And could I borrow the car you picked me up in?"

"For what?"

"I have to look for somebody. I can't call a cab to do that. That car, it looks like a thousand other ones. If the registration—"

"It's in my name. So is this property, matter of fact."

"You have a Xerox here?"

She just nodded.

"So I make you a copy of my driver's license. You give me a phone number that the cops can call if I get stopped. That's all the cover I should need."

"You don't know your way around."

"This town's not that big. I'll find the kind of places I want easy enough."

"What kind of places would those be, strip bars?"

"That'd be one kind, yeah. I don't need his picture; I'll know him when I see him."

"And then what?"

"Whatever Solly told you."

"Solly didn't tell me anything."

"There you go."

I guess she liked doing stare-downs. Probably practiced on her mirror. I got up and walked out.

Maybe fifteen minutes later, she stepped into the little suite she'd put me in. I'd noticed before there was no lock on the door—I left it standing open, so she'd know I had.

I was coming out of the shower, wearing this fluffy white robe I found in the bathroom. She strolled over to the closet. Went through all my stuff in about thirty seconds.

"None of this is going to work."

"Work? For what?"

"For you *not* looking like a stranger in town."

"What do I care about that?"

"You care because you already look like a bad guy. A *big* bad guy. A guy who wears sunglasses indoors. You put on that stupid *Sopranos* stuff of yours, you'll stick out a lot worse."

"I don't—"

"Sure, you do. What's *your* plan? Visit the kind of places where Jessop might hang out? Think you'll get lucky and spot him? Or maybe you just want word to get around? Leave your phone number, maybe he'll call?"

"You got a better one?"

"A much better one. I've got Albie's workbooks. His ledger, he called it."

"So he'd have this guy's contact info, right?"

"Probably. I never opened them."

"So why can't we just—?"

"Because you and me, we've got a problem."

"Do we?"

"How could we not, Wilson? All we know for sure is that Albie and Solly, they trusted each other. We don't know how much they trusted either of *us*."

"That's not my problem."

"Oh, I think it is," she said, walking over and sitting on the bed. I didn't see a cigarette in her hand. I guess I'd been expecting one.

I stood there, waiting.

"You'd rather try it your way?" she finally asked me.

"I'd rather look at those books. Only, you don't seem to want me to."

"I didn't say that. What I was talking about was trust, remember?"

"I remember. But I got no answers for you. I don't know how deep Solly trusts me, and I *damn* sure don't know how it was between you and Albie."

"Albie's not here."

I felt ice under my feet. Thin, slippery ice. I knew if I said the wrong thing I'd either fall down or fall through. But I didn't know what the *right* thing was. And if I just waited, I'd freeze to death.

She smiled like she could see the trap I was in.

"You trust *me*?" she said, real soft.

"I don't know you."

"Now you're getting the picture, Wilson." She looked at the clock next to the bed, one of those digital ones; 9:19, it said, a little picture of the moon next to it. "You're not going to find him tonight, anyway. You need new clothes, a clean phone, and—what else?—some protection you can carry around?"

"No."

"Think that last one over. This isn't New York. I can ID you up without ever leaving this house. Then you just walk into a gun shop and pick out one you like."

"They don't print you for that?"

"Uh, you think any broad with plastic tits, she's got to be stupid, is that it?"

"I didn't say—"

"You think I wanted *you* to walk into a gun shop? All I was saying, that name you're under, *that* person would do it. Get printed. And those prints, they'd come up clean as a vultured body after a month in the desert. Your picture, his prints. Jesus!"

"I don't know what *you* know, that means I'm calling you stupid?"

"Forget it. Maybe I'm just . . . super-sensitive since Albie's been gone. Anyway, travel throws your rhythm off. You don't want to be working unless you're sharp, yes?"

"I'm sharp enough."

"Just sleep on it, okay? We'll talk tomorrow."

Just like prison. I couldn't keep that out of my head. They're always telling you that you made bad choices. And then they put you in a place where *all* your choices are bad.

That digital clock said 11:24, with a little blinking picture of the sun next to it. I'd been sleeping a long time. But except for that little clock, there was no way to tell.

I took a quick shower, put on clean clothes, and walked down to where the kitchen was.

She was there. Sitting on one of those padded bar stools, watching another flat-screen. I didn't know there even was one in there; you had to open a couple of the cabinet doors to see it.

I took some more of her special water out of the refrigerator, sat down, and drank from the bottle, mixing it with bites of three power bars. Chewing real slow, like you're supposed to.

"You people eat special food?"

"What 'people'?"

"You know, like weightlifters or bodybuilders or whatever you are."

"I'm not any of those."

"That body built itself?" She kind of sneered, as she cupped one of her boobs and jiggled it.

I closed my eyes. Kept chewing and swallowing, chewing and swallowing.

"I hurt your feelings?"

"No," I told her. "But you're a bad listener."

"How do you know?"

"Because you answer your own questions."

"That's what happens when nobody else will."

"You actually want to know? You really give a rat's ass about me not being a weightlifter or a bodybuilder?"

"I *always* want to know things. New things, I mean."

More fucking word games, I thought. But I figured, if I want to ever get a look at Albie's books, see if the one Solly wants is in there, I have to go along. So I told her: "A weightlifter, he's trying for the most he can lift. He don't care how he looks. Could have a belly on him like a wrecking ball, it wouldn't matter. Power-lifters, they're pretty much the same, only they do different kinds of lifts. It's all about how much weight you can rack up, not how many times you can do it. But bodybuilders, *all* they care about is how they look. Weightlifters, they talk about leverage, position, *driving* the bar. Bodybuilders, it's all about definition. The look. How you're cut. Vascularity."

"What?"

"The more the veins pop out, the better. That's why they shave."

"Everywhere? Like . . . girls do?"

"Everyplace that shows. They put tan on, too. Not in the booths—that's bad for you—like a lotion."

"Are they all fags?"

"I don't know. I guess it's the same everywhere. Some are, some aren't."

"But you're not either?"

"What are you—? Wait, you mean, how come I'm not a weightlifter or a bodybuilder, right?"

"Sure," she said, flashing a big smile. She had perfect teeth.

"They're both all about . . . competition, I guess. It's not about lifting weight; it's about who can lift the *most* weight. The bodybuilders, they have contests, too. Those are about how they look. Like beauty contests."

"And you don't like to compete?"

"What for?"

"I don't know. I mean, people compete all the time, don't they? Women do, anyway. When I walk through the mall, I'll bet there's more women checking out my ass than men. Why do you think that is?"

"Men don't spend that much time in malls?"

She walked over to where I was sitting, stood over me, hands on her hips. "That was very sweet."

"I wasn't trying to—"

"That's what made it sweet, stupid."

I only had a little of the last power bar left. I chewed it, making it last.

"You need special food?"

"Not special. Just not certain kinds of stuff."

She walked over to the counter, grabbed a pad and a pen, and sat down next to me.

"Give me a list."

"Do they have, like, a GNC store around here?"

"They've got Florida State University, Wilson."

"I don't get it."

"Don't follow football, huh?"

"No."

"What I'm saying, this town is lousy with athletes. Every kind you can think of. Besides, I'm used to tracking down food. Albie, it had to be glatt kosher. You know what that is?"

"Jewish food?"

"*Extra*-Jewish food, yes. Now, come on, give me that list. I have to go out shopping anyway."

"I'll go with—"

"Let me show you something first."

"This must have cost a fortune," I told her. The place looked like a Nautilus showroom, a different machine for everything. Plus all kinds of free weights. Jump ropes, pull-up bars. A shower next to a wood-and-stone sauna. Even a lap pool.

"You're not so far off. After Albie had his first heart attack, I had this built. Not that I could ever get him to really *use* it or anything—he'd just sit there and watch *me* work."

"You—"

"Six days a week, honey. It's different for women. For us, the competition never stops. You might not always get a medal, but, you come in last too many times, you end up out of the next race."

"That doesn't sound fair."

"Aw, poor baby," she said, in a sad little voice, making sure I knew it was fake.

"Not fair to Albie, I was saying."

"What!"

"You're a gorgeous girl. But there's no way you look the same as you did twenty years ago, right?"

"Don't be so sure," she said, sticking out her chest again, like she was selling implants.

"The man stayed with you twenty years. He didn't leave you, he died, right?"

"Right."

"*And* he had a ton of money."

"He did."

"So how are you being fair to him, talking about all this competition stuff?"

She made some sound I couldn't understand, then just turned around and kind of stomped out.

The machines were incredible. Better than I'd ever used. Took me only a few minutes, and I had it down. Thirty minutes on, ten off. Three times.

I wanted to try that sauna, but I didn't know how it worked.

Didn't see a sign of her on my way back to that little suite.

"Wake up, tough guy. No way I'm carrying that load in here myself."

I'd heard her coming this time; so I'd kept my eyes closed, breathing regular, the way you sleep.

The trunk of the Lincoln was packed. Boxes and boxes. Like she bought out the store. A lot of stores. Took me four trips to get it all into the kitchen.

What's she think, I'm fucking moving in here? I thought. But I kept it to myself.

I figured she'd go off somewhere, but when I got back to my own space, I saw a bunch of clothes laid out everywhere, like a store window.

"I'm taking myself a nice long bath," I heard her say from behind me somewhere. "Try on this stuff."

When I turned around, she was gone.

Everything fit. Fit real good. Nobody's got that good an eye, specially for stuff like underwear and socks. She even had the right-size shoes.

Maybe she'd come in while I was sleeping?

That didn't feel right. Unless there was something in that water . . . but I'd picked it out myself.

And it was too big a risk for her, pull a stunt like that just to get clothing sizes.

More games?

I put on some workout sweats and went back to the gym. Three more sets. That's when I can think. When I'm pushing weight, my brain goes somewhere else.

Then I went back to the little suite. Took another shower. The one in the gym was better, but I didn't want to take a chance on her walking in.

Seven twenty-one, the clock said. With a little moon.

I didn't see her anywhere. And I wasn't going to test those new clothes until I knew she was out of the house.

So I went back to the kitchen and made myself a protein shake.

I wasn't even surprised to see the mixer, all laid out on the counter.

"I'm good at that, huh?"

"Good at what?"

"Shopping. Got you everything you needed, didn't I?"

"I . . . guess you did."

"That's my role. And I've got it down pat."

"What's 'role'? Like 'job'? Or like a role in a movie?"

"The last one. I'm the gold-digger the rich old guy married. I drive my fancy little car around and buy things, see?"

"Yeah. That's what you meant before."

"What are you—?"

"You work. But people who see you working, maybe even people who think they know you, they don't. Playing that role, it's just part of the job."

She reached behind her, laid her palms flat, did a hand-press to lift her butt off the counter, held it a good fifteen, twenty seconds, then let herself down slow. She hadn't been lying about using that fancy gym.

"So what was that before, more acting?"

She cocked her head to the side, like she was listening.

"When you acted like I thought you were stupid, remember?"

She smiled, showing off those perfect teeth.

"That must have hurt," I said.

"What? I do presses like that every—"

"The implants."

"Are you serious? You go to sleep, you wake up with new ones. A couple of weeks on the painkillers, you're good to go."

"I wasn't talking about—"

"How could you know that?"

"Know what? Look, you lost me a while back. I can't do this stuff."

"Stuff?"

"Talk in . . . code, like."

"Don't like dress-up, do you, Wilson? Okay, then, tell me how you could possibly know it *did* hurt. A lot. Most of the time, it's just like I said . . . no big deal. But the job Albie paid for, they had to take the old ones out first. Those were over the muscle, not under, the way you're supposed to have it done. But I was just a kid that first time. And the pig who ran the club said I needed them if I wanted to work the front pole, make some *real* money.

"It took me three months to pay off that bill. Five grand. Back then, I could've flown first-class for that much cash, but I didn't know that. I was even grateful to that sleazeball for fronting me the money. He probably split the fee with the cutter. Then he let me work it all off. Five hundred a week. Plus points, which is why I had to do the whole three months."

"I didn't know that. Any of that."

"But you *said*—"

"I was talking about your teeth. I know people, had that done. Not even their whole mouth, just a few. They said *that* hurt, so I figured, you got a whole new set, it had to hurt even more."

"Maybe I just have good dental hygiene."

"That keeps teeth white, maybe. But it can't make them perfect, like yours are."

"So maybe I'm wearing dentures."

"Like those things you take out at night? Not a chance."

"I suppose you're sure about that, too?"

"Yeah, I am. You work too hard at . . . everything, I guess. You don't take shortcuts."

"There wasn't one to take—my teeth were mostly rotted out, plus I had impacted wisdom teeth. . . . They had to come out anyway. So I guess I'm the one who should be saying I'm sorry, huh?"

"You don't have to say anything."

And she didn't. Sat there without moving until I finished. Then I asked her, "So can I borrow the Lincoln?"

"Now?"

"Yeah."

She hopped off the countertop and walked past me. I could hear her rooting around in that big white handbag she'd been carrying when she came in. Taking a lot of time to find the keys. I would have bet serious money she was bending over. I didn't turn around.

When her heels started clicking, I shifted position so I could see her coming. She put down a photocopy of the Lincoln's registration and insurance card. And a letter signed by her saying I was using the car with her permission. The letter was on some fancy stationery, said she was an interior decorator. It was even notarized. And I had a Florida driver's license, too. With my picture on it.

"This is *better* than perfect. Thanks."

"Hold on. First off, you understand that we're still in Leon County, but just barely?"

"Huh?"

"Ah, I mean, it's probably forty-five minutes to get into the parts of Tallahassee you're looking for."

"Okay, so how do I—?"

"See these buttons on the key fob? The yellow one turns off the sensors at the front. Always hit it *before* you go between those stone pillars. The red one opens the garage door. It's pretty long-range—you don't have to be close for it to work. The door'll be open; you just drive in. Press the red one again and the door closes behind you."

I nodded to tell her I got what she was saying.

"Good. Now take a look at this," she said.

It was just a drawing of the dashboard, black-and-white except for one big green button.

"You push that button and this screen here"—she tapped where she wanted me to look— "lights up like a big map. There'll be a thick red arrow, like one of those 'You Are Here' signs at the mall. It's preset. So, no matter where you end up, just tap that button again. All you have to do is follow the arrow, and you'll get right back here. You don't even have to look at it; there's a voice that'll tell you when to turn."

"Damn!"

"In the trunk, there's a lot of athletic equipment. Used equipment, years old. I'm pretty sure there's a couple of baseball bats. One wood, one aluminum, if I remember right."

"Okay."

She handed me a black knife, the kind that you can open with your thumb. The top edge was all ridges, like a saw. "In case you get a hangnail or something."

"Thank you."

She put her hands behind her back. It didn't look like she was showing off her chest that time; it looked like she wanted to make sure she didn't touch me.

The new shoes were as comfortable as if I'd been wearing them for years. Black lace-ups with a one-piece sole and heel. The chinos had a tongue-and-groove thing in front. The light-blue T-shirt felt like silk. The jacket was a darker blue, made of some kind of fiber that would breathe. It only came to my waist, so I tucked in the T-shirt.

I don't know much about cars, but I could tell the Lincoln had a real soft ride. I guess that's why everyone uses them for the baby limos you see all over New York. They're like cabs, only they don't have meters and you're not supposed to pick up passengers from the street, only off calls.

Three hours later, I still hadn't even seen a place that looked right. I didn't want to try the strip clubs yet—I figured I could run names past Rena and she'd be able to tell me something about them. Not what went on inside or anything, just their price range. I couldn't see this Jessop going into a place where you'd look wrong without a suit and tie.

I tried four poolrooms, but they were more like singles bars than the kind of spot I could see this Jessop in. The tables were all different colors, waitresses walking around between them, everything lit up, music playing.

The last one, I figured maybe I'd stay around awhile, see if anyone came over to talk to me. I can shoot a little. Not great or anything, but I wouldn't embarrass myself. If it cost me a few bucks to get some kind of lead, it'd be worth it.

I smelled them before they came up to me from behind, one on each side. A blonde in a yellow top, cut off just below her boobs. A Chinese girl—something like Chinese, anyway—with long black hair. She had on one of those outfits divers wear, only hers was red, and it zipped down the front. They must have used the same perfume.

The blonde kind of bumped me with her hip. I looked down at her.

"I made a bet with my girlfriend. Jasmine, that's her. I'm Angel."

I looked from one to the other.

"Your turn," the Chinese girl said.

"Wilson," I said.

"This is the bet," the blonde said. "Jazzy is always saying she weighs exactly a hundred pounds. Does she look like she weighs a hundred pounds to you?"

"I'm no good at that. Guessing, I mean."

"See?" the blonde said. "Didn't I tell you?" She jabbed her finger into my left biceps, like she was checking to make sure it was real. "You do free weights, don't you?"

"Sometimes."

"How much do you curl?"

"I don't pay much attention. I'm not trying to set any records."

"But you've got *some* idea. You must have. Like, benching a hundred pounds, that'd be a joke for you."

"I guess so."

"That's why I asked about curls, see? I mean, you could bench my girl here, even if she was a total heifer. But curls, like off a preacher bar, a hundred would be a serious lift."

"You know a lot about that?"

"I know a guy, built like you, walks in here and leaves his jacket on, he's not trying to impress anyone. That's not even a tank top under your jacket. So I say to Jazzy, 'That guy, he's the one to settle our bet.'"

"You want me to curl . . . her?"

"If you can. That's the bet. If you can curl her, she wins. If not, I do."

"I never curled a person. That wouldn't—"

"You're worried about where to grab her?"

"I . . . No, what I meant, a person, that's live weight. Not the same."

"But I'm wearing clothes," the Chinese girl said, like that would fix things.

The two of them were standing side by side, facing me. The blonde was way taller than the other one. I looked down to see if it was their heels.

"Can't you guess?" the blonde said.

"Not just by—"

She pointed at her chest. On that cutoff thing she was wearing, one boob had a little "R" over it; the other had a "G."

I just shook my head.

"Real," the blonde said.

"Good," the Chinese girl said, like they'd done this a hundred times.

"I wasn't—"

"Well, *now* you are," the blonde said. "Come on, big boy. One lift."

"How much did you bet?"

"Oh, we don't bet money. When you play pinwheel, the one who gets to go first has the best time."

"What's pinwheel?"

"If you stop asking questions and just try and curl this cute little slut, you'll see for yourself."

I held out my arms. The Chinese girl jumped up against my chest. I cupped the back of her neck in my right hand and wrapped my left around her calves. She made herself straight as a steel bar.

Then I kind of rolled her until she was at the end of my arms. I brought her down to the top of my thighs, sucked in a breath through my nose, and let it out as I pulled her all the way back to my chest. She nipped at my neck, so quick I didn't even feel it until I was putting her back down.

"Less than a hundred," I said.

They didn't want me to stay the night in the motel. "Why ruin it?" the Chinese girl said.

"She means, it's not going to happen again," the blonde told me. "Ever."

They didn't have to spell it out—I could see they couldn't wait to get at each other.

Crazy bitches. They thought they had everything covered:

Told me to follow them to a motel they'd never go back to. Didn't give me their real names or phone number. Even if I grabbed the license-plate number, it'd turn out to be a rental, under a fake name. Probably never pulled their act in the same place twice, either.

Like I said: crazy bitches. It was just a matter of time before they dialed a wrong number. They *had* to know that. Maybe that was part of the kick.

There's all different ways to be that kind of crazy. I knew this girl, she wanted me to choke her until she was almost out. "Edge-play," she called it. "That's where all the best things are, out on the edge."

Probably the same way the guy who killed her a couple of years later felt. It made all the papers, how he carved her up while he was doing her. That "sex game gone wrong" defense, it's no good when you play it with razors.

By the time I walked out of that room, it was real late. So much for my bright idea. I'd figured, after it was over, the girls would want to . . . I don't know, exactly, but . . . talk, or something. Me being a stranger, they might want to tell me about all kinds of places where I might look for this Jessop.

I was wrong about everything. And now it was way late. This Jessop, he wouldn't be a street guy. Even with it being so warm out, he'd be inside, someplace. Maybe a bar.

Rena was right. Small town or not, it was way too big for me to find anyone in it.

That map worked just like she said it would.

When the garage door closed behind me, I left the key in the ignition, so I wouldn't have to walk through the house looking for the right spot to put it.

The clock was showing 4:57 with a blinking sun when I closed my eyes.

When I opened them, the clock said 1:01 with a moon. While I was under the shower, I was thinking, this part was kind of like solitary, too. That's the only place where you can take a shower by yourself. You put your back against the cell door, hands through the slot. That way, they can box-cuff you before they have to open the door. Two guards walk you down, give you maybe five minutes, and back you go.

That's in Ad-Seg, not PC. The cons in Ad-Seg, they're supposed to be dangerous, I guess. PC, protective custody, the only way you get in there is if you ask for it, or if they decide you wouldn't be safe in Population.

Only, that isn't how it really worked. I was never in PC, but I know for a fact that the shot-caller of any gang, he can ask for volunteers to go there.

At least the Spanish ones can. I was still out in Population when this skinny young boy tells the guards he's afraid of getting raped. That's an automatic PC. But that skinny kid, he was in for murder. Not some drive-by, either; he'd used a blade.

Some of the weak ones, they run to a gang for protection when they get Inside. But this kid, he was already a Latin King on the street. That's where he picked up his charge. Word was, somebody owed money for dope, and the kid collected in blood. He was never going home.

Another reason to ask for a lockup is if you're a rat. A known rat. That skinny kid, he was in PC maybe two weeks before he shanked a guy who'd ratted on a whole bunch of Latin Kings.

He must have been quick—there's no blind corners in PC. And a real artist, too. Most of the time, a guy gets shanked, they can save him. I've seen guys stuck like a pincushion—two, three cons doing the work at the same time—and they still live through it. They know how to handle stab wounds in prison. But this Spanish kid, he hit the rat a perfect kidney shot, spun him around, and planted the spike in his neck before the guards could get to them.

I know the story because, by the time they transferred the kid to Ad-Seg, I was already there.

For me, landing in there was just pure luck. I don't know why those two black guys jumped me. I saw them coming in plenty of time to call for a CO, but I didn't do that. You can't do that.

I got cut a few times. Not stabbed, sliced. It's a big, big difference.

I wasn't dumb enough to think I was going to win that hearing they have to give you before they toss you into Ad-Seg. Everybody in the whole joint knew it was self-defense: What kind of maniac's gonna jump two guys, specially when they're carrying? But one of them had a fractured skull, and the other got a splintered rib that tore a lung, so they had to lock me up.

I still don't know why they went after me—it wasn't that I made some first-timer's mistake, like I had with the weights. They were real young, so maybe it was some kind of initiation. But a lot of the white guys thought it was me, representing.

And the guards—in Ad-Seg, I mean—they gave me a lot of play. Treated me good. Nothing out-loud special . . . maybe a few extra minutes in the shower, not tearing up my cell when they searched, calling me by my name. Doesn't sound like much, but in there, that's a lot.

Truth is, I kind of liked it. I didn't have any friends out in Population, and I wasn't going to make new ones.

"Do your own time," is what they always say, but that's no good anymore. Probably never was. I just caught a break, is all—if it'd been white guys who jumped me, I'd've been screwed.

Different color could mean a random shot. But a same-color hit, that couldn't be random. So it'd look like I was locked down for *some* kind of wrong reason—snitching, not paying a debt. Or, even worse, being what the Aryans call a "race traitor."

I just wanted the five years to go away. I didn't need to play dominoes or work some two-bit racket. I had a little radio, with earphones and all. And those books and magazines Solly had sent in.

I didn't even miss working out. You don't need equipment to do that, and I never skipped a day.

The only really lousy thing was the food. Even with my heavy commissary draw, I didn't have a whole lot of choices. I just stayed with what I knew, drank lots of water, and let every day fall into the night.

I woke up one morning when they key-slapped the slot and told me to roll it up, all the way. I guess they were a little surprised that I didn't get more excited about it.

That's prison for you. I'm too dangerous to be put in a population of nothing but criminals, but they kick me straight out into a much bigger population. What, I'm not dangerous to the public?

A couple of the guards wished me luck. The way they say it, it's always the same: "I don't want to see you back here, Sugar."

Like I'd be trying to break into the place.

I went down to the kitchen, but nobody was there. Not in the gym, either. The place was too big for me to go poking around on my own. And even if it wasn't, if I tried to find Albie's little book, I'd probably set off a hundred alarms.

So I went back to the kitchen and made myself something to eat. Killed another hour, doing that.

You don't want to work out right after you have food. Besides, something was gnawing at me, and I couldn't nail it down. Something about looking around . . .

That's when I went back to the place she'd put me in. But I didn't stay there. I went into the garage. If she was around, I could always say I hoped I'd done the right thing, leaving the keys in the Lincoln last night.

The Lincoln was still there. But not the little car. A Thunderbird, Rena had told me it was. A '57, like that was real special. All-original, like that was even *more* special. There was only one place in town that she trusted to work on her car. Maybe that's where she was.

Only, I couldn't see Rena sitting around while people worked on her car. For all I knew, she'd be back any second. Too many "maybe"s for me.

I broke it down into zones. Safe zones, like you do in prison. You have to learn them for yourself. Prison's a crazy place, and you better have it mapped if you want to move around and stay alive while you're doing it.

I figured it was the same way in Albie's house. The safe zone was from the garage all the way through to the living room or the kitchen. The gym was safe, too.

If you get caught in any place that's not yours, you always have to have a good reason. In that little suite, I didn't need to have a reason. Probably that was where they always put guests. But if I was in the kitchen, I'd better be eating. And if I was in the gym, I'd have to be working out.

The living room was no good at all. What would I be doing in there? The place I was staying in had its own TV.

I rechecked my map a few times before I got it. I already had all the cushion I needed. I don't know how to check for bugs on a telephone, and I wasn't going to use their phone anyway. I know you can hide those little cameras just about anywhere, but I didn't care about them, either—what was anyone going to see?

And even if they had cameras, they wouldn't have an X-ray machine. Nobody could see through the closet doors. And Rena, she had to have been in there herself, to get all those sizes right. Having a good eye, that would never be enough.

But by the time I went out the first time, I was wearing the stuff she'd picked out for me. So she'd already gotten in there, somehow.

With no windows, the place stayed dark all the time. I know there's cameras that can see in the dark, and I didn't want to make anyone watching suspicious, so I left the lights on when I opened the closet door.

I went through the clothes, all the new stuff. The closet was big, but I only used one of the two doors to get inside. What I wanted was to feel the wall behind the clothes. Just feel it, not look. I didn't take a flashlight. Besides, if there was a camera, the light would have given the game away.

The back wall wasn't wood. Or, if it was, it was covered in soft black stuff, like a layer of foam. I kept going in and out of the closet, every time bringing a different piece of clothing and laying it out on the bed, like I wanted to see how it looked in the light.

It took me a few tries, but I found it. Just a thin cut, but it went all the way down to the floor. Any decent burglar would have run across setups like that plenty of times: a fake wall, with a door behind it. The way this one was rigged, whoever was inside the closet couldn't use it, only someone on the other side. Probably had a pull-ring, so they could go into the closet, do whatever they wanted, and disappear back out.

A lot of work just to get clothing sizes. She couldn't know if I was a light sleeper, so she must have been *real* quiet.

For what?

I flopped back on the bed, stared at the ceiling until my eyelids got heavy.

Did Rena want to see if I was smart enough to figure out how she got the clothing sizes? Or did she want to see if I was smart enough not to mention it if I did?

The only thing I knew for sure was that whoever built that setup, they hadn't built it for me. I wasn't the first person to be in that suite. Maybe, for the others, it wasn't clothing sizes they wanted to check.

It had to be "they," because Rena knew about the deal before she put me in there. And the idea for it felt like something Albie would do—if he was that much like Solly.

Maybe there was something I should be doing, but I couldn't dope out what that might be. Fucking Solly. Go down there and nose around, huh? I haven't been that many places, but I didn't see why one place would be that different from another. *Somewhere* in this town, there had to be a joint where guys like me would go if they were looking for work—like a union hall for outlaws.

I don't mean a trouble bar, or a biker hangout. It would be a pretty quiet place. And they'd *keep* it quiet. The cops might know about it, but they could never put an undercover in there. I mean, he could walk in, all right—nobody was going to eighty-six him or fix him a Mickey Finn. But the place would go from quiet to dead silence, like the undercover had a neon sign over his head: COP.

A place like that, you have to come in the first couple of times *with* someone. And not just anyone. Not one of those "around guys"; it would have to be someone who was already in. And they'd do all the talking.

Someone says to you, "This guy, he's a pal of mine," that's one thing. But if he says, "Remember the time you and me . . ." you get up and walk away before he finishes the sentence.

So I was screwed. Even if there was places like that in Tallahassee, I couldn't walk in cold.

And this business of leaving my number around, that was bullshit, too. Like this Jessop was going to call me, right? Sure, whoever gave him a message would tell him what I looked like, and that would fit. But this Jessop, he knew me. That means he'd also know I'm not a guy who puts jobs together. So I'd come off as either a rat or a fool who wanted to talk him into some freelance work. Or even a guy who wanted more than his share.

Jessop, he'd just get in the wind.

That's when it hit me. I could make a call of my own. It wasn't even that late. If the lawyer wasn't in court, he'd be in his office.

I moved quick. Had the Lincoln back out of the garage and onto some road a few miles away in just a couple of minutes.

The parking lot of the Time Saver store wasn't full. I walked away from the car, in case it had some kind of wire on it. Then I called the lawyer.

It took another few minutes for that girl to put me through. All that control stuff she had going, she was going to end up costing the lawyer more than money. But I figured he knew that.

Turned out he knew a lot. "Let us be clear: this is an attorney-client conversation, in which I am reporting facts gathered by a person I employed to the person who employed me. That would be you."

"Sure. That's right."

"Abner Jessop," the lawyer said. "Would a DOB of 1961 work?"

"I guess so."

"Six-four, one seventy-five?"

"Perfect, so far."

"Priors back to '79. Convicted of armed robbery, served eight years at Raiford."

"That's in Florida?"

"It is," he said, like I should just shut up and listen. "Married in '89 to one Lily Lee Macomb. Age listed as twenty-eight for him, fourteen for her."

"How can you get—?"

"Parental consent," he cut me off, like it was my second strike. "He's got three children, none of them by the . . . woman he married."

"So he'd be paying child—"

"In arrears, all three. State took his driver's license in '02. Restored it in '06, when he got all caught up."

I didn't say anything.

"Prominent scar, left forearm. Confederate-flag tattoo over left pectoral."

"That's him."

"Good. Two assault raps: one in '91, the other in '96. The first was tossed; complainant withdrew. The other, he used a knife. Six years in on that one."

"So he would have been out on—"

"On parole, yes," the lawyer said, cutting me off in case I was dumb enough to say a date. I'm glad he did, because that's what I *was* going to say. "In fact, he still is."

All finished, so he waited for me to say something stupid. When I didn't, he gave me an address. It would be the same one his parole officer had, so it was probably just a drop, but it was a ton more than I expected.

"Thank you" is all I said.

The lawyer hung up without asking for more money, so I knew we were done.

When I got back, the Thunderbird was still missing. In my place, the clock said 4:54 with a half-moon. I changed into sweats, got a couple of bottles of water out of the refrigerator, and went to the gym.

Like always, when I work out *hard,* I get to a place where my mind is burning same as my body. Usually happens when I keep going even after I'm empty.

But the only thing I came out of that workout with was this: Rena was smarter than me. I wasn't going to be able to trick her into anything.

I might *make* her tell me something, but I don't have what it takes to do that. I mean, I could smack somebody around, scare the hell out of them, but for-real torture, the kind of guys who can do that, you don't want to be around them. I don't even understand how they can be around themselves.

I remember talking to one of them once. He told me, the worst thing in the world is when you have to go all the way, because the other guy's not giving it up. And then, after all that work, you find out later that he never knew in the first place.

Just listening to that guy made me feel like a fucking pervert.

Rena already said she knew where Albie's books were. But she said "work books," not "books." And she didn't say "stamp books," either. Maybe she didn't even know there *was* a book like Solly's, never mind where it was.

But I was just making excuses. When I told that cop, Woods, that if I found the guy who had really raped that girl I'd *get* him to tell me everything, I wasn't lying. But only if he didn't hold out too long. I never said that last part, because I wanted the cop to believe I'd do anything to get him the information *he* wanted. The truth is, I was going to skip all the stuff in the middle. If a broken arm or shattered kneecap would make him talk, great. But I wasn't going past that. I'd just jump right over to where I wanted to be in the first place—killing him.

I wished there was somebody I could talk to about that. Not about my feelings or anything, but how I could do it. Get that Rena to tell me whatever she knew, so I could go back and try to find the man Solly wanted dead.

I wondered why I'd never brought that up to Solly.

I was still thinking that over when the girl walked in.

"You really love this place, huh?"

"Who wouldn't? It's the best setup I ever saw in my life."

"You know what? I've been thinking. About what I told you before. You know, about how I couldn't get Albie to ever use all this, but he sure liked watching *me* doing it?"

"Sure."

"Well, I liked it myself."

"Working out?"

"No. I *hate* that. But being watched, that I liked. I know you think I stayed with Albie because of all the money. And I'm not going to say it didn't matter. At first, I mean. But I don't want you thinking Albie watching me work out was like some slobbery old pig watching me hump a pole.

"I got something from Albie that I never got from anyone. He . . . appreciated me. He was always telling me I was beautiful. To Albie, I was still a young girl, like when we first met.

"And not just that. It was always, 'Read this, Rena.' Or 'Come and watch the news with me.' We'd . . . talk about things. I got . . . I guess you could say I got an education. Not like college. I could have gone if I wanted, but I learned more from Albie. Being around him."

"Solly said he was a real smart man."

"Smart, that's nothing. Albie was *deep*. He'd say something; I'd say, 'Albie, I don't understand.' And you know what he'd say? 'So go and *think* about it, Rena.' And sometimes—a *lot* of times, in fact—I'd end up figuring it out. Then I'd go ask Albie if that was it . . . if I really understood it or not. And when I got it right, he was so . . . I don't know . . . *proud* of me. I can't even explain . . ."

She started crying then. Moaning like she lost something she could never get back. If she was faking, she fooled me.

I went over and sat next to her on the padded bench-press board. She turned into my chest. I just held her there until she stopped crying. I knew it was real, because she stopped little by little, not like she hit some ON/OFF switch.

I didn't know what to say, so I just stayed there.

"You know what else?" she said, after she got her breath. "Never once in his whole life did Albie raise his hand to me."

I didn't say anything.

"I know what you're thinking," she said. "An old guy like him, I could probably break him in half if he ever tried."

Fuck me, that *was* what I'd been thinking.

"You didn't know him. Albie was a *hard* man. People would come here to talk to him. Some of those people, you'd get scared just *looking* at them.

"I don't mean they were . . . big or anything. You can see guys like that in any club. You know, bouncers—just big guys with muscles. These men I'm talking about, they were like off a different planet. Their eyes. The way they moved. It felt like, if you touched them, you'd get freezer burn.

"In a way, they all looked alike. I can't explain it, but they really did. Very . . . controlled, I guess you'd say. But mostly it was the cold. You know how people get in bars? All mouthy, 'I can kick your ass' stuff. These men, you could see they'd never say anything like that. They wouldn't have to—they had those life-taker eyes."

"I've seen that."

"Wilson . . . that's not your name, right?"

"Right."

"You trust me enough to—?"

"Sugar. That's what people call me."

"Okay. Sugar, no disrespect, but I don't think we're talking about the same thing."

"I *have* seen those eyes, Rena. The same ones you're talking about."

"In prison, right?"

I just nodded.

"Tell me about them."

"Them?"

"The people who had those eyes. They weren't all the same, were they?"

"I don't know."

"You know what people are in for, don't you?"

"I guess so. Most of the time, anyway."

"So you don't mean murderers, necessarily?"

"For those eyes? No. There's people you know you can't fuck with. Just by looking at them."

"Guys like you?"

"No. I mean . . . ah, you can't tell by this," I said, flexing the arm I had around her. "It's not size. Or even strength. It's that . . . you said it yourself, a coldness, like. You know, someone like that, he *will* kill you, no matter what it costs him. That's what I mean."

"I understand. But that's not what Albie's friends were like. The men you're talking about, they'd kill you only if you did something to them, right? The ones who kill for fun, for the thrill or whatever, they *didn't* have those eyes?"

"No," I said, thinking about this psycho locked in Ad-Seg the same time I was there. I don't remember his name, but he was always shouting out the names of the girls he'd killed, saying this one was better than that one, because it took her longer to die. I passed right by him one time on the way back from the shower. His eyes were like a foaming mouth on a dog.

"Albie's friends, you could see it. And not just in their eyes. Everything about them. They'd kill you if they were . . . I don't know, if they were *supposed* to. And it wouldn't mean anything to them. They wouldn't get a kick out of it, and it wouldn't make them upset, either. They'd just do it."

"They were all like that? Albie's friends, I mean."

"Every single one. Albie was very polite about it, but I always knew they were going to speak Jewish—Yiddish or Hebrew, I mean—and I wouldn't understand a word. Maybe that's why they didn't care if I was around. Or not."

"Were you scared of them?"

"No. No, I never was."

"That *is* different from the guys I was talking about."

"So you understand? What I said about Albie never hitting me?"

"Yeah. I do—now."

"You sure? Because I'll tell you something: I don't care if you think I'm some minor-league Anna Nicole. But you can *never* think Albie was some old fool."

"I wouldn't ever think that. Solly said—"

"Well, now *I'm* saying. And we never got married, anyway."

Later, when I was alone, *never got married* kept running through my head. Solly said he had Albie's will, but he never said who was supposed to get what.

If Albie took care of Rena with his will, she wouldn't see a penny unless Solly showed the will in court or whatever they have to do.

Rena, she had to know that. So why didn't Solly just put it on the line? Just *buy* that little book?

It had to mean Rena didn't even know there was a little book, the twin to the one Solly had. Because, if I just told her there was money in it for her, why would she care if I tore up the whole house looking for it?

It was a real mess to start with. And now I had to think about those friends of Albie's showing up, too.

I don't do good like this. If you tell me what my job is, I'll do it. And if I get caught doing it, I'll never tell on you. But I'm not one of those guys who can just work things out as they go along.

Maybe I couldn't find this Jessop, but I found a place to buy a prepaid cell easy enough—I didn't want to use any of the ones in that suite.

"I'm still down here," I said.

"You called to tell me this?"

"I called to ask you about that . . . paper you have. The one that says where all your friend's stuff is supposed to go."

"Why?"

" 'Cause if there's enough of that stuff going to the person I'm staying with, and I could *say* that, then maybe I could get permission to look for it. You know, even if I had to bust through drywall or something."

"Meaning, nobody there can tell you where what I want is, because they don't know themselves? Or are you getting held up?"

"I can't tell. Not for sure."

"So?"

"So, if nobody *does* know, then I got to smash up stuff. And I can't do that unless they *let* me do it."

"I get it. And I got a trump card, too, it comes to that. But you try and find out first, understand?"

After Solly hung up on me, I used that bat—the aluminum one—in the trunk of the Lincoln to splatter the cell phone.

Then I drove back to where she lived.

The Thunderbird was in its slot.

It was late. I figured I'd try the next morning.

I was taking off my clothes when she walked in. Wearing a bathrobe, with a towel around her hair.

"I thought I heard something."

"The garage door. When it opens, you hear that?"

"I . . . guess I do. I was never inside by myself at night when it did before. So maybe that was it."

"I'm glad you're up. 'Cause I want to ask you something. And it's real important."

She sat down on the bed. I zipped my pants back up and made sure I stayed as far away from her as I could.

"Albie's books?"

"Yes?"

"Remember you telling me about them?"

"Yes, I remember," she said, like her voice was a wall between us, and she had to use all her strength to keep holding it up.

"What you said was, you knew where they were but you never even looked at them, right?"

"Yes."

She was like a big talking doll. A doll that could only say one word. I knew she'd just say it again and again if I kept asking those same kind of questions. I was stuck. So I just shut up.

A little time went past. She never moved. Then she said, "I told you, it was a matter of trust. Didn't I do that?"

"Yeah," I said. But even as it came out of my mouth, I realized I was going to end up sounding just like her. Two parrots, who only knew one word between them. I had to take some kind of shot. "Did you know Albie left a will?" I asked her.

"No." Just like that. Maybe she didn't even want to think about it. Maybe Albie had family somewhere. Maybe she didn't know that; maybe she was afraid to find out. Everything out of this broad's mouth was a "maybe."

"Well, he did," I told her.

"Where did he leave—? Wait. I get it. Solly, *he's* got it, right?"

"Yes. I called him earlier tonight. I wanted to make double-sure before I said anything to you."

"So you're saying . . . you want to trade?"

That's when I knew she was lying about Albie's books. His "ledger," like she told me. Telling me she never opened them. She'd opened them, all right. And she couldn't find one thing in there that would pay her a dime.

I just looked at her, waiting.

"How do I know you're not just saying this?"

"If I can prove that, prove I'm not making it up about a will, you'll show me Albie's books?"

"If you can *prove* it? There's only one way you could do that, Wilson."

That's when I got my idea. I thought about it for a minute. She didn't move. Then I said, "I need to go out again. I need to make a call."

"Just stay right where you are," she said. Then she got off the bed and walked out.

By the time she came back, she had changed into one of those silly outfits you see in gyms all the time. Fit her like blue paint, with white stripes down the sides of the legs. And she had a cell phone in her hand.

"Yes, it's clean," she said, handing it to me. She stood there with her hands behind her back, telling me she wasn't leaving.

Okay.

I dialed Solly again. When I heard the click, I said, "What if I had to prove that there really *was* this certain paper? Is there any way I could do that without actually holding it in my hand?"

"She's standing right there, huh?"

"That's right."

"Good!" he said. Which surprised the hell out of me. "Ask her, does she know what a partners desk is?"

"Do you know what a partners desk is?" I said.

She just nodded.

"Yes," I said to Solly.

"Then tell her to go sit on it. Tell her you'll be there in five minutes."

I told Rena. I couldn't read the look on her face, but she turned around and walked out.

Then Solly told me what I had to do.

I walked through the house, cursing myself for always being such a fucking dope. And just when I thought I had played it so smart, too.

See, I knew Rena was sitting on a partners desk. And what I was supposed to do with that desk. Only, I didn't know where the damn thing was.

I knew where it *wasn't,* because I hadn't seen anything like what Solly described. But I didn't want to walk through the whole house. It was dark. Maybe she was thinking Solly knew she could hear what he was saying, so he'd used some code. Like "tell her to go sit on it" was really telling me to kill her.

It wasn't just that I didn't want to scare her; I was scared of what she'd do if she thought I was coming after her.

"Rena?" I called out. Not loud, but strong enough to carry.

Nothing.

I turned on the TV in the living room. Maybe the sound would tell her where I was.

But then I shut it right off. For once, I wasn't going to mess something up. If I'm Rena, maybe I think the TV is just a trick. So I could trap her instead of trying to hunt her down.

So I went to the gym.

I was doing lat pulls, front and back. Ten front, ten back. Over and over, until I lost count. I don't even know what I set the weight for. I wasn't tired. And nothing was coming to me.

Except Rena. She came into the gym and stood in front of me. She had on that same blue outfit, but now she was holding a pistol. She handled it like she knew what it was for.

"What happened?" she said.

I let the bar go back up. Slow, the way you're supposed to.

"I'm stupid," I said.

"Meaning . . . ?"

"I tell you, go sit on the desk. Only, I don't know where that damn desk *is*, okay?"

She made a pretty sound in her throat. It made every part of her wiggle a little. Except the hand holding that pistol.

"Go that way," she said, pointing with her other hand.

I walked. She was behind me. When she said to turn, I turned. Finally, we were in a little room. The desk was just old dark wood with a couple of drawers, little glass knobs. The only weird thing was that it was facing the wall.

"Stand still," she said.

I saw her walk around from behind me. She went right up against the wall, then she turned around and faced me. She sat down so her elbows and wrists made a triangle, with the pistol centered on my chest.

"You get it now?"

"A *partners* desk. So one partner sits facing the other one, right?"

"Yes. This is Albie's den. For his special, private stuff. Not his *work* stuff, understand?"

"Yeah."

"I've been in here *plenty* of times," she said.

I remembered hearing a girl say something like that, a long time ago, when I was still in school. The other girls were really stabbing her. With words, I mean. Not like playing the dozens—

really vicious stuff. Like, her mother must be a real whore, 'cause the girl didn't even know who her own father was. "I do *too*," the girl kept saying, like she was a little kid.

That's how Rena sounded now.

Back then, I'd waited around after school until the worst one came out. I didn't know her name, but I could see she was with her special friends.

When they saw me coming, they didn't know what to do. A guy like me, I wasn't supposed to be around people like them. I stepped close to the leader girl. Before she could say anything, I slapped her, hard enough to make her fall down and start crying.

"Tell your boyfriend I did that," I said. "He's not gonna do nothing. You know why? Because he don't give a fuck about you. He's only with you because everyone knows you give the best blowjobs in school."

I never did find out what happened at school. I never went back, and they never came looking for me. But I was on the same corner every night, and people knew it. Her boyfriend, that pussy could have found me anytime he wanted.

Only he never showed. So I never found out what happened in school. I wanted to call the girl they'd been torturing, but I guess I was afraid that I'd only made things worse.

I wasn't going to do that this time. So all I said to Rena was "Sure, *you* have. But I know something about that desk you don't. . . . At least, I think I do."

"What are you talking about?"

"The desk. The proof you need is in the desk. Only, Albie had it fixed so's it takes three people to get at it."

"There's only two of us."

"I know. But I can do what two of the people are supposed to. You do the other part."

"Like two partners?"

"I . . . I guess so. Maybe that's right. All I know is, that desk has to be lifted up. *Way* up. All four legs have to be off the ground. *High* off the ground. That's the two-man job.

"Then the third one stands underneath. There's like this water stain. On the underside, I mean. You have to look real close to even see it. Then you have to tap right on it. Not hard, just, like, with your knuckle."

She got out from behind the desk. "Give me that phone," she said.

I handed it over. She tossed it onto this old couch. It was some dark leather, and it didn't look comfortable. But it had a bunch of rugs and stuff on it, so the phone didn't make a sound when it landed. Neither did the pistol.

"Let's do it, Sugar."

I crawled under the desk. It would have been an easy lift, only I couldn't get my head free to take the weight on my shoulders. I crawled back out.

"What?" she said.

"It's probably not all that heavy, but I can't lift it like you do a squat. And I don't think I can hand-press it from my knees."

Rena went over to the desk. She looked at it a long time. Then she said, "It has to go up, but it doesn't have to go up *level.* Just lift one end, okay? When you get that up, slide your left shoulder underneath. Put your left palm up, like you were getting ready to press. Then just slide your palm more to the left. Slow, just a little at a time. When you get it far enough over, you push with the one hand and I'll haul up on it, too. Then you'll be able to get your right hand inside."

She showed me with her hands what she was telling me to do. I could see it.

"Okay? Now, when you get both palms under it, just *push.* Like it was a . . . I don't know what you call it, but I saw you do it. In the gym, I mean."

She was right, too. Once I got one end up, the rest was easy. I got my palms under it, bent my knees, drove it up, just like doing a squat-thrust. One with serious weight to it—the damn desk felt like it was made of lead.

Only one rep! I kept saying to myself. *I can hold this up all night.* For a minute, I thought I might have to. I couldn't look around, but I could feel Rena wasn't in the room anymore.

But then I felt her against me. Smelled her. Her, not her perfume. I couldn't see what she was doing, but I could see a flashlight, so I knew where she'd run off to.

I heard a couple of little taps against the wood, and something dropped on my head. It didn't knock me out or anything, but the surprise almost made me drop the desk.

"I've got it," I heard her say. "Let it down *easy*, okay? I'll help."

In the living room, I watched her unwrap something in white tissue paper. She did it like she was disconnecting an alarm. Inside all that paper, there was a little bag. It looked real old, like it was once red but faded to a brownish color now.

Like the thumbprint in Solly's book, I thought to myself. I knew that little bag had to be Jewish. There was a gold star embroidered on the front with Jewish writing inside it. Underneath, there was like a whirly thing, also in gold, and two green-leaf things coming out of each side. The bottom was all gold fringe.

"It's his *tallit*," she said, real soft.

"His what?"

"His prayer shawl. That's what's inside that bag. You get one of these when you're bar-mitzvahed. On your thirteenth birthday. For Jews, that makes you a man. In the temple, you wear it over your shoulders."

"How come you know all this?"

"Albie told me, what do you think?"

"You went with him? To the—?"

"No! And Albie didn't go, either."

"Well, Solly said this was something Albie left to you. In his will, I mean. Doesn't that *prove* Solly has it?"

She didn't say anything. For a long time.

She was still sitting there, with that little bag in her lap, when I got up and walked back to that suite.

It took me a while. By the time I got there, a whole set of books was on my bed. Big, thick ones.

Albie's ledgers, I guess. Because that little blue book Solly wanted, it wasn't there.

It was still nighttime when she came back to where I was—3:51, with a blinking sun. There was enough light from the hall for me to see she only had her underwear on.

She lay down next to me. Before I had a chance to even think about what was going on, she put her lips against my ear.

"We have to get out of here, Sugar."

"Now?"

"Right now. Pack up your stuff. *Everything,* understand?"

"What about your—?"

"The keys are in the Lincoln," she said, stepping over what I wanted to ask her. "Put all your stuff in the trunk. Then come back to the living room. I'll have stuff, too. A lot more than yours. If it doesn't fit in the trunk, we'll just throw it into the back seat."

"What hap—?"

She put her finger over my mouth. Then she jumped up and ran out the door.

It was easy for me to pack. The only problem was that new stuff Rena had bought for me. I didn't have a suitcase for that, so I just threw it in the back seat, loose.

In the living room, there was Rena. And about half a dozen different bags.

"If I had a strap, I could—"

"Just make a couple of trips, Sugar. I'll be carrying some of them, too."

The garage was dark. She got behind the wheel of the Lincoln and hit the button for the door, then hit it again as soon as we rolled out.

Only, Rena didn't take the driveway. She turned and drove out behind the garage. It looked like a damn forest, but she drove through it like there was a road somewhere.

A few minutes later, she stopped.

"Unload it all," she said. "Don't worry about being neat—just get *everything* out of the car."

It only took us a couple of minutes. When Rena saw my loose stuff, she popped one of her suitcases open and stuffed it all inside.

"Wait right here. Don't *move.*"

The Lincoln went back the way we came. When she came back to where she left me and all that stuff, she started snapping off sentences like she was firing jabs.

"It's about a half-mile from here to the road. You stay here. *Right* here. But lie down, like, okay? I don't know how long it's going to take, but I'll be back for you."

She looked at me the way you look at a pawnbroker, trying to get him to believe you really *are* coming back to claim what you hocked. I didn't know what the deal was, but I didn't know what else to do except sit there and listen.

"Keep this cell on," she said, tossing a new one at me. "Then you'll know it's me coming." She handed me a big plastic bag. "There's your bars and drinks in there. Now *wait.*"

She threw some of her stuff in a little carryall and disappeared.

Waiting never bothered me, but I didn't like being in those woods—I wasn't used to places like that. When it finally got light, I could see why she picked that spot—it was almost like a cave of trees.

The fucking bugs were making me crazy. I had to take my mind off everything. I had to do that or go nuts. I still didn't know what was going on.

So I opened one of Albie's books—that tiny flashlight Solly gave me was enough for me to read by. After a while, I could figure some things out. Like the dates. They started in 1966, and they went all the way to a couple of months ago, probably just before he died. Every page was laid out the same. I couldn't understand much more than the dates, but I knew all those words and numbers had to stand for *something*. I just couldn't make any sense of them.

I took a few deep breaths, then I started over. Albie was in the same business as Solly, right? I used that. Looked at the capital letters in blocks, like initials. Some I found over and over again. Like, whoever JBR/H/C was, he had the same phone number for years. The first number, it was inside a box. Not crossed out, just this box around it. Then nothing for a long time. Then a *different* number. With no box around it. So that one, it was probably still good.

I'd picked up on that because I was looking for a "J." Like in "Jessop." I kept trying. Found "AJ/WT/X."

Whoever that was, Albie kept his record the same as he had for the other one. Phone number started in 1978, all in those boxes. Nothing until 1985. Then a new one.

Only this one was different from the others. The phone number was still the same, but the name, there was a circle around it, starting in 1990. And just the number "100." In the very last book, "AJ/WT/X" had a line drawn through it. Not a line, more like an arrow. Pointing down.

The cell went off. It didn't ring, just kind of throbbed. I opened it up, but I didn't say anything.

"I'm coming in," Rena said. Then she cut off.

Maybe ten minutes after that, I heard her crashing through the woods. At least I thought it was her.

It was. She had on jeans and boots. Work boots, not show-off things; lace-ups, with heavy soles.

"Hurry! I'm parked on the shoulder. Some cop could come by. . . ."

It took three trips. It wasn't the weight, it was all those different little bags. She didn't have any big suitcases, like for traveling.

The car was a white Cadillac with a monster of a trunk. Everything fit.

Rena stomped on the gas, and we got out of there. After a few turns, she kind of calmed down. I could tell, because she lit a cigarette.

We drove for a while. She was on her third smoke when she finally said something.

"All we've got to do now is *not* get a ticket."

"Where're we going?"

"Tampa. It's, I don't know exactly, maybe three, four hours from here."

"Okay."

"'Okay'? That's it, 'Okay'?"

"What do you want me to say? I figure you'll tell me whatever you want to, sooner or later."

She kept on driving. She looked like she hadn't been to sleep at all, but I didn't offer to take over. I could see she was locked on, concentrating.

We went through little clots of traffic, but it was mostly trucks. Rena was a good driver, smooth with the wheel. I felt my body easing. If she didn't want to talk, maybe I'd just . . .

"This isn't fair," she said.

"What isn't?"

"What I'm doing. There's no reason you have to go where I'm going. They've got bus stations in Tampa if you don't want to get on a plane."

"I want—"

"Yeah. I know what you want. I'm sitting on it."

I felt bad when she said that. Not that she was wrong, but she wasn't exactly right, either. I don't know why I felt bad, but I knew for sure that I did.

I looked out my window. There was nothing to see.

A long time passed. I kept looking out the window.

"I'm sorry, Sugar."

"What?"

"I said I'm *sorry*. What I said, you took it wrong. But that's not your fault; it's mine. I've been playing a role so long that I don't pay attention anymore. That's over now. All over. Everything. It's over."

"I don't get what you—"

She shifted in her seat, twisted herself below the waist so I could see the right cheek of her butt. Her jeans were so tight that I could see the outline of something in the back pocket.

"I can't keep driving like this. Just take it, okay?"

I didn't even try and get my fingers inside the pocket of her jeans. I could see the only way I could get it out was to push it up. It came out slow. But as soon as I saw the top of it, I knew what it was. I got my finger and thumb around it and pulled it free.

The twin to Solly's book.

"What you came for, right?" she said, staring through that windshield.

"Half of it, anyway."

"What else do you—?"

"This Jessop guy, remember?"

She made a funny sound, like laughing and spitting something out at the same time. Then she went back to staring out the windshield.

I opened the little blue book. It was all in the same kind of Jewish writing that I saw on that bag Albie had hidden in that desk.

"Nothing in English, right?" she said.

"No," I said. But I knew it was the right one for sure—the old bloody thumbprint was right where Solly said it would be. I looked a little closer. There *was* some English—that thumbprint was stamped over "Goliath, 22/7/46," whatever that was supposed to mean.

"Yeah? Well, *this* is," she said, reaching inside her shirt and pulling a folded-up piece of paper out of her bra. "Be *careful* with it, Sugar."

I unfolded it the same way I had seen her unwrap that prayer-bag thing. I knew by then that she wasn't just being careful, she was showing respect. So that's what I did, too.

The paper wasn't any bigger than a dollar bill. The writing was so small, I had to move my hands a little away from my eyes to make it out.

My Rena, if you are reading this, it means I am gone and Solly has told you he is holding my will. To prove this, he

*would read you the part that led you to my desk. You must lis-
ten to me now. Listen and obey.*

*GET OUT OF THE HOUSE. GO NOW. NEVER
COME BACK. They will come soon. They will be afraid an
old man babbles in his sleep. They will never believe you
know nothing. I told you this time would come. You know
where to go. Go now! Do not call Solly. For you, there is no
will. Disappear, Rena. You can do that. With me, you started
your life over. Now you must do that again.*

*Know this, child: my life began anew when you came into
it, but also know that my life had already been pledged. I
apologize for nothing. What I did, I did. I never told you of
these things, because knowing would be dangerous for you. I
was always true, my Rena. To you, and to the oath I swore
many years before your birth. I could never allow a conflict
between my oath and you, because my oath was given to a
greater thing than any person could ever be.*

*You have my love, forever and always. It would be no
betrayal for you to be with another now. In truth, it would be
my wish. But, whatever you do, you tell Solly NOTHING. If
you must speak with him, lie. Once you are gone from him,
STAY gone. Never contact Solly again. I write this with a
prayer that someday you will be reading it. If you never read
this, it means you have already rejoined me. If any other person is reading this, I have been betrayed.*

*So to whoever is reading this, I say: YOU MUST SHOW
THIS MESSAGE TO ARI! Show this to Ari BEFORE
you act.*

*Ari, this woman knows nothing of our business. Now you
have the proof you sought. SOLLY IS THE TRAITOR. This
girl does not know my book exists. Solly has my book. He will
deny this, but I sent it to him months ago, when the doctors
told me I had little time left. When Solly says he does not have
my book, you will know the truth. Ari, if you hurt this girl,
you will learn nothing. Worse, you will dishonor your own*

father and the cause for which we both pledged our lives. Go see Solly. And finish this.

Then there was some Jewish writing. Maybe it was more words, but I could only read the English part. I did that, over and over again.

I shook my head, like maybe that would change the writing. I'd probably still be staring at that paper if Rena hadn't stabbed me in the side of my neck with a long fingernail.

"What the—?"

"There's nothing else to say, is there? You got what you came for."

"Except for—"

"Just stop, okay? I don't care anymore. I'm going to obey my husband. You want to run back to Solly, do it. You want to talk to Jessop so bad, I can tell you where to find him too."

"How could you do that?"

"Easy," she said, like there was a foul taste in her mouth. "On paper, *he's* my husband."

Rena pulled the Caddy into a marked-off slot right in front of one of those little up-and-down houses. She had the key for the front door.

The place was like brand-new clean, but it had a musty smell. *Like Solly's unit,* I thought. *Only his smelled good, because Grace came in every week.*

I got all our stuff inside. Rena went around turning things on. "Don't open the blinds," she said. "I want to get the car into the garage. It's out back. We have two slots. One's large enough for an RV. That's a big thing in time-shares."

Then she was gone. At least, this time, there weren't any of those damn bugs to keep me company.

"What's a time-share?" I asked, as soon as she sat down. She looked like she didn't have much left in her, and I wanted to be sure I knew what the deal was. "Time-share" didn't sound good to me.

"The owner is a corporation," she said, between puffs of her smoke. "You buy shares that entitle you to use the place one month out of every year. Summertime, the shares are pretty cheap. In the winter, they go for a lot."

"So you own one of those shares?"

"I own them all. One corporation, twelve shareholders. But they're all me, just different names. The corporation has a bank account. The mortgage company gets a check every month from that account. Automatically, I mean—they just go in there and take it out. Same for the condo association. You have to pay them fees, on top of the mortgage. Also the cable TV.

"There's no phone. The account for the corporation always has enough in it to carry the place for a few years, even if no new deposits show up.

"I handle all the deposits into the corporate account. I just made one last April. Nobody's going to be asking any questions for a long time. And I'll be gone a much longer time by then. That's the way Albie set it up.

"The same for the car. I own it. In the same name I use for my driver's license and insurance. Down here, a white Caddy's like a palm tree—anyplace you look, you see them."

"Are you going to—?"

I stopped when I saw she was already asleep. Just passed out on the couch. I snubbed out her smoke in the ashtray, then I kicked back in the recliner.

But I didn't go to sleep.

It was way past midnight when she came around. At first, she looked scared, like she woke up in the middle of a bad dream. Then she shook her head hard, put her nose under her armpit, made a face.

That's when she saw me there.

"I need a shower, Sugar. Then you can sleep, okay?"

I didn't say anything. Just kept sitting there, with her pistol in my lap.

She made it quick. I guess she knew I was running on fumes. I don't even remember going out.

When I opened my eyes, I was in a bed. Rena was next to me. She must have taken off my shirt and shoes and socks. She smelled fresh and sweet. I didn't.

I found the shower easy enough. Draped over the hamper, all the fresh clothes I'd need, except for my shoes.

I just kept going, like I knew what I was doing. But I didn't even know what day it was. Didn't know the time until I went back into the living room. It had those tiny little blinds, the kind you open and close by twisting a rod. I pushed one up with my finger. Daylight.

The kitchen was nothing like the one in Rena's house, but it was still all high-end. Looked new. I opened the refrigerator. Bottles of water were all I saw. But there was a whole mess of my power bars on the little round table.

I was still eating when I felt her behind me. I started to turn, but she put her hand on my face and pushed it back to where it was.

"Finish first, then we'll talk," she said.

In the reflection from the hood over the stove, I could see she wasn't wearing anything.

When I went into the front room, she was waiting. Dressed in a set of baggy gray sweats, barefoot. Her hair was down, looked wet, like she'd just walked out of the shower.

With the blinds drawn and only a little lamp going in the corner, the room was all dark and smoky. Like an after-hours joint, except for the quiet.

"You'll have to cut this later," she said, pulling at her hair. "I can dye it myself. I'll pick up what we need when I buy some real suitcases."

"You're going to, what, disappear?"

"I already have. Rena Rosenberg is gone. I'm Lynda Leigh. On this unit, on the car, on my license. Even on my birth certificate. Which you need to get a passport. And Lynda Leigh has a credit history, too."

"You've been ready for this to happen, huh?"

"For a long time. Albie knew it would come someday, and he never let me forget it. You know something else? I made all this ID myself. Me. Albie taught me. Perfect ID isn't just copying a photo on a license, like I did when you took the Lincoln. It takes research, equipment, and technique. That last one, I don't know if I can explain it. But Albie said I was a natural.

"I learned from the best. Albie told me that the fatal flaw in buying ID is, you're giving the person you bought it from more than just the money; you're giving him something he can sell. But when you learn to make your own, you never have to trust anyone, ever."

"And this Jessop . . . ?"

She lit another cigarette. "I lied," she said.

"You lied about what?"

"Everything. I'm not thirty-nine; I'm thirty-five. I married Jessop in 1989. That was to keep him from going to prison. He paid my mother to sign some paper so we could get married."

That's what the lawyer told me about Jessop, I thought. *He got married to some girl who was fourteen.* She wasn't lying about that, anyway.

"I'd already been with him for almost two years then," Rena said. "I'd probably still be with him except he once brought me along to a meeting with Albie."

"At that big house?"

"No," she said, like only an idiot would even think that. "In a restaurant. I already had the first implants by then, and Jessop, I think he wanted to show off. Show *me* off, I mean. I was all slutted up: four-inch heels, raccoon eyes, a little skirt I had to fight to fit into.

"Albie had two men with him. The same men who are coming for his book now. Not them, necessarily, men just like them, I mean.

"They started talking about some job. Right in front of me, like I was a piece of furniture. All of sudden, Albie says to Jessop, 'This is the way you work? You bring a little girl along, let her listen to everything?'

" 'She's dumb as a fucking rock,' Jessop says. 'By the time we get back home, she won't even remember she's been here. How old do you think she is—twenty-two, maybe? Well, she's fifteen, and she's been stripping for a couple of years already. You got nothing to worry about.'

"Albie just looks at Jessop. 'I drove a long way for this,' he says. 'Did I say you could bring anyone?'

" 'No,' Jessop tells him. 'But what's the—?'

"That's when Albie cut him off. 'You take any risk you want. But you don't make me take them with you. So this girl, she stays with me until it's over.'

"The way Albie said it, you could see he wasn't asking. I'd never seen Jessop like that before. Scared, I mean."

"He left you there?"

"Sure. Far as he was concerned, this was just a long trick. Like a rental. I think he even expected Albie to throw a bunch of cash at him when the job was finished."

"But . . . ?"

"But Albie brought me to the house, the one you stayed at. He told me I was going to stay there until I was old enough to make intelligent decisions."

"Weren't you scared?"

"Not for a minute. Albie told me to take a shower, scrub all that *shmutz*—that was the word he used; I still remember—off my face. Put all my clothes in a plastic bag. He didn't have any women's clothes, so I had to wear men's stuff for a couple of weeks, until he brought all kinds of things back. I didn't know *exactly* what the stuff was, but I could tell it was good."

"He never—?"

"Don't you even *think* it! I had to read all the time. Books, magazines, newspapers. And watch TV; that was okay, too. Anything I didn't understand, I'd ask Albie. Some things he'd tell me. Sometimes, he'd say I was just being lazy, go look it up. An education, Albie called it. The first time he said, 'Rena, you are a truly intelligent young woman,' I thought I would die, I was so happy.

"All I know is that Albie met with Jessop again. After the job, I mean. I don't know what they said, and I know they kept doing business, but Jessop never came around the house. None of the people that Albie set up jobs for *ever* did. Just those other men; the ones I told you about.

"So, one day, I asked Albie if he'd bought me from Jessop. 'Cause I knew Albie had money, and Jessop loved money.

"You know what Albie said? He said he told Jessop he'd *disposed* of me. I knew too much; I'd seen too much. *That's* when Jessop wanted to get paid—he must have told Albie he had a lot of money invested in me. But I know Albie told him he wasn't getting a dime, because it was Jessop's fault in the first place, for bringing me along."

"Jesus."

"I know. I . . . never really believed it, not for a long time. I remember, once, Albie told me to stop being such a little brat. I knew what he wanted then. To spank me, you know what I mean? A lot of guys are into that, especially with a young girl. Only, I was wrong. You know what he wanted?"

"For you to stop being such a little brat?"

"Yes!" she said, smiling for the first time since . . . I didn't even remember the last one.

She lit another smoke. "I was with Albie twenty years, that much is true. But I wasn't his wife until the millennium came. The year 2000, that's what everybody called it.

"I was Rena for ten years, but only by name. One day, I just marched into his den—that's where the partners desk was—and I told him I was old enough to make intelligent decisions. And I'd made one."

"That's almost like this old movie I saw once."

"If you say *Baby Doll*, I'll spit in your face. I saw that movie.

We've got a satellite dish, with like a million channels, so I know what you mean. And it was *nothing* like that. Albie wasn't waiting until I turned legal, and he damn sure knew I was no virgin. And I didn't walk around shaking it, either."

"I'm sorry."

"For what? You've got no idea—"

"I'm sorry for saying something that hurt your feelings, Rena."

"Rena's gone."

"Lynda, right?"

"Yeah. Albie always told me this day would come. That's why he replaced the implants."

"I don't under—"

"After Albie . . . went, I was supposed to go, too. I *always* had Albie's little book. I was supposed to take that with me, and hide it where I could always find it. A life-assurance policy, Albie called it."

"Life insurance?"

"*Assurance.* Something I could trade for my life if any of . . . those men found me. And that isn't all. Anyone can get paper ID. Only the implants, they were like this secret weapon. Plenty of women change their hair, but how many have implants taken *out*?"

"I know a girl who did."

"A stripper, right? And she went jumbo on them?"

"That's right."

"The size *I* got, it makes me . . . stand out, I guess. But they're not the kind that would herniate my spine."

"They don't . . . pull on you?"

"Not a bit. I wasn't lying about the working out every day."

"So, if you got . . . smaller, you wouldn't look like yourself?"

"Depends on where you're looking."

"I get it."

"Good," she said, like she was a little annoyed. "You have any more questions, Sugar?"

"Yeah, I do."

She turned a little straighter, facing me like she was making sure I still had the different-colored eyes.

"So?" is all she said.

"You said you could find this Jessop. That can't be just because he was on some paper as your husband a long time ago."

"What's your question?" She sounded a lot colder than before, but I didn't have any choice. So I asked her: "Have you . . . seen him since you—?"

"Your whole mind is dirt, huh? No, Sugar, I haven't 'seen' him since he brought me to that meeting. He brought in a piece of poor white trash, a . . . thing he could do whatever he wanted to with. If I'd just been dumped by the side of a road, I'd have been happy, just knowing I'd never have to see that . . . filth again. That answer your question?"

AJ/WT/X, I thought. *Abner Jessop, White Trash, maybe? But what was that "X" for?* I knew I couldn't ask her about that; I had work to do. So I only said, "Then how could you know where he is?"

"Albie's ledgers. It's all in there."

"You can read them?"

"Every word."

"I didn't see any addresses. Some phone numbers, maybe, but . . ."

"We have to unpack anyway," she said. Not icy anymore. More like bored. "When we find the ledgers, I'll show you."

By the time we dug out the ledgers, it was late. "It's not like you need this stuff tonight," she said. "I'm tired and I'm hungry. I know every take-out spot around here—there's a lot of them. You probably don't know how to . . . ah, never mind, what do I know? Just tell me what you want. Asian, Indian, Mexican? Hamburgers? What?"

"I'll eat whatever you bring back."

"Thai, then?"

"Sure."

"Wake up." Rena, kneeling on the carpet so she could whisper in my ear.

Damn! is all I remember thinking. Nobody should be able to sneak up on me, specially if they had to open a door to do it.

The food was good. Crisp and clean. She brought so much that there were leftovers, even though we both ate like pigs.

"We have to let the food settle first," Rena said. Sitting back in the living room, lighting a cigarette.

"Sure," I said, although I didn't know what she was talking about.

A few minutes later, she said, "Go take a shower, Sugar."

I was standing under the steam when the idea that she might be calling Jessop right that minute hit me.

I was still thinking about that when she got into the shower with me.

"Don't be rough with me," she said in the bedroom. "It's been a long, long time."

That made me mad, like she had to warn me. "Can't you do *any* damn thing without making it some kind of deal?" I said.

She raised her hand to slap me. I didn't move.

Then she was crying and kissing me at the same time. I don't even know how I ended up inside her.

"I said don't be rough, not play dead!" she hissed in my ear. But I could tell she wasn't mad at all.

The first time she woke me up that night, she was a little rough herself. The second time, she was just right.

I don't mean she was good, like an expert or anything. She was just . . . right, is the only way I can say it.

"This is my breakfast specialty." She was standing in the kitchen, talking over her shoulder at me. "Warmed-over Thai."

I didn't say anything.

"Trust, remember?"

"I do," I told her. She was sitting on the floor with her legs crossed, the ledgers in her lap.

"I'm not going to ask you why you want to find Jessop."

"If you want to know, I'll tell you."

"That isn't what I meant by trust, Sugar. He doesn't live in Tallahassee. Or Tampa, either. It's way east of here, damn near in the middle of the state."

"So?"

"The middle of this state, it's another world from the coasts. Plus, where he lives, it's a *tiny* little town. They probably pay attention to anyone who even stops for gas."

"Were you ever there?"

"Not there, exactly. But in that part of the state? Sure. That's where I was born."

"So you met—?"

"I was a runaway, Sugar. I hitched a ride and I was gone. I didn't meet Jessop until I'd been on my own for a few weeks. And that wasn't so far from here. Tampa's where he took me.

"If he hadn't gotten busted for underage . . . I didn't have any fake ID, and I wasn't even . . . developed yet, not really. This was before I got the implants. The way the cops explained it to me, if we got married, they'd drop the charges on Jessop. But I'd need my mother's permission. I never even went back myself. Jessop went over there, paid her the money, and she signed. Like he was buying a used car."

The address she got from Albie's ledger wasn't the same one the lawyer told me. I figured Albie paid closer attention than any parole officer would. The Law might know where Jessop got his mail, but Albie would know where he lived.

A lot of good that did me. If Jessop had any sense, he'd stay close to his home base between jobs.

"He'd see me coming a mile away."

"You are difficult to hide," she said, kind of smiling at me. That's when I realized I must have said it out loud, instead of just thinking it.

"So far, nobody's seen me here, though. Do you think you could go out and get some more food? Enough we don't have to go out for every meal?"

"Sure," she said. I could see from her face that she knew why I wanted her out of there.

"Wait. Come here for a minute, Rena."

"Lynda."

"I'll get it."

She came over and dropped into my lap. "You *have* to get it, Sugar. Before I was Rena, I was someone else. Jessop never put a hand on Rena. And you never have, either. Understand?"

"Lynda," I said. And kissed her hair.

She snuggled against me. I kept thinking about trust. "Do you know this town?" I asked her.

"I *used* to know it. Now all I know is what I told you: take-out joints, pharmacies, one mini-mall. I looked them up before we came down here. I even have a little map. But that's about it."

"Damn."

"What?"

"I thought maybe there was a way to get this Jessop here. Not *here*, here. In Tampa someplace, I meant."

"Oh."

"Can you sit here and listen?" I said.

"Of course I can."

"No smoking."

"Sugar . . ."

"You want to smoke, sit over where you were. I still want you to listen."

She wiggled in my lap. Not like she was teasing, like she was making up her mind. Then she kind of settled in.

"Why didn't you take off the minute Albie was gone?" I asked.

"I didn't know I was *supposed* to do that. I called Solly, and he sent you down empty. Without any will, I mean. How come?"

"Because he read it."

"Oh."

"And he wanted Albie's book."

"And he didn't care if I . . . Yeah, I get it. I get it now."

"I'm supposed to be down here looking for this Jessop. But, really, I'm supposed to get that book."

"That was the deal?"

"That was it. Only, Solly, he didn't know what was in that partners desk. He probably thought it was a stash of gold. That's something Solly always was a fanatic about, gold. 'Jewish Traveler's Checks' is what he called it."

"How does this help us?"

"You have to help *me* first, Lynda. I don't mean a trade or anything like that. I mean, you and me, we have to help each other. You're smarter than me about some things; I'm smarter than you about other things. We have to put that together."

"That's what Albie always told me."

"I don't—"

"Add everything up. Always add everything up. If you do that right, whatever's missing, that's what you're looking for."

"Okay, but—"

"Sugar, just sit here for a couple of hours. You can think while you're sitting; I can think while I'm running around stocking us up. When I come back, that's when we can sit down and do the adding up. Together, okay?"

"Okay," I said. I was a little disappointed she hadn't noticed me calling her Lynda. But then I thought maybe that meant she didn't think I was dumb.

I didn't want to disappoint *her,* so I really did try and think over everything we had. But all I could really think of was what we didn't.

"Let me do it," she said, when I got up to help her unload the car. "There's no reason for anyone around here to get a look at you. That's what the slot in front of each unit is for. Your guests, or if you want to drive right up to the door to off-load stuff."

It took her a lot of trips, but not much time—it was only a few steps to the door, and she left it open. She'd bought some real big suitcases, too, but they were empty.

When she—when *Lynda*—got back from putting the car away, she closed the door behind her.

"Hungry?"

"I guess so."

"I thought you guys had to have a ton of calories every day."

"You don't get a ton of calories in prison."

"But you still lift weights and all?"

"If you can. It all depends. And if you have enough money on the books, you don't have to eat mainline, either. The problem really isn't calories, it's getting healthy food."

"Well, that's my specialty. Salads and stuff like that, I mean. What I got was either fresh or frozen. I'm a killer on the microwave, but I'm not touching an oven."

"You want me to—?"

"I want you to sit there like a good boy and let me put some plates together for us."

I liked how she put everything away, even the plates and glasses in the dishwasher. Not the way she did it, just that she did it before she had a smoke. Most smokers, they finish eating, they light up.

"Can we do this, Sugar?"

"What you said before? Sure, I think we can. We have to try, anyway."

That's when she fired up a cigarette, and said, "Me first. I'm going to say things. Each one, you tell me if I'm right, if I'm wrong, or if you just don't know, okay?"

I just nodded.

"Albie and Solly were like brothers. They go back to before either of us was born."

"That's what Solly said. I don't know if it's true."

"It was, once, anyway. They each had a book. Those little blue books. And they each had a will."

"Solly said that, too."

"When Albie . . . died, I called Solly. He told me he was sending a man down. He said he'd call again, first. I thought you were bringing Albie's will down with you."

"Only, I really came for that little blue book."

"I know. But you didn't say a word about it. That's why I . . . acted like I did. I never talk like that now, but that doesn't mean I don't remember *how* to. And I didn't want to just come out and ask you. About the will, I mean."

"I get it."

"But you looking for Jessop, that was real?"

"Now, sitting here, I don't know anymore, Lynda. All I know for *sure* is that Solly wanted Albie's book."

"I knew that all along."

"You knew? Then why didn't you just—?"

"Albie told me not to."

"What? You mean, like, some kind of . . . I don't know what to call it, but you know what I mean."

"A voice from beyond?" She smiled. Sweet and gentle, just like Grace did when I met her. "No. When he told me, I was standing in his den. He was at his desk. He said if he went before Solly I should call Solly. Just tell Solly, then just listen.

"It used to upset me, him talking like that. But I knew it was just him getting me ready. Albie always used to say, if a train is coming at you, closing your eyes won't save you . . . but if you look right at it, you at least have a chance to jump."

"He was right about that. That's me, perfect—I never saw it coming."

"What are you—?"

"I'll tell you what I am, Lynda. A dope. I didn't mean to knock you off the track."

She took a long, deep drag of her smoke. "Was that a pun?"

"A what?"

"Sugar, I swear, you've got some kind of mind. Where was I? Ah! I told you what Albie said: the minute he goes, I should call Solly, right?"

"Yes."

"Only, what he said was, 'You just speak *once,* Rena. Then you listen.' I remember that like it was engraved in stone. You know what a litmus test is? No? Like the test the cops have: pour some liquid into white powder, shake it up, see if it turns blue?"

I just nodded at her.

"If Solly came himself and brought Albie's will with him, I was supposed to give him Albie's little blue book. Just hand it over. But if Solly *didn't* bring the will, I should never say a word about that book." She took a long breath in and held it, like she was getting ready to lift a heavy weight. Off herself. "The only problem was that Solly didn't come himself; he sent you," she said.

"I never had the will."

"I know. I . . . checked. So what would Albie want me to do?"

"Play me so I got Solly to show you the will?"

"That's what I thought. And that's what I was going to do. But it didn't take long for me to see you'd already *been* played."

"So either Albie never trusted her, or, now, you don't." My own words to Solly, ringing in my head. Albie had trusted Rena, all right—it was *Solly* he didn't trust.

"Damn, he was slick," I said.

"Who?"

"Albie. He had it all figured out. That will. Solly telling me he'd have to go see a lawyer, make out a new one. Total bullshit. I bet there never was any will. Not the kind you'd show in court, anyway. Just a list of where stuff was. If Solly went first, this girl, Grace, she was supposed to send *his* will to you. And she would have done it. She would have mailed it off, without ever looking at it."

"You're that sure? Maybe she—"

"No. Stop whatever you're thinking. This Grace, I met her. She couldn't even tell a lie. She's like, I don't know, a saint or something. There is *no* way Solly was anything to her but 'Uncle Solly,' understand?"

"That's what *you* thought, anyway."

"Check yourself, girl. You don't know everything. You think the same thing doesn't happen to me? Guys stare at your chest, think that's all you are, the joke's on them, right? You think people don't take one look at me and decide I gotta be stupid?

"Well, you know what? About *some* things, I'm real smart. And I'm telling you, I know Solly. He's . . . superstitious, I guess you'd say. He once told me, if he didn't take care of Grace, her father, this guy Ken, he'd come back and haunt him. Not 'Boo!' like a ghost; like a hit man. Wait a minute . . . like a *golem,* is what he said."

"A golem, that's like a devil in human form. Albie told me about them."

"See? Grace, she's like . . . You know what Down syndrome is?"

"Sure. It's when—"

"So here's Solly, paying off his debt to Ken because he's afraid Ken could come back and be this golem thing. *That,* he believes. And he knows what Ken the golem would do to him if he ever . . . did anything to his little girl."

She stood up. Walked around in a little circle. Stopped in front of me, hands behind her back. "I want to sit in your lap, Sugar."

"Yeah? Well, you can't do it from there."

She snuggled in. But it wasn't like before. "Tell me again. About Albie being so smart, Sugar. I think you might know more about that than me. Really. I won't say a word until you're done."

I took a deep breath, like I was getting ready to drive a lot of iron. I let it out slow, no burst. That's showing you've got control of the weight.

"If Solly showed you whatever Albie left with him, it would have been all about money and property and stuff, Lynda. Probably where a lot of money was stashed, too. But it would have *also* had that thing about looking in the partners desk.

"I don't think the whole bit about the partners desk was in any will, Lynda. You know what I think? What I think *now,* I mean? I think that whole partners desk thing came in when Albie knew he was going. *That's* when he would have told Solly about it. I don't think there ever *was* a will. Not from Albie; he wouldn't want you going near any court. And why would Solly leave one? Dead is dead—what would he care?"

"But what about all his . . . property and stuff?"

"What about it? Solly knew Grace would do whatever he told her to do. He could make sure she had money without any will. He probably did that. But no more."

"Solly would tell her to mail his book to Albie?"

"No. Look, I had to think about this as hard as I ever did, Lynda. About everything. Solly knew Grace, sure. But he didn't know *you*. Albie, he must've told Solly you were supposed to send him that book. When you didn't, *that's* when Solly knew something was wrong. He was right about that . . . but he was wrong about you, see? He thought what you wanted was money. When you didn't send the book to Solly, or even *mention* it, he figured you were holding it hostage."

"Okay, but—"

I slapped her bottom, real light, so she'd know I wasn't mad. "You said you'd let me finish," I told her.

"I'm sorry." She sounded like she really meant it.

"So Solly sends me down to get it from you. When I told him I came up empty, *that's* when he played his trump.

"No way men like Solly and Albie would trust a typewriter. They'd know each other's writing. Albie knew the *only* thing Solly could ever tell you about some bullshit 'will' without actually show-ing it to you was that partners desk. Like I told you before; Solly probably thought there was gold or diamonds or something like that in there.

"So you open that secret compartment in the desk, now you *know* Solly's righteous. He just proved it, right? So you hand over that little blue book. If you have it, that is. If you don't, it's in that house somewhere. See?"

"No," she said. "No, I *don't* see. What was Solly going to do, come down and tear the place apart?"

"Lynda, let's say it *was* gold or diamonds or whatever in there. How are you going to turn it into cash without going through Solly?"

She shifted a little, like a fighter taking a real hard shot but refusing to go down.

"When Albie set that trap, he couldn't know who would go first, him or Solly. But he knew, if Solly told you about the desk, you'd have a chance to get in the wind before he could send someone."

"To kill me," she said. Like she was tired of living anyway.

"Unless you gave it up, yeah. Probably even then, from the way Albie's message sounded."

"Solly sent you."

"To talk to this Jessop."

"And get Albie's book."

"Yeah. He was always a step ahead, Solly. He knew you'd get me to . . . Wait! Wait a minute. No, he couldn't know that. It's just like I said. Solly didn't know you; what he knew was *me*. Sure. When I called and asked him to prove you had this 'will' of Albie's, Solly, he was *expecting* that."

"So how come you didn't kill me, then?"

"I wouldn't ever have done that. Solly, he knows that, too. Listen, Lynda. Solly, he's every kind of tricky you ever heard of, and plenty that you haven't. And I'm not trying to get you to change your mind about him, but he *never* told me to do anything to you. That's why I was kicking myself, looking for the room where the partners desk was. I was afraid you'd think I was hunting you."

"I thought you might be, Sugar. I didn't want to, but I was . . . taught better, you know?"

"Yeah. And you were taught right, too."

"So this whole Jessop thing, that was just—what?—a convenient excuse?"

"I don't know. I for damn sure don't know. But now there's no choice."

"That's why you asked me about getting him to Tampa?"

"Yeah," I said, glad she couldn't see my face when I said that.

I kept waiting for her to say something. I felt her body get softer and softer, her breathing change. She was asleep.

I guess I must have gone out, too. I heard her say, "Oh, Sugar!"

"Huh?"

"I dropped off, like a baby taking a nap. And you couldn't even move for . . . jeez, almost four hours! I even got your shirt wet."

She looked embarrassed when she said that last part, so I made like I didn't hear it.

"We just needed to rest," I said.

She jumped off my lap and started doing stretches on the carpet. I took off my shirt and worked the kinks out of my neck. I was finished way before she was. But when she got done, she jumped up and ran out of the room.

Before I could even think about why she did that, she was back.

"This is Albie's phone," she said, handing a cell to me. "It's got a 305 area code. That's Dade County. Miami.

"Every town in the part of Florida where Jessop's supposed to be living, that would be an 863 area code."

"Would he recognize your—?"

"Not mine. Albie's."

"What good does that—?"

"Wait," she said, "see this?" Holding up a little metal case. "Watch."

She hit some button. The case she was holding said, "New work. Same place. Tomorrow night at eleven. Leave message, in or out?"

The voice sounded like it was in the room. Thin and strong at the same time, like piano wire.

"That's Albie," she said. "I've got a couple of dozen different messages from him on this."

The next afternoon, we kept arguing all the way back.

"If he recognizes you—"

"He won't see me, Sugar. Just you."

"Yeah? And how are we going to get that Lincoln out of the garage?"

"Just drive in and take it. What's the big deal? We're not doing anything illegal."

"Albie told you to get out of that house and never come back."

"I *won't* ever come back."

"What if they're waiting?"

"They wouldn't do that. They only come after dark, and they never stay long. To them, it'll look as if I already disappeared."

"I don't like it."

"You don't know them. They're . . . machines, not people. And I know things have been going wrong the past couple of years. Things they planned, I mean. Not crime stuff, like Albie did with those others. But . . . something. Something bad. I don't know why anyone would want Albie's blue book, but that note—*that* says Solly's a traitor, straight out. I'm sure, if I showed them that, they'd know who'd been talking to the wrong people."

"I still don't like it."

"We already agreed to do it, Sugar."

"Me, *I* agreed to do it. I didn't agree to do anything with you."

"Would you *listen* for just a second? If Jessop doesn't see that Lincoln, he's going to spook."

"I know."

"Do the math, damn it! Two cars, we need two drivers."

"You got stubborn confused with smart, Lynda."

"I don't have *anything* confused."

"Yeah, you do. Starting with me."

She sulked all the way. But when I told her she had to park the Caddy in the airport lot, way in the back, and lie down in the back seat with the windows up and the doors locked, she turned into a fucking volcano.

"If I don't fry to death, I'll run out of oxygen."

"You'll be uncomfortable, that's all. This thing's not airtight. You can even crack the far-side window a little bit, if you want. But once you get down, and I throw these jackets and stuff over you, you have to *stay* like that, understand?"

"You think, just because it's dark, I can't bake to death? It must be over a hundred, even now."

"Stop all the damn drama, Lynda. You've got a water bottle, and I'll be back before you know it."

"What if—?"

"I don't know what this Jessop's going to be driving. But if he doesn't see Albie's Lincoln, he's going to turn around and make tracks, right?"

"Yes," she snapped at me.

"So, if that happens, you just climb into the front seat and go back to Tampa."

"Sugar—"

"Zip it. I've got the key to the Lincoln and the button for the garage. That's all I need, except for one thing."

That one thing was the address of a little mall not so far from where the house was. The cab driver didn't even try and make conversation. He was an older black guy, and I guess he figured it wasn't worth working a guy who looked like me for a tip.

I went into the mall with my carry-on bag in one hand and walked through until I found the last exit.

The bar was a couple of blocks away. I went in. And, like Lynda said, it was full of just what I told her I needed. Albie probably had the whole town mapped for people like them.

I sat down at the bar, ordered a beer. It was loud: some kind of crash-pound-boom noise from the jukebox, people trying to shout over it.

All the punk with "88" tattooed on the back of his shaved head knew was that I was there to do a job on some kikes who were contributing *way* too much money to the wrong people. He was down with the cause. RAHOWA all the way, bro. But he still snatched the C-note I offered him for a ride on the back of his cycle.

When we got close enough, I slapped him twice on his right shoulder. He pulled over and rolled the cycle into a thick clump of bushes, just like I had told him in front.

I also told him that a car was coming for me in half an hour, after I got finished doing whatever I was going to be doing with whatever I had in the carry-on.

He gave me the White Power fist, saying goodbye. By then, I already had my left forearm around his neck, so I said goodbye, too.

I left him there. I wasn't worried about prints, not with the leather gloves I'd been wearing.

If there's one thing I know, one thing I've studied all my life, it's how to be a thief.

And that's me. Maybe, at first, I only got in on jobs because I was good muscle, and I'd stand up if the wheels came off. It was Ken who told me, and I never forgot: "This life of ours, where you stand isn't about how much weight you can lift, kid. It's how much weight you can take."

That's all I ever wanted to be: a man like Ken. Maybe "all" isn't the right way to say it. Ken was a legend. A legend with witnesses.

I was getting there, I hoped. I was still a young guy, but I'd proved in by doing everybody's time on that first robbery, so I could hang out in this bar where Ken did business. In fact, I was sitting right next to him when it happened:

This guy, Eugene, he was good-sized, and he was supposed to be a shooter, too. Reliable, people said about him. Never turned. But he'd never been Inside, either, so I always wondered about that.

Plus, he was twisted in his head. Always bringing his girlfriend in with him right after he finished working her over. Most guys, I think, if their woman had a big black eye and a split lip, they wouldn't want her to be showing her face. But Eugene, he *liked* that.

This girl, she was kind of good-looking, but you could see she was . . . dull, or something. Ken and I were at the bar. Eugene, he drags the girl in by the back of her hair, throws her across from him, and sits down in a booth.

We could see the whole thing in the mirror. The girl was trying to hide her face with her hands. Eugene must have told her to get him a drink, 'cause she got up and walked over to where we were. Her blouse was ripped; you could see her bra. And her bruises. She was trying hard not to cry, like she was afraid to.

I turned my shoulders. I don't know exactly what I was going to do, but Ken stopped me from ever finding out. He put his hand on my arm. "Not like that, kid," is all he said.

"I was just gonna—"

"You know what happens when you slap a woman-beater around? He takes it, like the bitch he is. Then he goes home and makes *her* pay for it."

"Then what should I—?"

But Ken was already gone. I reached out and pulled the girl into my chest. Not to hurt her, or to make a play for her. Just to keep her close enough to me so she couldn't see anything.

In the mirror, I could see Ken walk up to this Eugene. When he got real close, Ken pointed at the wall next to the booth. Eugene turned to his left to see what Ken was pointing at. Ken stuck something in Eugene's ear. There was a little noise, like a dry twig snapping.

Eugene's face hit the table. Ken walked back to where I was still holding on to the girl.

"Eugene went to the dice game out back," he told her. "He left me a message for you: When he's done shooting craps, he's going back to his wife. From now on, you're on your own."

She looked over at the booth. From where she was sitting, it looked empty.

"I didn't even know he was married," she said. "What . . . what happened?"

"I dunno," Ken said. "I was walking by when he got up. Told me to tell you what I just told you."

"Oh Jesus."

"He got his clothes at your place?"

"Sure. I mean, we—"

"His wife's in Boston, so you know he's not coming back for them," Ken said. Then he turned his back on her and started talking to me.

It took a few minutes for her to walk over to the empty booth. Only by then it wasn't empty anymore. Four guys were sitting there, playing cards.

She kind of stumbled out, still crying.

Ken slid a red handkerchief across the bar. There was a little lump in it. The guy behind the stick swept it up so smooth you'd have to be watching close to see it. One of the guys who'd been playing cards, a skinny guy in an old brown leather jacket, he walked over and handed Ken a shell casing. A real small one. Maybe a .25; I don't know much about guns.

"About those arrangements for your beloved aunt?" he said to Ken.

"Ah, you wouldn't think so, but what she always said she wanted was to be cremated. Said it was the cleanest way to leave this earth. Only her spirit left behind."

"Aye," the man in the leather jacket said. He shook hands with Ken, pulled his cap down low over his eyes, and walked away.

That's why I never wanted to be a hammer; I never wanted to work for anyone but me. And I wanted people to talk about me after I was gone. The way they talk about Ken now. A true hard man. Always true. And hard to the core.

Only, now that I'd met Grace, I realized there was more to being a hard man than what I'd always thought.

By my thinking, I was getting closer all the time. Everyone knows: Sugar, he's a real thief. Not just stand-up if he gets caught, but good at *not* getting caught.

I know when someone's been in my place. I was going to say "house," not "place," only I never had a house. That's what convicts call their cell: "my house."

Anyway, it doesn't matter. I can take one look and see if something's wrong. Things don't move themselves. I can always see this picture of how I left things. If the new picture doesn't fit *right* over it, I know.

If these guys Lynda told me about were as good as she said, no point trying to sneak up on them. The bike was noisy, but it was quick. I hit the garage button while I was still riding up to the door.

The garage was exactly like we left it. But maybe they had another way in, so I took a few seconds to check down the hall. The place I'd stayed in, nobody had been in there since we'd left.

I jumped back on the cycle and rode it over the bumpy trail Lynda had shown me when we first took off. I didn't even try and find the best spot, just laid the bike down flat and ran back to the house.

The Lincoln fired right up. I backed it out, clicked the garage closed, and took off.

Part of being a good thief is not needing a map to a place you've already been. And not writing anything down. The clock on the Lincoln said 10:15. Plenty of time.

I drove careful. Not *too* slow. And I was still twenty minutes to the good as I backed the Lincoln into a slot all the way across from where Lynda was. I could see the white Caddy, but nothing else.

Lynda didn't know how these airport meets were supposed to go— Albie never told her details. Probably only told her anything at all so she wouldn't get worried when he went out late at night.

Albie wouldn't have a bodyguard. Or even a driver. So Jessop, he'd be looking for Albie behind the wheel. I eased the passenger-side door open, ready to break any bulb that lit up . . . but none did.

I thought of waiting in the back seat, leaving the door cracked. But it was too risky. Jessop might open the door, but he'd check the front seat before he climbed inside.

A man like Albie, he tells you eleven o'clock, you're not there by one minute after, he's gone.

Running through my mind: Was this Jessop smart enough to get there way early? No. If Albie saw a strange car, he'd just pull off.

I had Lynda's pistol in the carry-on, but a gunshot in that open space would be loud. And the way airports are today, the place would be swarmed with fifty different kinds of cops in ten seconds.

Plenty of darkness, but if Jessop's headlights picked me up . . .

I settled for crouching behind the trunk, all the way over to the right. The tire would give me a little cover—best I could do.

The tool I was carrying looked like a long, thin canvas bag with a loop on the end. It was filled with ball bearings, weighed about thirty pounds. I put my hand through the loop. Then I started hyper-tensing different muscle groups. Tense, hold, release. Tense, hold, release. Not as good as stretching, but it would keep me from getting stiff.

A wash of headlights. I heard a car door open and close.

Footsteps.

I snuck a peek. A man, walking straight toward the Lincoln. His hands were empty, but that didn't mean anything—if you're expected, you don't walk up on a man with a gun in your hand.

Heavy shoes, but light-footed, not much noise. Little crunching sounds from the parking lot, louder as he got closer.

I could hear him breathing. Calm and relaxed. Probably did things like this a hundred times before.

One more and . . . yeah, it was Jessop, all right. He was reaching for the door handle as I came around the back of the Lincoln.

Damn, he was *fast*. But by the time he whipped around and reached for the gun in his belt, the lead-shot club was already on its way. Instead of the back of his head, I caught him full in the face.

The way he went down, I was pretty sure he was already finished—flat on his back, eyes wide open.

I took out a crowbar. Knelt down and held it across his throat with both hands. Then I rammed it down with everything I had.

I heard some kind of sound, but it wasn't coming from his mouth; it was the little bones crackling in his neck. One of his eyeballs came way out of his head. I didn't need the smell to tell me he was done.

I kicked the door shut and popped the trunk. Dragged Jessop's body around to the back by his belt. Heaved him inside. Stuck the key to the Lincoln and the button for the garage in the outside pocket of his jacket. Closed the trunk.

I pulled the gloves off my hands as I walked over to the Caddy, moving easy.

"Jesus, I am *rank*," Lynda said.

"You're fine."

"Sure. It wasn't you who was back there. I could hardly even breathe."

"You're not back there *now*, okay? Just tell me where to turn."

By the time we got to the highway, she was a little calmer. But she *was* rank, for real.

Then she started shaking. Real bad. I had to light the cigarette for her.

"I guess I'm just a fraud," she said, an hour later.

"How are you a fraud?"

"I'm supposed to be . . . I'm supposed to be what Albie taught me to be. He said, he said over and over, 'Rena, a man has to believe in something bigger than himself, or he can never truly be a man.' I thought I understood that. I thought I was *doing* that. But . . . what was he telling me, that it's only *men* who have to do that?"

"It's just the way people talk."

"I . . . I guess that's true. I mean, the Israelis, they have women in their army. In combat, I mean. And I know they had a woman Prime Minister once. But all I could do was . . . *hide*. That's all I could do. Like a little kid in a closet, afraid of the monsters in the house."

"What the fuck did you *want* to do?"

"Why are you mad at me, Sugar?"

"Why? You're saying I'm nothing, and I'm supposed to just—"

"How could you even think—?"

"You're better at things than me, right?"

"I never said—"

"Yeah, you did. And you are. But you're not better at *everything*. This . . . this work that had to be done; you did your part, then I did mine. That's what happened. And what's coming out of your mouth? Ah, you're such a piece of crap because you didn't handle the whole thing yourself, like you're *supposed* to, right?"

"I . . . I see what you mean. I was just being a bitch, Sugar."

"I don't think so."

"All right, I was *scared*. Is that what you wanted to hear?"

"No."

"You won't even say my name, will you?"

"Which name do you want?"

"You *bastard*!" She tried to reach over and slap at me, but the seatbelt held her in place.

It was another hour before she spoke to me again.

"He's . . . dead? You're sure?"

"Which one?"

"Oh. Jessop, I guess."

"You *guess*? Jesus."

"Sugar, please, stop. You're thinking, 'That's the one she cared about,' aren't you?"

"What if I was?"

"And that makes you mad?"

I didn't say anything.

She unbuckled her seatbelt, turned so she was kneeling on the cushion, and leaned over. To kiss me on the side of my face.

"Don't be mad, Sugar. You'd be mad for all the wrong reasons."

"I don't know what you're talking about."

"Yes, you do. You think I still have feelings for Jessop, don't you?"

"I don't know who you've got—"

"Stop! I had feelings for Jessop, all right. I was *terrified* of him. When Albie died, the first thing that hit me was, Jessop's going to come for me now. I think that's why Albie kept him on. Working, I mean. So that when he . . . when he *died*—okay?—*I'd* know where to find him. Jessop. And kill him, like I should have done.

"That's what I was so upset about before. I shouldn't have been hiding under those coats, trembling, trying not to whimper. I shouldn't have been hiding from him; I should have been hunting him.

"It wasn't that I didn't have confidence in you. Not for a minute. I knew Jessop was as good as dead from the minute you . . . took over. I was . . . ashamed, okay? I put up this big front, but it was all a lie. I *wanted* you to do it, Sugar.

"You know what I did, under those coats? Sucked my thumb. Like a baby. You think I didn't believe you could take care of things, but the truth is, I knew you could. And the worse truth is, I knew I couldn't."

"All you can ever say is you *thought* you couldn't. You'll never have the chance to find out now. He's not coming back."

"I love you," is what she said.

It was around four in the afternoon when I finally woke up. Lynda was still next to me.

"About time," she said. So I knew she must have been awake for a while.

"You been watching the news?"

"Yes. Not a word."

"There's gonna be."

"That depends," she said.

"On what?"

"Tactics."

"You're giving me a headache."

"Then go take a shower and I'll get you something to eat."

"They may never find that motorcycle," she said, watching me as I ate. "Who's going to report it missing? So why would they be looking for it at all, much less on the property?"

I shrugged my shoulders, chewing slow, like you're supposed to.

"That skinhead, him they'll find. But so what? People like that, they get killed every day. For all kinds of reasons. By all kinds of people."

I nodded. They're always talking about wiping out every mud on the planet, but they spend more time on killing each other. Saw it plenty of times in prison. Sometimes it's because they find out something about the guy, like he's got the wrong blood in him. Or sometimes it's just to be doing it.

"And Jessop?" Lynda said. "Ex-con found dead in the trunk of a car he stole in Miami, with a pistol in his belt. Who knows what *that's* about? The gun won't be registered. All they'll ever be able to do is trace the car and find out the owner's a person who doesn't exist, a man who lives at an address in a neighborhood where nobody knows nothing. And they won't be lying about that, either."

"Your prints are in the—"

"In the Lincoln? Sure, baby. But not in the system. Without a match, they hit a wall. And I had the car detailed after that first time you used it."

The way Lynda ran it down, I sounded like a criminal mastermind. But I knew better.

"Traces of me could be in that car, too, girl. Maybe not prints, but *some* kind of DNA. That's all they'll need, if they decide to go that route."

"What good would DNA do them?"

"If you're a convicted sex offender, they take a DNA sample from you. And there's a national database."

"How could *you* be a—?"

That's when I told her how me getting railroaded had started this whole thing.

I don't remember what I said. I don't even remember when I finished. All I remember is Lynda holding me before . . . I guess I don't even know before *what*, but when I woke up, the side of my face was against her chest, and my arm was all the way across her body. She'd probably fallen asleep when she realized she couldn't get out from under all my weight.

For a minute, I thought I was losing it: every word made me think of another word, like this . . . chain, or something.

Weight. I *did* take the weight.

Wait. I *had* waited, just like the rules say.

I got my money from Solly. I made sure Jessop was never going to roll on anyone, ever. Just like Solly wanted.

Solly couldn't do time, not at his age. But that book. That's what Solly *really* wanted, wasn't it? And I had that book now.

Solly couldn't do time, and I had the book . . . so everything was back where it was supposed to be. All I had to do was go back, give Solly everything he wanted: the book and the news about Jessop. Lynda, she'd go . . . wherever she wanted, I guessed.

What I really wanted was for her to go with me. But where was I going? Where the *fuck* was I going?

I had to see Solly. Albie had it right. Solly was a traitor. And not just to whatever those hard men were doing. He sent me down to Florida to tie up a loose end. That was a lie. But now I had a loose end of my own. As long as Solly was alive, I'd never be safe.

I couldn't bring Lynda with me for what I had to do.

Big Matt, he got himself out. But he knows how to do legit things. The only things I know how to do, I could only do until I got caught doing them.

I couldn't bring Lynda to Solly, and I couldn't take her to prison with me, either.

"Sugar?"

"I didn't know you were awake."

"My . . . head is awake. But I can't move my arm."

"It's just cramped, girl. You're not built to have that much weight on you. I can put the . . . feeling back in it pretty quick, but that would hurt. Could you just, like, lay there for a couple of hours? With the weight off, your arm'll come—"

She looked like a little girl trying to be tough. "I'd like to do that," she said. "But I have to . . . use the bathroom, okay?"

Before she could say anything to stop me, I scooped her up and carried her into the bathroom. I put her down there, but I held on. Good thing—she couldn't stand on her own. I pulled off her underpants with one hand, put her on the toilet.

She looked pretty steady. Her right arm was working, and she braced herself with it.

"I'll be close enough to hear you," I told her. Then I backed out of the bathroom without closing the door. I moved a few steps away.

When I heard the toilet flush, I went to her. But she was already sort of standing against the sink, holding herself with that one good hand and arm.

I stepped behind her. "I've got you, Lynda." I turned on the water. It heated up quick, so I dialed it back. Then I held her at the waist. "Use your good hand to wash the other one."

When she was finished, I put her on the couch so her arm was stretched out along the top.

"Wet heat, that's best. You stay there."

"Okay, boss," she said. Smiling.

I felt good, too. Doing something I knew something about. I put a whole layer of dry towels under her arm, then one of the steaming-hot ones over it. Then I put some dry ones over everything, to keep the heat in.

"How long will it take?"

"Can you feel anything?"

"Not . . . not really."

"When you start to feel something . . . the towels are too hot, or even if they're all cold, as soon as you can feel them, it won't be long after that."

"Could I have a—?"

I was already there before she finished. She held the lit cigarette in her good hand, and took a deep puff like it was a painkiller.

"You should put something in your stomach, Lynda."

"Don't be such a big nag."

All of a sudden, her face changed. "I was just teasing you, Sugar. Soon as I'm done with this, I'll have soup, okay? Just take one of the cans from the—"

"I know how to make soup."

"Stop pouting, you big baby." The way she said it, it felt like a kiss.

By the time she got back to herself, it was dark out. I had made myself some soup, too. Then I found enough ways to get a decent workout. Made me feel better. But not that much.

I took a quick shower. When I came out, she was on the couch. "I don't know what to do," I told her.

"We've got to make a decision, Sugar."

My mouth got all dry. "We." Was that, we *each* had to make a decision, or we had to make one together?

"How many sets of clean ID do you have?" she asked me.

"Besides my own?"

"You have real——?"

"What I mean, I *am* Tim NMI Caine, for real."

"NMI?"

"No middle initial. That's what it says on my record. Timothy NMI Caine, a.k.a. Sugar."

"Not counting that one."

"All I've got is the one Solly fixed me up with——" I stopped myself even before I saw her mouth move. "I know," I told her.

"I've only got that one clean set," she said. "Lynda Leigh. There's others, but those were for living with Albie. And after that note . . ."

"How old is it?"

"What?"

"Lynda Leigh. That set."

"Oh. Well . . . I've had it for a long time. That makes an ID really strong, when you use it for things. Like credit cards."

"Albie taught you to make ID, right?"

"So? What are you saying, Sugar?"

"I wonder how clean that Lynda Leigh stuff really is."

"How can you even *say* that? Albie——"

"I know, you made it yourself, sure. But that was when Albie was still teaching you, right? So maybe, by the time he was teaching you, he didn't have the . . . technique to do it himself anymore."

"Yes, he did," she said. Her eyes burned me like the tips of two cigarettes. "I made the ID, with him watching. He could lose his perfect touch, maybe, but he'd never lower his standards. *That* I know for sure."

"I'm not saying this right, Lynda. I'm just saying, behind that note he left and all, isn't there a chance those men who come to visit, they've got a copy of it all?"

"Then they'd know how to find me, Sugar. And Albie never would have left that note then, would he?"

"He couldn't say two things in the same note."

"But he *did*. He couldn't know who'd see it, don't you understand?"

"Sure. He could say *some* things. But, like you said, he couldn't know who'd see it first. So he couldn't tell you, 'Nuke that Lynda Leigh ID,' see?"

"You're the one who doesn't see! There's a thousand ways Albie could have said that without them knowing what he was talking about."

"You're sure?"

She walked off. Came back in a minute and sat down in the same place. Only, she had a little piece of paper in her hands. I knew what it was. She motioned me to look over her shoulder, pointing with a red fingernail.

"Hah!" she said. "See?"

"See what?"

"See where he says, 'You know where to go'? Albie *never* would have told me to come here if he'd shown that ID to those men. *Never*."

"You're right."

"What? Just like that, you turn around and—"

"Didn't he also say something about there *was* no will?"

Her long red fingernail moved. "Yes! Just like you said, Sugar. Right here. He says—"

"You see that? Albie was the smartest player in the whole game. Solly never had a chance."

"What in God's name are you talking about now?"

"Where's Albie's stamp collection, *Lynda*?"

"What stamp collection? Are you crazy? What would Albie want with collecting stamps?"

"Yeah," I said. "Yeah, that locks it down. Solly thought he had it going both ways. And he'd take either one."

"What?"

"What if I'd just asked you, when I first showed up, I mean, 'Where's Albie's little blue book?' You'd say you didn't know what I was talking about, wouldn't you?"

"Yes. I already told you what—"

"Wait. I ask you, and you say you don't know what I'm talking about. Fine, that's what you already told Solly by *not* mentioning it. So *then* I say, 'Okay, then, what about his stamp collection?' Now you *really* know something's wrong, see?"

"Sugar, if you don't tell me—"

"I will, if you'll shut up a minute. See, all that time you'd be thinking I'm lying. Me, I'd *know* you're lying.

"Be Solly for a minute. You send Sugar down to get a blue book. He *has* to come back with that book. You know Sugar. If he says he'll do it, he'll do it.

"Sugar doesn't get a charge out of hurting people. He looks scary. You, you're a girl Albie . . . keeps. Probably all Sugar has to do is lean on you a little bit. Only, you say there's no book.

"That might be true. To Sugar, I'm saying. It might sound right to him. You're a live-in girlfriend, the guy's old enough to be your grandfather; why tell you any real secrets? And you made *sure* to play it that way, too. Remember that, Miss Plastic Tits?

"So, in Sugar's mind, you might not know about that book. Why would Albie trust you that much? But there's no way you wouldn't know about the stamp collection. Which means you're a stone liar. And you *do* know where that little blue book is."

"So *then* Sugar wouldn't mind hurting me, is that what you're saying?"

"Wouldn't mind tying you up and taking the house apart, piece by piece. The book'd *have* to be in that house, somewhere."

"And if he still didn't find it . . . ?"

"In Solly's mind? Sugar, he'd either make you talk or make you dead."

"What a purely evil man."

"Not evil enough, girl. I was the best Solly had, and I never had a chance against Albie, not even against his ghost. He had it set up so Solly'd play himself out of position, no matter what. Remember, you said those guys who came around, they were the real thing. Hard men, you called them."

"They were."

"That's what Solly always said about Ken. That he was a hard man. If it was Ken coming around to see you, you know what he'd do? He'd find out the truth before he did anything. He'd look real close. And Albie, he left his mark on Solly. Put him right on the spot."

She started to open her mouth, then brought her lips together.

"You know what Albie's mark is, girl? That 'will' he was supposed to have sent to Solly. If the hard men showed up and found Albie gone, they would have called Solly, right? And Solly, first thing out of his mouth, he'd tell them all about the partners desk. But once the hard men saw that paper Albie left, he's cooked. Solly's getting himself some visitors. When they show, no mattter what story he tells, he's a dead man.

"Solly, all those years, he still had Albie figured wrong. That's why he'd tell those hard men about the desk in a flash. That's a prove-in, that he knew Albie's secrets. Only, it was Albie who knew *Solly's* secrets. See?"

"Oh God."

"Yeah. And now that we know *that,* we know what we have to do. It's easy."

"*What's* easy?"

"Making choices. When you've only got one, I mean. My ID, it's not worth crap to me, but it's gold to Solly. My credit card's a goddamned tracking unit, like it was stuck under my skin. Solly could find me, no matter where I went."

"So what can we do?"

"We're gonna burn my ID."

"And I make you a new—?"

"Not burn it with a match, Lynda. Burn it by using it."

"Sugar, I'm not keeping up."

I can't really explain how her saying that made me feel. I wasn't trying to confuse her or anything, but I could see that it was me who knew what to do. Me, not Lynda. I knew what to do. So I told her:

"We're going back to New York. You and me. We'll rent a car. And not just so the Caddy's plates won't show on any turnpike scanner, either. It's a long drive. We'll have to stop along the way. In a motel, like. That's two ways to use the card. And there's others, too. Like buying gas. Or food.

"I'm gonna tell Solly I got it done. Which I damn well did. He wouldn't expect me to use the phone he gave me, so it wouldn't spook him that it's not signaling.

"But he can track me through the card; he'll see I'm headed home. That's perfect. He wouldn't expect me to say what he wants to hear on the phone. And the book, that I'd have to hand over to him in person, anyway.

"So, before he even knows I'm in town, I slip back into the bank, take my money out, and stash it with you, before I go to see him." I knew it couldn't happen like that—I'd have to do Solly before I went near that bank. It wasn't that I didn't trust Lynda. I guess it was that old pass-the-polygraph thing in my head coming up again.

"Are you going to—?"

"After I see Solly, I don't need any new ID. I just go back to being me. I even got a plan how I can do that. You, you'll be Lynda Leigh."

"We'll see."

"What?"

"I said, 'We'll *see*,' didn't I?"

"I get it. You mean, you'll make me a perfect new ID anyway, just in case, right?"

"What part of 'We'll see' didn't you understand?"

We got started early the next morning. Lynda dropped me off a block away from a cabstand, then took the Caddy back to its garage. By the time she got to the American Airlines terminal, I'd been waiting almost an hour.

We used my Stanley Wilson credit card to rent one of those big SUVs. Then back to the condo, where we loaded up.

By lunchtime, we were on the road.

The SUV had this gigantic navigation screen. With Lynda reading it for me, we didn't even need a map.

Everything was going fine. I thought I had it pulled off, but Lynda caught wise.

"What the *hell* are you doing?"

"Seeing if you trust me."

"Sugar . . . what?! This isn't where we should be—"

I pulled into one of those rest stops. Stopped the SUV. Turned off the ignition.

Lynda wasn't saying anything, but her breathing was tight and fast, like a boiler getting ready to blow.

"Do you trust me?" I asked her again.

"Sugar, how could you even *ask* me that? After all we've—"

"I'm asking you, Lynda. There's only one way to make this work without having to look over our shoulders for the rest of our lives."

"What makes you think you—?"

"Did you hear what I said? *Our* lives. You want to go your own way, now's the time."

A cigarette appeared in her hand like magic. She took a puff, blew a stream of smoke at the roof, tapped her nails on the dash. Not saying anything. Not *going* to say anything. Okay, then: time to find out.

"I need Albie's note, Lynda."

"*You* need it? For what?"

"So Albie could finish his last job. That note, either you'd find it, or these other men would. Albie couldn't know. That's why he tried to cover you from both sides."

"He *did*."

"No. No, he didn't, girl. He did the best he could, but there's more than two sides to cover. Tell me, that tiny little writing, would you recognize it?"

"You mean, would I know it was from Albie? Of course I would. And if you look close, you'd see it was torn right out of his book. And his *tallit*—you know how old that must be? How many places it must have been?"

"All I know is, you have to give it up."

"Give it up?"

"All of it."

"Sugar, you're scaring me."

"You never got mail at that house, right?"

"Of course not. There was a box in—"

"And, like you said, the bills got paid by themselves, from this computer thing."

"So?"

"So how's anyone gonna know Albie's dead? It's not like it would be a news story or anything. Maybe they had some signal you don't know about, but—"

"Who's 'they'?"

"The men who visited Albie."

"Oh. Well, if they did, I can't see what it could be. I mean, we had no phone, just the cell. I've got Albie's cell. It hasn't rung once since he—"

"Okay, when these men would show up, did Albie ever tell you they were coming?"

"He . . . no. No, he never did. I don't think he knew himself. We'd just be, I don't know, sitting in the living room, having tea, and they'd just . . . *be* there. The first time it happened, I thought they were robbers or something—I was so scared they'd hurt Albie."

"Good. That means we got a shot. Solly knows Albie's gone,

but he wouldn't pass that info along until he was sure he was covered. That's what he was using me for, see?

"The window's wide open, Lynda. But it could drop closed any minute. If it drops before we get all that stuff back inside, it'll be like one of those guillotine things, chop off our heads like *this*," I told her, snapping my fingers.

"You want to leave Albie's things back there? Albie left them to *me*!"

"What he left you was *protection*. Only, you're not using it."

"What are you saying?"

"I'm saying, Albie, he didn't leave you fucking *keepsakes*, okay? What he left you was tools. And you've gotta *use* them, not hang on to them."

"I'm not giving up my—"

"You don't have to, Lynda. Just give me Albie's blue book. I'll drive you back to your condo, and then I'll go back to where I came from."

"Sugar . . ."

"I came down here for two things. I was supposed to check out this Jessop and get that little book. I have to tell Solly I got all that done if I want to get close to him again."

"What's that got to do with anything? You can *have* the little book, all right?"

"If that's the way you want it."

"What I *want* is what you said. We were going back to New York just long enough for you to show Solly you got the job done. That's 'we,' as in *both* of us. Why can't we still do that?"

"Because I have to get back into that house, Lynda. I have to leave Albie's stuff right where we found it. That's the only way those men who come to see him will ever understand what happened."

"You're losing me, Sugar."

I probably am, I thought. But what I said was, "You already said it. Those hard men, they're going to come, sooner or later. They won't find Albie. Or you. What could they do then *except* call Solly?

"First thing out of his mouth, he's gonna tell them about that partners desk. If we don't get that stuff back where Albie had it stashed, they'll find an empty space."

"But if—"

"You're wasting time, Lynda. And we don't have much. You know what Solly's gonna say was supposed to be in that desk? Come on. *What?*"

"Albie's book," she said. She bit her lower lip to stop herself from crying.

"Yeah. And when they find that slot empty, they'll naturally think *you* cleaned it out and took off. They *want* that book, girl. People like them, you think they won't be able to find you just because you got some nice new ID?"

She was quiet for a second. When she opened her mouth, I could see a drop of blood on her lower lip. She must have bit down real hard.

"What if they're already there, Sugar? At the house. Waiting."

"You said they always come at night, right? We've still got plenty of daylight left."

"Not *that* much. And what if—?"

"If they're waiting, then I'm the one they grab. But so what? I'll have what Albie left you. I'll tell them you paid me to sneak in and put it back.

"Whether they'll buy it, who knows? But they'll know *I* didn't write that note. The way I've got it worked out, no way you come into it. Ever."

"It'd never work."

"It'd work *perfect*. They'd pound on me, just to make sure they got all the juice out of the orange. When I've taken enough to convince them, I'll tell them the whole truth."

"The . . . what?"

"The truth. Solly sent me. To get Albie's book. And I did that. They'll see that for themselves. Solly told me to get that book no matter *what* I had to do.

"Get it? Me, I had to hurt you pretty bad to make you talk.

Solly was on the phone all the time I was doing it—he could hear everything. When you finally told me where to find Albie's book, Solly told me, make sure I don't leave anything behind.

"So I killed you. Then I ran out and mailed Albie's book to Solly. Only reason I went back in was to wipe the place down, make sure there wasn't anything there that could trace back to me. That's why I had the prayer bag on me. Only, Albie's note, it's going to be *inside* the bag, get it?"

"That *is* where it was."

"It doesn't matter. They're never going to think a thug like me would open that bag. I'm just a guy Solly hired. Hired to get the *book,* see? That's why I'd have to let them work on me for a while, because telling them who paid me, that'd be like ratting him out."

"Why would you care? About Solly, I mean."

"I don't. But you don't rat. That's the rules."

"The what?"

"Never mind. It's too . . . complicated to explain now. But those men, *they'd* understand."

"They'd kill you, Sugar."

"They might. But they wouldn't *have* to. There's no reason for them not to believe my story. How else would I know about Solly? Or Albie? Or the book?"

"They'd still—"

"Maybe not. Maybe they wouldn't want to make a mess, I don't know. But that's all downside. If I can get in there and leave Albie's stuff without being caught, now *that's* a message they'd get for sure."

"Which is . . . ?"

"*You* found the note. And *you* left it for them. They'd know Albie's handwriting. They'd think you did what the note said to do. Albie made sure they'd know there's no reason to hunt you now— they'd already have everything there was to get. Why be mad at you? You played it square all the way. You didn't *have* to leave anything for them, but you did."

"I don't like—"

"It's not for you to say."

"Why? Because you're the man."

"Because you've got all your . . . feelings in this, and I don't. Right or wrong, those men, they'd know Albie wouldn't just leave his prayer stuff behind."

"Of course he wouldn't! I . . . oh!"

"So, if I don't put it back, and if they can't find it, they'll know *you* have it. They wouldn't care about that—what they'd want is that little blue book. With Solly telling them his story, they'd go right for that partners desk. They find it empty, they have to find *you*, understand?"

She lit another smoke. I hadn't even noticed her finishing the first one.

"Which means they'd be looking for you, too."

"If that's what you believe, if you think I'm going back in there to cover myself, don't say another word. I'll go back and tell Solly I had to take you out, too. That'll make him feel safe, back in control. Albie's gone, and he's holding both books. He never knows about the note. So, soon as he has Albie's book, he contacts those hard men himself.

"He can tell them any story he wants. Long as he's got both little blue books, he's golden. He'd have to admit he sent me down for the book, sure. But that just proves you're in the ground, so *you'll* never be talking, see?"

"I hate you."

I felt like smacking her. "You fucking *must*, you think I'd be going back in that damn house to cover my own ass, bitch."

"Sugar, can't you see what I'm *really* afraid of? Believe me, if those men got their hands on you, all those big muscles wouldn't mean a thing."

"Only one way to find out."

"Sure. And if you guess wrong . . ."

"No. I mean, find out if you want to be with me, Lynda. 'Cause if you do, you got nothing to say about anything I *ever* do to keep you safe."

"That's why you killed Jessop? You thought he might—"

"No. I killed him for me, Lynda. Not for you."

"For you? You didn't even know him."

"I know what he did. And I know who he did it to."

"You mean, selling me to Albie? That was the best thing anyone ever—"

"And Jessop, he fucking *knew* that, huh?"

She was either going to have another smoke or start crying, I thought. But she just turned and looked at me.

"I was glad you did it, Sugar."

"We can't keep sitting here, girl. There isn't much daylight left."

I knew Lynda had cut all the alarms off before we left the last time, so I just jammed the pry bar under the window as deep as I could, then I jacked it up, slow and strong, like I had with the arm-wrestler. The locks popped and the window went up.

I went in without the gun. If the men Lynda was afraid of were already there, no gun was going to help me. But if cops ended up in the picture, a gun would cook me.

I get pinched, I'd say the owner hired me to break in because there was valuable stuff inside and he wanted to run an insurance scam. It would be pretty lame, since I'd be describing a guy I never met—Lynda didn't know *what* name was on the deed to the place. Better than nothing. Not much better, but . . . something, anyway.

I didn't prowl. If they were already waiting, I wanted to make sure they could hear me.

The place was empty. Or, if it wasn't, I couldn't tell.

Were they already there? Waiting to see what I'd do before they did whatever *they* wanted to do?

So many rooms in that house. So many places they could be.

I could feel it getting darker, like the sun was dropping inside the house.

The rule is that you never work scared—if the job's too risky for you, pass.

I tried, but I couldn't seal my mind off from those hard men.

I knew exactly where I was going, so I moved fast. That'd fit my story, too.

The house was so big that I knew it had rooms I'd never seen. If they were coming for me, I'd never hear them. Even the shadows were full of . . . I don't know what.

I left Albie's prayer bag on top of the partners desk. Propped the note he'd left for . . . for Rena, I guess, up against it.

The hard men wouldn't expect the little blue book, not with what that note said. They'd know Solly had Albie's book.

And soon enough he would.

I ran back to the window like somebody was chasing me.

When I got back to the car, Lynda wasn't there. And it was already dark. I was still trying to decide what to do when she came out of the bushes, holding that pistol.

From there, we drove straight through, taking turns behind the wheel. About five in the morning, we found a motel somewhere in Maryland, just a few miles off the highway. I wanted to be sharp when we hit New York.

The kid behind the counter looked all fresh-scrubbed and neat, but his eyes were the kind you see in a porno store. He told me that checkout was eleven, so if we stayed past six hours we'd be charged for another whole night. Looking at Lynda all the time, like he knew something.

"We have an excellent room, sir. You and your wife'll be in 321."

"I don't want that one," I said.

The clerk's skin turned blotchy. "The only other vacancies are on the first floor, sir. It's *much* noisier there, especially in the morning."

"Three, two, one, that sounds like a countdown. Got to be an unlucky number."

"I'm sure you—"

"Give us another room."

His skin went pinto again. I covered my mouth like I was yawning, handed over my credit card. The jerkoff artist was still going on about "incidentals" as we walked away.

The room reminded me of the front-desk kid: looked all neat, but you could feel dirt no maid would ever get out.

"Sugar, come here. Did you ever see anything like this?"

She was standing in the tiny little bathroom, pointing at the toilet. The seat was down, covered with a thin film of clear plastic, stretched tight. A yellow tag said it was "Sanitized for Your Protection."

Actually, I *had* seen that kind of thing before. Never thought twice about it. But with Lynda being so amazed, I kind of looked at it different.

"You're saying you don't believe the sign?" I asked her.

"Do you?"

"I . . . guess not. But it's a good thing they put that big sticker on, anyway."

"Why?"

"Uh, well, if you were, I don't know, drunk or something, you might . . . I mean, if that sticker wasn't there, that plastic, you might not even notice it was there."

"You're so cute," Lynda said. She made a little motion with her finger. I moved my face close to hers. She kissed me. "Now get out," she told me.

I knew she wasn't going to be quick, so I flopped down on the bed.

Next thing I remember was Lynda, smelling like thick flowers, straddling me, pushing down on my shoulders.

Woke me out of a nasty dream. That night clerk was in a little closet, door closed behind him, watching a man and woman go at it on a TV monitor. The feed from the camera he's got hidden in 321.

"It's all yours," Lynda whispered.

When I came out of the shower, Lynda was lying facedown on the bed, dead to the world. She was wearing a sweatsuit, with socks on her feet. I could see the bedspread in the corner, where she must have thrown it. One of my T-shirts was between her face and the pillow.

There was a T-shirt over my pillow, too.

We were back on I-95 by six the next night. I turned the rental in at Newark Airport. Lynda waited on a bench around the corner.

That's the same reason we took the PATH train to Penn Station. Lynda did the best she could, but I was still loaded like a pack mule when I checked into the nearest hotel I could find.

The girl at the front desk worked real hard to convince me, doing her job even when she saw I'd walked in with all that luggage. So I told her, "Yeah, I sure could use some help getting all this into my room."

"Suite," she said.

I almost said something stupid until I realized what she meant.

The bellman helped me get all our stuff into the room. Suite, I mean—it was like another little apartment. No point being cheap with that credit card now.

I sat there waiting. It wasn't long before my cell phone made a noise. I didn't bother picking up the call, just went by the door and opened it a crack. Lynda already knew what room I was in—I had texted her the number. She came down the hall like she owned the joint.

I locked the door. Lynda was strolling around the place, checking it out. "Very nice," she said.

"Don't get used to it," I told her.

I ordered for two from Room Service, letting the girl who took the order hear me ask Lynda what kind of dressing she wanted on her salad.

I let the guy who brought the food up get a good look at Lynda while he was working me for a tip, describing each dish as he pulled off the metal tops like he was doing a magic trick.

"They really give you the tips off credit cards?" I asked him, looking at the leather-covered bill he'd handed me with a little flourish.

He didn't say anything, just shook his head.

"Guys like you and me, we know how things work, right?" I told him, shifting my eyes over to where Lynda was posing in her high-class-hooker outfit. I handed him a pair of twenties.

"Yes, *sir*!" he said. "When you want the tray picked up, just call Room Service. I'll make sure—"

"Uh, I'm gonna be kind of busy, pal. I'll just leave it outside when we're done, how's that?"

"Oh, absolutely, sir. Why don't I leave the serving cart right here? That way, you can just push it outside whenever you wish."

The hotel had entrances on two different blocks. The front desk was on the fancy-street side. I just walked down the stairs to the fifth floor, rang for the elevator, and stepped off to my right. Nobody paid any attention. People who want to be noticed make sure they hang out in the front lobby; it's all set up for that, with couches and a little bar and everything.

The subway was perfect. Like in any bad neighborhood, nobody sees nothing.

"You got the—?"

"I got it all."

"How far away are you?"

"Too far to walk. But on the subway, maybe forty-five minutes."

"So I'll see you soon, Jerome?"

"That was my plan, too. Only I have to stop by the office first."

"This place is completely—"

"Maybe for you. Not for me."

I hoped Solly was thinking about all those security cameras in his condo that he'd told me about.

"What say I meet you at the office, then? I can make it all . . . suitable. We can have a drink there, talk things over?"

"I'm on my way."

I watched the alley for almost an hour. No sign of Solly. So he'd been in his office all the time, just like I figured.

Okay.

I played blackjack on the door. When I heard the heavy clunk of the deadbolt, I stepped into the darkness.

A soft light came on. Solly, behind his desk.

"Sugar!" he said, standing up.

I came around the desk so he could give me a hug. Then I sat down across from him in the guest chair. It wasn't a partners desk.

"So?"

I took out Albie's little blue book. Slid it across the desk like I was dealing out a card.

Solly scooped it up while it was still moving. Took a quick look. "You never miss, Sugar," he said. "This is perfect."

"There's more."

"You mean . . . ?"

"Show me the tape first."

"Tape? What tape?"

"I know you've got me on video, coming here. Time and date stamped, all that. So I figure maybe Solly's got his office miked, too. Like you're always saying . . ."

He smiled like he was proud of me for being such a good listener.

"You didn't get what I said about making the place suitable? Or you didn't believe it? Eh, *macht nit*. Go over to the bookcase on your left. The one with the thick pillars for sides."

I got up and did that. The pillars had Jewish writing carved into them, like on Albie's prayer bag. They looked real old, like they were made before people nailed boards together.

"Crouch down. Second shelf from the bottom. See the green book, *Basic Accounting*? Pull it out. Good. Now reach in and feel around for a little bump. Yeah? Just push on it, kid."

I heard a *thunk!* on the side of the bookcase. I went over there. The right side of the whole pillar had dropped. *Same way Albie had his desk rigged,* I thought. Bolted to the wood was a pair of metal boxes.

"Top one is video, bottom is audio."

"This is fucking amazing, Solly."

"Well, now you know my secret, kid. I trusted you with that, I hope you'll trust me when I tell you that, knowing you were coming, I turned everything off a half-hour ago, just like I said I would. You're not being taped now, and every tape I ever had of you, it was shredded a long time ago."

"I trust you, Solly," I said. Then I walked back to the desk.

"That means a lot to me, Sugar."

"Besides, I'm going to tell you what happened down there. How I did exactly what you told me to do. So, even if there *is* a tape, it's not gonna be one you'd want to show anybody."

"You're a real piece of work, kid. How about something to take the edge off your nerves?"

"No thanks, Solly."

"I wasn't talking about booze. For your nerves, I got something much better."

"I don't want any—"

"Jesus. You think *everyone* don't know you're a health freak? All you got to do is *listen.* You can do that, right?"

"Sure."

"Try this, then. I, me, Solly, I planned the jewelry heist. When you got out, I asked you to do a couple of things for me. So, if this Jessop got his ticket punched, that's on me, too. Think I'd put *that* on tape, kid?"

"I sure don't. Okay, Solly. But what you said, that's only half."

"You had to—?"

"Kill the broad? Yeah, I did. You told her about that desk. What do you think was in it?"

"A few mil."

"Just a note, Solly."

"A what?!"

"A note. From Albie to her. Something about how she had to run away. Fast. *With* the book. The book, it was supposed to prove you were some kind of 'traitor,' only that part wasn't for her. I couldn't make any sense out of it."

"So? Give it to me and—"

"That's what I said to her, Solly. Only she wouldn't."

"So she's . . ."

"I didn't have any choice."

"I understand. I would have done the same thing. Albie, he must have been going soft. In the head, I mean. Like Alzheimer's, you heard of that, right? Crazy old man, he could have said damn near anything."

"I didn't want to do any of that."

"Jessop, he didn't give you any choice, either?"

"Choice, *fuck*! You know where he lived? Right in that same town. And you know who told me that? Rena."

"Her and him?"

"You got it. They were playing Albie like a fiddle."

"I *knew* he was over the edge. *Had* to be. What a lousy way for a man like him to go out, wearing the horns."

"I guess. Anyway, once I got her to tell me where I could find him, the minute I—"

"Wait," Solly said, holding up his palm like a traffic cop. "Why did she tell you all this?"

"As soon as that note popped out, she knew she was going anyway. Come on, she knew who sent me, right? So I told her I could make it easy . . . or real, real hard."

"She didn't try to—"

"Sure. Probably thought it worked, too."

"Ah! You're a lot deeper than people take you for, Sugar."

"Nobody needs to know that besides you, Solly."

"Nobody ever will, kid."

"Anyway, I go over to where this Jessop was living. Cheap dump. I wait for him to get back from wherever he was. Can't miss him. He drives a red Corvette. Some pro, huh? As he's getting out, I walk up to him. I got my hands open at my sides, so he can see I'm not carrying.

"*He* was, though. I got to him just as he was reaching for it."

"Not much of a conversation, huh?"

"He won't be having *any* conversations anymore. That's what we wanted to be sure of, right?"

"Right," Solly said, showing me again that we weren't being taped.

"That note," I said, getting up to dig a little piece of paper out of my jeans, "the writing is so tiny, I could only make out some of it."

I was around to his side of the desk by then, holding the paper in my left hand to spread it out in front of him.

When Solly looked down, I slammed my right forearm across the back of his neck. Like I was a machete chopping cane. His forehead hit the desk on the way down. It was like breaking a broomstick over your knee—he was dead before he hit the floor.

I knew Solly had this big freezer bin in the back. For unstable goods, he told me once. I never asked what he meant by that—if he wanted me to know more, he would have said.

For once, I got lucky. All that was in there was a few little bottles, with corks in them. Looked like frozen water, but when I took them out, I put them down real careful.

Something else, too. A big Ziploc bag. When I wiped off the frost, I could see what looked like something wrapped in a black cloth. I pulled it open. The cloth wasn't cloth at all—some kind of plastic weave, with a thin layer of foam under it. When I peeled that off, I found what looked like an old-style address book, the kind with the little rings along the spine. The blanket must have been insulated; the book was hardly even cold.

With the freezer empty, I didn't even have to cut Solly up—just kind of folded him over and shoved him around until I could close the lid. Breaking those bones *felt* loud, but I knew it wasn't really.

I snatched that address book and slipped it into my coat. I took the Ziploc and the wrapping, too. A good thief knows you never leave empty spaces; that's the same as telling the owner someone found his stash. If everything still looks the same, it might take him a long time to look inside and find out he's been robbed.

I looked at my watch. Lynda would be pushing that serving cart outside our door in five minutes.

I was back in the hotel by two in the morning, sleeping with my alibi.

Yeah, my prints were all over Solly's basement. But if I'd known about that place for a long time, other guys knew, too. And I know, from listening to B&E pros, that the cops can't tell *when* a fingerprint was left.

I could have gone in with latex on my hands or something, but Solly, he would have sniffed that out before I could get close to him.

It's already done, is what I was thinking, just before I fell asleep. *Fuck it.*

I checked out early. Got one of those guys they have out front to find me a cab. He hit something on his cell phone. A minute later, a black sedan pulled up.

I handed the doorman a five and piled into the sedan like I didn't know what he'd just pulled on me. A few blocks later, I handed over what the driver said was the "flat fee" to JFK. Sixty bucks.

Lynda was waiting for me at the United terminal. I stacked the luggage all around her. Then I just walked over to the cab line.

The "flat fee" back was a lot cheaper.

At nine on the dot, I walked into the bank. I didn't speak to the manager, just emptied my safe-deposit box.

I caught the LIRR outbound. At that hour, it wasn't even half full.

From the station, I walked over to the lot where I had the Toyota stashed. The guy was a little surprised to see me so soon, but I told him the job had gone sour, and acted like I wished there was someone around for me to hit.

He got a little jumpy then. But when I didn't ask for any money back, he even smiled.

I drove the Toyota to JFK, parked in the short-stay lot.

It took me two trips, because I wanted to move fast and look normal. Lynda went along on the last leg. She barely fit, and the Toyota's back window was completely blocked, but we didn't have far to go from there—I knew a motel that took cash.

We transferred everything to the room. Place like that, you can't leave luggage in a car. Even the trunk, you'd be taking a chance. But out in the open, it's as good as gone.

When that insurance spook visited me Upstate, he'd left his card. I tore it into tiny pieces, then I got rid of the pieces in different spots. But the number that he wrote on the back, I put it in the one place they can't search.

He answered on the second ring.

"You came to visit me once," I said. "That offer you made, is it still good?"

"Absolutely."

There wasn't a trace of . . . anything in his voice.

"It's really that important to you, Sugar?" Lynda asked me.

"Yeah. Yeah, I guess it is. It's never really . . . gone from me."

"What if she still believes that you—"

"That'll be her choice. I'm no head doctor, but I figure, girl's been through what she's been through, just getting to *make* a choice, that'd be pure gold to her."

Lynda looked at me for a long time. Like she was trying each eye on by color.

"You're right," she finally said. "Only, what if they don't manage to convince her? Sure, she gets to make that choice. But if it really goes the way you want, won't she think the man who . . . did that to her, won't she think he's still around?"

"I never thought of that," I told Lynda. "But what can I do? It's one package. No bargaining. I'm not asking for much, considering what they put on the table the last time."

"That was years ago, baby."

"I guess I'll find out, then."

"*We'll* find out," Lynda said, putting her little hand on top of where I'd made a fist out of my right.

He was where he said he'd be: a booth way in the back of this diner on Queens Boulevard, far away from any windows. "You can't miss it," he'd told me. And he was right; it was the biggest diner I'd ever seen in my life.

"You're looking good," he said, shaking my hand. "And those glasses, that's a very fine touch."

"Solly fixed me up with them. And a bunch of other stuff, too."

His face was almost a perfect mask, but when I said "Solly," he'd given it away. So they probably knew all along, but didn't have a shred of proof.

I hoped they had. Known it all along, I mean. Being a thief doesn't just mean stealing, it means knowing who you're stealing from—my first fall taught me that. If the insurance people knew that jewelry job had been Solly's, they hadn't bothered to tell the cops.

Or maybe they had, for all the good that would have done them. From where they'd look at it, Solly's been in the business longer than I've been alive, and the Law has never touched him, not even once.

"You said the deal was still good?"

"Conspiracy charges have a statute of limitations just like robbery. Only difference is, the time doesn't start to run until the conspiracy is *discovered*. And that's exactly where the case is now—in discovery."

"It takes that long?"

"It can, depending on who you—"

"Okay, I get it. Only, I don't want the same deal."

"Because you already did the time and—"

"No. Just listen, okay? I don't want your money; I want your protection."

"From who?"

"Solly. He's probably got spotters on the street looking for me right now."

"I don't suppose you want to explain that?"

"Good guess. There's a few other things, too."

The waitress came over. The menu was as thick as a damn dictionary. I got a Caesar salad with chicken, no dressing; he got a steak, fries, onion rings.

Soon as she left, I told him the rest of what I needed. "I'm not going to give you a statement. If you're recording this, you'll have to edit out the part where you offered me a quarter-mil to lie in court so you could get the case against your company thrown out. And you'd also have to—"

"I'm not recording anything, Mr. Caine."

"At least that's my real name, Mr. Robert Johnson."

"How long do you want to play this out? All you've given me so far is a list of what you *won't* do."

And Solly's name, I thought. That's when I was sure they'd known all along.

"I'm not going to testify," I told him. "But I can give you enough to prove that jewelry-store job was a setup from jump. It was the owner's idea. *He's* the one who found Solly, not the other way around. I know how much we got away with, and it's nothing close to what he's suing you for."

"You know this how? Whatever you got from a fence doesn't mean you got the actual value."

"That's right. That'd always be right. But I've got the *actual* value."

"You mind telling me how?"

"Solly. You know what a GIA certificate is?"

"Yes."

"Well, I didn't. But Solly did. Solly always knows what things are worth. That's why he gets half off the top: he sets up the jobs, he moves the loot—even cash money, you have to sell at a discount; it could be marked, see? And he supplies everything you need to do the work, too."

"This 'Solly' would be?"

"Solomon Vizner."

He was on the hunt now. But he didn't want to spook the canary before the song was over. "That name doesn't mean anything to me, sorry."

"I don't think he has a record. But I have his address."

"And you think if someone were to go and speak with him . . . ?"

"Not a chance. Solly, he's the smartest guy I ever met. But I got something better."

He didn't say anything, but I could see he was drooling. And not for that steak he'd ordered.

"I got his book."

He made a "What's that supposed to mean?" move with his face and hands.

"His crime book. Solly's name isn't in it. No names are, just little . . . codes, like. But it's in his handwriting."

"I still don't see—"

"Solly wouldn't put his own name in the book. Who makes evidence against himself? And he wouldn't put in the names of the guys he hired for different jobs, either. He's no rat, Solly. Not even in secret. But you know what he *does* put in there?"

"Whoever hired *him*?"

"Bingo. Plus the dates, the take, the split, everything."

"And you have this book?"

"That's what I said."

"You didn't just happen to find this book lying around."

"No. And that's why I need what I'm going to ask you for. See, I thought Solly was . . . like an uncle to me. Solly always was a guy who took care of things. I guess I thought I was one of those things. Like Grace."

"Grace?"

"You wouldn't understand. She's . . . special."

He tapped the side of his head.

"Not like you think. I mean, you can tell she's got this Down-syndrome thing just by looking at her. And the way she talks. But she's smart as hell."

The food came. We ate like two guys sitting across a mess hall table. Two guys who didn't like each other. Kept our eyes down—to watch the other guy's hands.

"How does this Grace fit into what you're telling me?"

"She's got a key to Solly's place. I do, too. I thought we were the only ones. Now I'm not so sure."

"What difference would that make?"

"Right after I got out, I went over there. Solly introduced me to the doorman. The parking lot guy, too. Said I was his nephew. Jerome. Anyway, while I'm sitting there, going over the job—you know the one I'm talking about—this Grace walks in.

"She calls him 'Uncle Solly.' Turns out she's the daughter of . . . one of us. He's dead. Been gone a long time. Solly tells the building people that she's his maid. Comes in once a week to clean. And he pays her for it, too. Five hundred a week."

"Money he was holding from—"

"Nah. He's just doing the right thing. See, that's what we—all of us, I mean—that's what we'd expect him to do. Solly's not the boss, he's more like the . . . like I said, the man who takes care of things. Even people, he takes care of."

"All right," he said, making a little move with his fork, like he was pulling me over to him.

"Okay, here's what happened," I told him. "I'm there with Solly. Grace walks in. She sees he's busy, so she goes into one of the bedrooms.

"Solly, he's telling me there's going to be a little wait for me to get my money. From the jewelry-store job. He sees I don't like hearing that—he's had five *years* to get my money in a good safe place. But he tells me he's got me all set up: bank account, a car, even a place to stay. So it sounds pretty good.

"Now, Solly's an old man. Grace is a very sweet girl. She worries about him. So the fridge is always full of stuff that's good for him. Juices and that. Solly, he has to use the bathroom a lot. Especially when he's drinking a lot of juice, and he always does that when Grace comes over, he says.

"So Solly's in the bathroom, and I get up. Just to move around, not get cramped. I walk past Grace. She's got her nose in a book. Then I remember Solly telling me that she's not really a maid; he just tells the building managers she is, so they don't expect him to use their own people.

"Remember, I'm a thief. A good one. I can tell when a place has people living in it or not. That place, Solly probably only used it for a front—it wasn't just clean, it was like nobody ever sat on the furniture.

"His book was taped to the back of the night stand in one of the bedrooms. It looked like one of those old-fashioned address books. Kind of thick, with rings all along the binder.

"I took the book. I don't know why, but something told me to grab it, and I did. Just slipped it into my coat. Solly never suspected a thing.

"But by now, he knows. And he knows *I* know, too."

"And you believe yourself to be in danger because the book ties him to . . . ?"

"I'm not sure what it ties him to. But I know what it means when there's a black 'X' over someone's name."

"Something that the statute of limitations would never run out on."

"Yeah. But that part wouldn't have made *me* worried, unless I was in Solly's ledger—if he even has one—and I was already X'ed out."

"Why would Solly want you . . . eliminated?"

" 'Cause he's fucking insane. You'll see. That's what Solly's been doing all these years. Putting out hits on people he worked with. Like he's cleaning up behind himself.

"Maybe he's gone paranoid, I don't know. But by now, he's got to know I've got his book. With the money he's got, he could hire the best. So I'm a dead man unless I can get out of here. Disappear. Start over."

"We can certainly take care of that."

"Putting Solly in jail won't make me safe."

"I understand."

"And I'm not going in any Witness Protection bullshit."

"Fair enough. Now, when do I get this book?"

"When you make a promise."

"I already said we'd be able to—"

"Not that. Before you visited me in prison, you spoke to the cops, right? Detective Tom Woods?"

"That's right. Among others."

"And they told you, flat out, that they *knew* I never raped that girl?"

"Of course. Why else would I have—?"

"Yeah. Okay, here's the promise I want. You go and see the girl, and you tell her the truth."

"The girl who was—?"

"Yeah. Her. Get Woods to go with you, if you can. But all that really counts is that she knows it wasn't me."

He closed his eyes for a few seconds, so I couldn't see the battle going on in there.

Then he let out a little breath, like he'd made a decision.

"I can't do that," he said. Flat, not bargaining.

"What? Why the hell not? It's the truth."

"It is. And where would that leave *her*?"

"Huh?"

The gray fog around him went from pale to almost black, bright streaks flashing, like lightning at night. "I'll tell you where I'm going, Caine." Even his voice was different. Not . . . neutral anymore. "This is all about you, isn't it? Your 'rep.' You ever know a woman who's been raped?"

"I . . . I guess I don't know. Nobody ever said that to me, anyway."

"I have. And you want me to tell this woman, 'The man who raped you never went to prison at all. The man you've got a

Permanent Order of Protection against, he's not the man who raped you.'"

"You mean, she wouldn't want to think she sent an innocent man to prison?"

"You don't feel anything outside yourself, do you, Caine?"

"Me?"

"If you can't understand why it would terrify her if I told her that story, you're either a miserable reptile or as dumb as a rock."

His words were like a blast of wind, blowing me back against a wall. I couldn't move.

"So let me spell it out for you," he said, like a bucket of ice cubes tumbling out. "It's easy enough to explain to her that you *weren't* any kind of innocent man—you *should* have been in prison, only for a different crime. But if she hears that story you want me to tell, she'll think the man who raped her is still out there."

"Christ!" I said, thinking, *You fucking moron. Lynda even* told *you that!*

"Oh, it gets worse, believe me. She thought it was over. And now you want me to go and tell her the man who did that to her, not only is he on the loose, but the man she put in prison is out now. And *that* man has a long history of violence. You think she'd ever be able to sleep through the night again? Nah, you don't give a fuck. You know what, Caine? You can just *keep* your little book."

He pushed his plate away from him, like he was getting up to leave.

"Wait," I said.

He looked at me.

"Please."

He just kept looking at me.

"I'm not what you think. It's not that I don't give a damn. And it's not that I'm stupid, either. And I can prove it to you. Right now."

He just sat there.

I could hear that cop, Woods. In my head, like a message. *"Or maybe he's already doing time on one of the others."* So I told the dark cloud: "What if you told her the man who *really* raped her is still in prison? Never coming out. All you need is a rape-o who was on the street when it . . . happened. One of those pieces of shit who rape for fun. And now he's behind bars forever, 'cause he got dropped for a bunch of *other* ones."

He was quiet for a minute. Then he said, "I suppose that *could* work. But there's still . . ."

I could hear Lynda in my head: *You think any broad with plastic tits, she's got to be stupid, is that it?* I knew what to say then.

"You think any guy looks like me, he's got to be stupid, right? Muscles and brains, they, like, cancel each other out. You fucking 'suppose' it could work, is that right? Maybe you're too busy looking down your nose at me to see I might know some things.

"Well, here's one of those things: You go to any joint in the country, most of the cons will tell you they're innocent. They were framed, the cops flaked them, their lawyer sold them out—you know. And a lot more than you think would be telling the truth."

"What does this have to do with—?"

"How about if you just let me finish, okay? Convicts, they got a different way of looking at things. In their minds, crime, that's a game with *rules*. You go out and hold up a bank. If they catch you, you lose. If you get away, you win. Get it?"

"It's not complicated."

"Yeah? You sure? See, you're missing what I'm telling you. The joints are loaded with guys doing time for a crime they never committed, all right. But those guys, they actually *did* enough crimes to box them for life if they *had* been caught, see?"

"So you think this . . . scenario would have the ring of truth?"

"For all you know, it might *be* the truth, that's what I'm telling you. The guy you want doesn't even have to be in a New York pen. Could be federal, another state, doesn't matter. All he needs to qualify is be a big white guy doing a long stretch for rapes, a guy who was out when . . . it happened to her. Now, tell me you can't find one guy who fits *that* frame."

He looked straight at me for a couple of seconds. Then he said, "You're right. That *would* work. She wasn't raped in her own place, so—"

"Don't tell me anything about it. I still have that polygraph card. Maybe it don't mean nothing to you, but it's precious to me. You never fucking got that, did you?"

"I do now," he said, as he sat back down.

I felt a weight come off me. "You can tell her something else," I said to him. "Tell her *you* spoke with the man who went to prison for raping her. The innocent man who really isn't so innocent. A bad, dangerous man. That's me, right? You tell her not only did I do that guy's time, he hung a sex-fiend jacket on me, too. Tell her, if that scumbag ever crosses my path, he's dead."

"That I do believe, Mr. Caine. If she hadn't been raped, none of this—"

"I don't care what you believe, Mr. Johnson. All I care about is, *she* believes it. Can you get that done?"

"I can."

"Okay. That's one piece. Remember what you promised?"

"We've been all over—"

"No. No, we haven't. You said you could get me immunity, remember?"

He just nodded.

"I know it's too late for that. But when you offered it, that was the same as telling me you know some connected people. High-up connected."

He just stared at me.

"Seeing how long you managed to drag this insurance thing out, I figure you must still know people like that. *Permanent* people, like. So what I want now, it's something I know you can do."

"Which is?" he said. His eyes were half closed, like when you squint to see something better.

"I don't want to be a sex offender."

"But that's all—"

"Fuck if it is. I'll take your deal, but I'm not letting anyone keep me on a leash."

"What are you talking about? You're not on parole. Nobody's got any 'leash' on you."

"Just make the conviction into something else. *Anything* else, I don't care. With that sex-offender tag on me, I have to tell them every time I change my address. I can go back to prison just for moving without doing that. I can't have that hanging over me."

"Did you get the notice? The one that tells you—?"

"Yeah. They gave it to me as a going-away present."

"All right. Have you registered yet?"

"No."

He nodded, like he was agreeing with himself. Then he said, "Will you settle for the conviction standing? On paper, I mean. But your name never goes in the registry?"

"I can't."

"But that's all you—"

I heard the voice of that writ-writer, cluing me in. It echoed in my head: *It's pure bullshit. "Sealed," all that means is they can't put it in the newspapers.*

So I told him, "Whoever you can . . . talk to, they'll tell you how it *really* works. There's all kinds of paper floating around. Paper that says I did a rape. I'll never really be out from under with that over my head."

"Even if we could . . . arrange to go back and erase every trace, it could take years. And finding every *single* trace might be impossible."

"You don't need that," I told him. "I don't care about the arrest. Even the charge. Or the indictment. This isn't some trick for me to slide out from under two priors. In fact, it'd be fine with me if you made it another manslaughter."

"Another?"

"I'm on paper for one, but I pleaded it out to misdemeanor assault. But any *felony* assault, that'd be a violent crime. You pick it; I'll take it, so long as I don't have to keep checking in, like I was on parole for life or something. I won't wear that jacket."

"Just sit here for a few minutes, all right?"

"Sure," I said.

He got up and walked away. I didn't even turn my head. If he was going to pull something, I didn't *want* to see it coming.

⊢●⊣

"I've got something for you," he said when he came back. "That misdemeanor you told me about?"

"Yeah?"

He waved his hand like a fly was after his food. "How many times do you think you can slide on serious crimes? You'd think a guy with your record would know better than to go down on a possession charge."

"Possession? Possession of what?"

"A firearm, of course."

"For real?"

"It's already done. Ask your lawyer. One Hector Santiago-Ramirez, I believe? He must have done a hell of a job getting the DA to let you plead down to a possession charge instead of what you deserved, an ex-con carrying around a loaded handgun, like you were."

He leaned in closer to me. "Understand, you've *still* got two felony convictions. Robbery, age seventeen; criminal possession of a weapon, age thirty-three."

I took off my glasses. I wanted him to see what I was doing. He didn't flinch. And he had to know he was swearing on his life.

"Then I've got something else for you," I told him.

"What?"

"I did the jewelry job. You already know that, and you already know I'm not rolling on anyone else who was in on it. Only, now I'll give you the planner. Solly. Him I'll give up in a heartbeat. I'll tell the truth: Solly and the jeweler, they put the plan together. Solly *told* me that.

"I couldn't understand why he'd tell a guy at my end that kind of stuff. But now I get it. He was pulling me closer, so it'd be easier to have me hit. And that was his plan all along."

"You'll make that statement?"

"Yeah. Right now, if you want. And if I ever get hooked up to that polygraph—"

"I know."

"No, you don't. Listen for once: If I ever get questioned, the *truth* will be that I didn't get a dime from rolling on Solly and that jeweler. Not from you, not from anyone. All I asked was for some protection, and for you to tell that girl I didn't rape her. All true. What's *that* worth to you, pal?"

"Everything you asked for," he said. "And now it's my turn."

"I thought you said it was already—"

"I apologize," he said, holding out his hand.

His grip felt just right.

Lynda took the Greyhound to Chicago. Took her only a couple of days to find a place. For her and her husband. He was coming after he cleared up all the paperwork at his office. Their plan was to buy a home, so they were really only looking for something for maybe six, seven months. So she could just pay the whole thing now, if the landlord wanted.

She'd have to pay cash, because she didn't have a Chicago bank account yet. She hoped that was okay with the landlord. He turned out to be a real agreeable guy.

While Lynda was setting up, I got put on videotape. And everything I said was the truth.

I asked the cameraman to come in real close. In case they wanted to show the girl who'd gotten raped what my face looked like when I said the part about doing time for another man's crime. And my promise to kill him if I ever found him.

The guy who sold me the used Ford Crown Vic in Youngstown didn't mind cash, either. I told him I'd bring back the plates as soon as I got it registered. The way he shrugged, I could see the plates were already NFG—probably his insurance had run out or something like that.

I left the Toyota in a mall lot. Nothing was open that early in the morning. And I could see a lot of them weren't *going* to open—the place looked like a ghost town. I left the keys in the ignition.

It was Lynda who showed me how I could read the *Daily News* without buying a copy. Or even being in New York.

I wouldn't have asked her, myself. I knew I'd never trust any planner again, and I wasn't ever going back home, either. So I didn't care about checking to see if anything looked ripe for a one-man job.

Lynda, she liked the *Times.*

"Honey," she said one day, "come here. Take a look at this."

Her voice was quiet, but something else was in there. The headline said:

EXPLOSION IN EAST SIDE BUILDING
TERRORIST ACTIVITY SUSPECTED

The address was Solly's. Solly's office, I mean. The story said there'd been what they called a "targeted explosion" in the basement. Nobody hurt, but the first two floors had to be evacuated while they checked to see if they would hold.

I didn't know if one of those glass bottles was something that you had to keep cold, or if the hard men who visited Albie had found his last note.

But *terrorism?* That was so weird, I kept reading.

It was a long article. Whoever wrote it, they must have been on the trail a long time before the explosion happened.

Started off about how a guy named Morales had blown his own hands off while he was trying to put together a bomb for the FALN back in '78. They took him to Bellevue for surgery, but his people busted him right out.

Morales made it to Mexico, but he got caught in a shootout down there. They hit him with a long sentence for that, plus he was supposed to be sent back here when he maxed it out. Only, Mexico pulled a fast one. They cut his time in half, and then shipped him to Cuba.

The article said Morales is still there, and some woman who'd been busted out around the same time was, too. Only, this woman was supposed to be a Black Panther, and she'd been busted out of a prison in New Jersey.

Another woman had been convicted of being part of both escapes—a white woman who they said was the "armorer" of the Black Liberation Army. She was still in a federal pen.

The same year they bagged Morales in Mexico, the FALN took down an armored car for around seven million. ·

The reporter didn't come right out and say it, but you could see he thought some of that money went to Mexico, because it was that same year Mexico shipped Morales to Cuba.

"Does this make any sense to you?" I asked Lynda.

She printed out the story, sat down, and read it a bunch of times.

"I don't know, Sugar," she told me. "I guess it *could* all be tied together."

"Just because—?"

"Well, remember, there were a *lot* of bombings back then. You read about them, maybe?"

"Not me."

"Well, I did. My teacher said it was important to know those things."

That's what she called Albie now: "my teacher." She never spoke his name.

"I was just a little kid when all this stuff happened. And I didn't go to school much, anyway."

"Stuff happened *before* this," Lynda said. "There was a brownstone in Greenwich Village, I think. It exploded when some of the people there were trying to make a bomb."

"White people?"

"Rich white people."

"Were they Jewish?"

"I don't remember. But we could find out easy enough."

"Nah. I just wanted to make sense out of it. It doesn't matter what they say in the papers. If they want to think Solly blew himself up trying to make bombs, that's fine with me."

"They don't say *anyone* was killed, Sugar."

"So I guess we'll never know what happened, girl. But bet on this: no way Solly was some 'terrorist.' Where's the money in that?"

"How far back did you go with him?" is all she said.

Maybe I couldn't connect all the dots in that story, but one thing I knew for sure: Solly wasn't going to be explaining anything to anyone.

I didn't go outside for months. But that was fine. Lynda made it fine.

Funny, huh? This all started with me being railroaded. And now I'm on the Amtrak, headed for someplace west.

My name is Henry K. Lynch. Height/weight: six three, two fifty-five. Hair: blond. Eyes: blue/brown. Born: March 3, 1972; Alton, Illinois. The "K." is for "Ken."

The scar's impossible to see now. Where there used to be a space in my eyebrow, there's a black tattoo.

The woman with me, her name is Lynda Leigh Lynch. We got married in Chicago, six months ago.

If I have to go back to work, I will. But on my own. No more planners, no more partners.

Crime wasn't on my mind, not the way it used to be. I have to make up my own rules now.

But I won't have to do that alone. Never again.

ABOUT THE AUTHOR

Andrew Vachss has been a federal investigator in sexually transmitted diseases, a social-services caseworker, and a labor organizer, and has directed a maximum-security prison for "aggressive-violent" youth. Now a lawyer in private practice, he represents children and youths exclusively. He is the author of numerous novels, including the Burke series, two collections of short stories, and a wide variety of other material, including song lyrics, graphic novels, essays, and a "children's book for adults." His books have been translated into twenty languages, and his work has appeared in *Parade, Antaeus, Esquire, Playboy,* the *New York Times,* and many other forums. A native New Yorker, he now divides his time between the city of his birth and the Pacific Northwest.

The dedicated Web site for Vachss and his work is www.vachss.com.